❥ The ❦
Spirit Woman

**Center Point
Large Print**

**This Large Print Book carries the
Seal of Approval of N.A.V.H.**

ॐ श्री गणेशाय नमः

The
Spirit Woman

Margaret Coel

Center Point Publishing
Thorndike, Maine · USA

Compass Press
British Commonwealth

This Center Point Large Print edition
is published in the year 2001 by arrangement with
G.P. Putnam's Sons, a division of Penguin Putnam, Inc.

This Compass Press edition is published in the year 2001 by Bolinda
Publishing Pty Ltd., Tullamarine, Victoria, Australia by arrangement with
Jane Jordan Browne.

The text of this Large Print edition is unabridged.
In other aspects, this book may vary from the original edition. Printed in
Thailand. Set in 16-point Plantin type by Bill Coskrey.

US ISBN 1-58547-063-5
BC ISBN 1-74030-378-4

Library of Congress Cataloging-in-Publication Data

Coel, Margaret, 1937-
    The spirit woman / Margaret Coel.
        p. cm.
    ISBN 1-58547-063-5 (lib. bdg. : alk. paper)
        1. O'Malley, John (Fictitious character)--Fiction. 2. Holden, Vicky (Fictitious character)--
Fiction. 3. Wind River Indian Reservation (Wyo.)--Fiction. 4. Catholic Church--Clergy--
Fiction. 5. Indians of North America--Fiction. 6. Arapaho Indians--Fiction. 7. Wyoming--
Fiction. 8. Large type books. I. Title.

PS3553.O347 S65 2001
813'.54--dc21

                                                                                    00-047362

Australian Cataloguing in Publication Data

Coel, Margaret, 1937-
The spirit woman / Margaret Coel.
(Compass Press large print book series)
ISBN 1740303784 (hbk.)
    1. Large print books.
    2. Catholic Church Wyoming - Clergy - Fiction.
    3. O'Malley, John (Fictitious character) - Fiction.
    4. Holden, Vicky (Fictitious character) - Fiction.
    5. Indians of North America - Wyoming - Fiction.
    6. Arapaho Indians - Fiction.
    7. Wind River Indian Reservation (Wyo.) - Fiction.
    8. Detective and mystery stories.
I. Title
813.54

Acknowledgments

Robert Pickering, Ph.D., forensic anthropologist, Buffalo Bill Historical Center, Cody, WY.

Todd Dawson, special agent, Federal Bureau of Investigation, Lander, WY.

Detective Sergeant Bob Campbell, Lander Police Department, Lander, WY.

Zelda R. Tillman, director, Shoshone Cultural Center, Fort Washakie, WY.

Mary Keenan, chief deputy district attorney, Boulder, CO.

Judge Sheila Carrigan, Boulder, CO.

Barbara Paradiso, longtime advocate for battered women, Boulder, CO.

Anthony Short, S.J., Denver, CO., formerly at St. Stephen's Mission, Wind River Reservation.

Ron and Laura Mamot, St. Stephens, WY.

Virginia Sutter, Ph.D., member of the Arapaho tribe, Auburn, WA.

Karen Gilleland, Beverly Carrigan, and Mary Hill, Boulder, CO; Mary and Ron Dunning, Louisville, CO; and John Dix, Washington, DC.

George and Kristin Coel, and Lisa and Tom Harrison.

Sacajawea never liked to stay where she could not see the mountains, for them she called home. For the unseen spirit dwelt in the hills . . .
—Tom Rivington, Wyoming pioneer

For Samuel Coel Harrison

⇒ 1 ⇐

Father John O'Malley pulled up the collar of his jacket and dipped the brim of his cowboy hat against the hard wind whirling little pellets of snow into the air. Thick gray clouds scuttled overhead and rolled through the cottonwoods like a dense fog, nearly obscuring the snow-covered path that ran between the trees and the Little Wind River. He could see his breath ahead of him. The rhythmic crunch of his boots on the snow punctuated the sound of water gurgling over ice. It was November, the twelfth month in the Arapaho Way, the Moon When the Rivers Start to Freeze.

Walks-On-Three-Legs bounded toward him out of the trees, and Father John coaxed the red disk from the golden retriever's mouth and gave it another toss. It sailed down the path into the fog, a streak of red in the grayness. The dog loped after it and, pivoting on his only hind leg, snatched the disk out of the air and darted back. Another toss, another snatch. Was it really three years ago that he'd found the dog in the barrow ditch? It seemed like yesterday. He'd rushed him to Riverton, where the vet had amputated the dog's smashed left hind leg and saved his life. Father John had brought him back to St. Francis Mission.

He tossed the disk again, putting some real spin on it this time so that it veered into the cotton-woods. He would leave Walks-On at the mission.

11

Even if the new pastor didn't like dogs, Elena, the housekeeper, was fond of Walks-On, no matter how much she proclaimed otherwise. "Just more work around here, which I don't need, thank you very much," she'd told him when he'd carried the dog into the priests' residence and laid him on a rug in the corner of the kitchen. Hers was the same protest his mother had made when, as a kid in Boston, he would come home with a stray dog. He'd seen how Elena slipped the dog the best table scraps, and more than once he'd popped into the residence in the middle of the day to find her seated in a chair with her beading, Walks-On curled at her feet. She would take good care of him when he left.

When he left. The words echoed in his mind, a counterpoint to the sounds of his footsteps. He'd been at St. Francis Mission on the Wind River Reservation now for nearly eight years, but he'd been pastor only half that time. Six years was the usual term for a Jesuit assignment. He'd hoped the provincial would date his assignment from the time he became pastor. It wasn't to be. The call had come less than an hour ago. He'd stared at the phone jangling into the quiet of his office in the administration building, a sense of foreboding sounding in his head. Finally he'd reached across the desk and lifted the receiver. "Father O'Malley," he'd said, his throat tight with dread.

"John? Good news." The familiar voice of Father William Rutherford, the Jesuit provincial. For one crazy moment he'd allowed himself to believe that he was about to get a new assistant. He needed an assistant. He'd been alone now for almost two months, ever since Father Joseph Keenan had been murdered, shot to death when he went out on an emergency call. Everywhere he looked were stacks of papers demanding his attention. Next year's budget, next semester's religious-education classes, liturgies for the Christmas season, speakers for the new parents' group. There were shut-ins and people in the hospital to visit and a never-ending round of meetings to attend: Alcoholics Anonymous, men's club, women's sodality. He was hopelessly behind.

"I've found a new pastor for St. Francis." The provincial had blurted out the news. "Kevin McBride. You know him?"

Father John had snapped a pencil in half and shot the pieces across the desk. So this was it, the news he'd been dreading for two years. He had muttered something about never having heard of the man.

"Recent doctorate in anthropology. Anxious to get some fieldwork among the indigenous peoples."

"Fieldwork?" He'd heard the sharpness in his voice. "St. Francis Mission isn't some kind of laboratory. The Arapahos need a pastor."

The line had gone quiet a moment. "Perhaps I phrased that badly. Kevin will make a fine pastor. To be perfectly honest, John, I expected you to welcome the news."

He'd drawn in a long breath, struggling to control the disappointment that flooded over him. It was as strong as the mountains, as big as the sky. He heard it in his voice when he said: "I've started a lot of things here, Bill. I'd like to finish them."

"You don't have to worry. Kevin will step right in, take up where you leave off, finish things before he starts his own programs."

"Look, Bill"—a different tack—"I'm not ready to leave St. Francis. I was counting on another couple of years."

Silence had hung on the line like an eavesdropper. Finally the provincial said, "Frankly, John, you've been on the reservation long enough. I've seen other men like you. They start feeling too much at home. Go Indian, if you will. Start thinking they are Indian. When they finally leave, they have a hard time making the transition into the outside world."

"I know who I am," Father John had said in an impatient tone. A Boston Irishman, with red hair fading to gray at the temples and blue eyes, taller than most men at almost six feet four. A recovering alcoholic. A struggling priest. How could he forget?

"I didn't want to bring this up, John, but . . ." The provincial hesitated, then plunged on. "I've heard the rumors."

"What rumors?" Father John's stomach muscles tightened. He knew the answer. O'Malley, stuck on an Indian reservation in the middle of Wyoming, probably drinking himself into oblivion.

He was about to say that he hadn't had a drink since he left Grace House eight years before when the voice crackled over the line: "The woman, John."

He'd been wrong. The rumors weren't about alcohol after all. They were about Vicky. The long, un-relenting lines of the moccasin telegraph had reached all the way to the provincial's office in Milwaukee.

He said, "Vicky Holden's an attorney. We work together on adoptions, DUIs, juveniles who get picked up by the police, divorces, a lot of different cases. We're friends, that's all. I hope I have a lot of friends here."

The provincial had drawn in a long breath that sounded as if he were sucking air from the receiver. "There's always the danger . . ."

"She's back with her ex-husband." The explanation was sharp with anger and a sense of violation. What in heaven's name had gone out over the moccasin telegraph? "There's no danger," he added, stopping himself from saying, There's no longer any danger.

"I hope that's true," his boss had said in a tone that suggested he didn't believe it. "In any case, it's time for you to move on. You've been stuck at St. Francis long enough."

"Stuck? I don't consider myself stuck."

"You're an academic, an historian. Have you forgotten? It's time you got back to teaching and finished your doctorate. A position has opened up in the history department at Marquette University. You'll teach a couple classes in American history next semester and finish the last of your course work. Should only take another couple years to write your dissertation. Maybe you could do something on the history of the Arapahos. Make use

15

of your experience on the reservation."

Father John pressed the cold receiver hard against his ear and stared out the window at the clouds drifting over the Wind River mountains, gray in the distance, and the sweep of the snowy plains disappearing into the fog. This was home. He loved the place; he loved the people. He couldn't imagine leaving. "Let me think about it," he'd managed.

"Think about it? There's nothing to think about. This is in your own best interests, believe me. Take a little time and get Kevin up to speed. I'll expect you in Milwaukee in two weeks."

Father John didn't remember asking when the new pastor might put in an appearance, but the provincial had volunteered the information. "Kevin should arrive any day. He's on his way." The entire conversation reverberated in his mind, like the electrical charge of a lightning storm. He'd hung up, grabbed his cowboy hat and wool jacket, and set off for a long walk. Walks-On had come loping along, disk clenched in his jaw.

Now Father John jammed his gloved hands into his jacket pockets against the cold and kicked at a stone, sending it skittering over the riverbank and pinging against the ice. The vow of obedience was the hardest to live by; he'd always known that would be the case. "How you gonna do it, lad?" His father's voice. He could still see his father at the kitchen table, shaking his head in disbelief, pouring the whiskey into a tumbler with the fine, musician's hands that spent the days adjusting the knobs of steam furnaces beneath Boston College. "An Irishman vowing to be obedient. Ha! We can't even spell the word."

"Give me the grace to obey," he prayed. "Please, Lord, the grace . . ."

Suddenly he realized Walks-On hadn't returned. He walked a little way farther on the path before turning in to the cottonwoods where he'd sailed the disk. The sound of his footsteps mingled with the hush of the wind in the trees and the in and out, in and out of his own breathing. "Here, boy!" he shouted. There was no sign of the dog, but he heard a faint scratching noise. He stood still a moment, listening, then started toward the noise.

The dried bushes and undergrowth snapped under his boots as he ducked past a low-hanging branch, peering through the trees for the dog. Finally he spotted him, nose to the ground, front paws feverishly digging out a narrow trench in the earth. The red disk lay at his side. The dog had found some buried bones, he thought. Cow bones, perhaps. "Come here, boy," he called.

Walks-On kept pawing, shoulders hunched to the task. As Father John moved closer he saw something, light brown colored, partially submerged in the trench. He grabbed the dog's collar and eased him back a few feet. The dog gave a little yelp of protest. "Stay," he ordered.

He moved closer. Wild animals had been here before Walks-On, judging by the snow and soil pushed into ridges here and there. Scattered in the freshly dug trench, like hard pieces of snow, were tiny bone chips. Stooping down, he brushed away some of the loose soil. What looked like a femur began to emerge. Brushing harder now. Another bone appeared, small and gnarled, like a joint. He reached across the trench and scraped at a ridge. His fingers found something hard and round, and he pulled it free. A human skull, wisps of brown hair still clinging to the bone. His heart thumped against his ribs.

He laid the skull back in the earth and stood up, eyes fixed on the burial place. "Whoever you are," he said, "may God have mercy on your soul."

Nearby he found two dead branches, which he pushed into the ground at each end of the grave site. Then he snapped a thin branch from a tree and jammed it between the others, bending the tops together in the form of a tripod, like the skeleton of a tipi. He set the red disk on the branches. The wind would probably blow the whole thing over, he knew, but it was the best he could do.

He glanced about, trying to get his bearings. The fog was thick and icy, wrapping the trees, seeping around him and the dog and the bones. The muffled thrum of an engine sounded in the distance. Rendezvous Road was probably only a half mile away, which meant they'd come about two miles from the mission. He had to get back and call the police.

"Come on," he said, taking Walks-On by the collar again and leading him through the trees, counting the steps until they reached the river. The dog stared forlornly in the direction they had just come as Father John tied his handkerchief around a low branch. Then he started running along the path, Walks-On loping at his side and finally bursting ahead, breaking the way, as if this was some new game. For an instant the fog parted and Father John caught a glimpse of the white steeple of St. Francis church rising above the trees in the distance.

He ran on.

⇒ 2 ⇐

Sacajawea: The Hidden Life
by Charlotte Allen, Ph.D.
Foreword by Laura Simmons, Ph.D.

A Frenchman Squaw came to our camp who belongs to the Snake nation. She came with our Interpreter's wife and brought with them 4 buffalow Robes and Gave them to our officers.

> — Sergeant John Ordway,
> the Corps of Discovery,
> Captains Meriwether Lewis and
> William Clark in command,
> Fort Mandan, November 4, 1804

Thus Sacajawea walked into history.

A Shoshone girl not more than sixteen years old, captured by the Minnetarees and sold to the French trader Toussaint Charbonneau. Or perhaps the wily old trader, already in his forties, had won the girl in a game of chance. The record is unclear. At any rate, when she appeared at Fort Mandan on the Missouri River in present-day North Dakota, she was one of Charbonneau's wives. She was six months pregnant with his child.

She had accompanied her husband to the triangular-shaped fort built of cottonwood logs where Lewis and Clark were spending the winter before continuing the expedition to the Pacific Ocean. Charbonneau hoped to hire on as an interpreter, but the captains quickly took the trader's measure: an arrogant man, unreliable and brutal. They declined his services. Yet they hoped to purchase horses from the Shoshones, and the trader's young wife could speak Shoshone. Finally they agreed to hire the man on the condition that Sacajawea accompany the expedition.

On February 11, 1805, after an extremely difficult labor, Sacajawea gave birth to a son, Jean Baptiste. Scarcely two months later, April 7, the thirty-three members of the Corps of Discovery set out on a journey through the wilderness to the Pacific Ocean about 2500 miles to the west. They would traverse rocky canyons and almost impenetrable forests and navigate the rushing rivers in canoes and pirogues. They would encounter Indian tribes that had never seen white people. They would endure torrential rainfalls, freezing temperatures, and snow as high as a horse's neck. They would know hunger and thirst and, at times, despair, but they would go forward.

Sacajawea would go with them, the only woman on the expedition, her infant son strapped to a rawhide cradle on her back.

S o here you are."
Laura Simmons stared at the tall granite
marker, a silent sentinel looming over the grave.
SACAJAWEA was carved into the smooth section of
stone. Beneath the name: *Died April 9, 1884. A guide
with the Lewis and Clark expedition. 1805-1806.*
Scattered about the grave, intermingling with
bouquets of plastic flowers, were tiny packets
wrapped in fabric—prayer bundles, she knew,
offered for the spirit of Sacajawea.

On either side of the granite marker were two
shorter markers. The one on the left, a memorial
with the inscription BAPTISTE CHARBONNEAU,
*papoose of the Lewis and Clark Expedition, buried in the
Wind River Mountains.* The stone on the right
marked the grave of Bazil, Sacajawea's adopted son.

The wind was cold and unyielding. Laura hugged
the fronts of her white coat close and stamped her
boots to restore the circulation in her legs. She realized
she was the only one in the Shoshone cemetery.
Sloping away were rows of graves with small wooden
crosses and red and yellow plastic flowers that poked
out of the bare dirt and patches of snow. The Wind
River Reservation crawled eastward along the valley of
the Little Wind River. In the near distance, the framed
houses and tribal buildings of Fort Washakie seemed
to shimmer in the wind. Fort Washakie was where
Sacajawea had spent her last years.

The mountains rose on the west, peaks upon

peaks floating into the clouds: Bold Mountain, Mount Windy, Knife Point Mountain, Mount Sacajawea. Stretching north and south along the horizon were the farther ranges of the Rocky Mountains, which had been heaved out of the earth in some ancient cataclysm.

"You crossed the mountains, you went to the Pacific, and you returned to your people," Laura said out loud, as if Sacajawea were beside her. The idea made her laugh, a thin, brittle sound in the wind. That would rattle her colleagues, shake them to the very roots of their academic complacency, were she to announce at a Western history conference that she had visited the grave site of Sacajawea and had *felt* the truth. The real Sacajawea was buried here, not in some unmarked grave in South Dakota.

"And how do you explain the documentary evidence, Dr. Simmons?" her colleagues would demand. " 'This evening the wife of Charbonneau, a Snake squaw, died of a putrid fever. She was good and the best woman in the fort . . .' John C. Luttig, clerk, Fort Manuel Lisa, 1812." To counter this evidence, she would smile and present her colleagues with irrefutable evidence—Sacajawea's memoirs, recorded on the reservation in the 1870s and 1880s by the wife of the Indian agent. The crowning glory of the unfinished biography that Charlotte Allen had left when she died. Laura had already edited the manuscript and written the foreword. She had only to locate the memoirs to complete the biography.

The wind caught at her coat again, wrapping it

around her legs. She shivered and, raising a gloved hand, dabbed at her cheek—an automatic motion now, like an old habit. She'd been checking the bruise for two weeks. Still tender, but the color had begun to fade. It had seemed hardly noticeable in the mirror this morning, after she'd applied a second coat of makeup. She badly wanted a cigarette. She made herself take a deep breath—two, three breaths—gradually feeling confident again, like her old self. Professor Toby Becker was a nightmare that had finally ended, and she was free. She had her work: the classes to teach in the history of the American West at the University of Colorado, the Sacajawea biography to complete.

She threaded her way among the graves to the blue SAAB parked in a narrow dirt path. A trace of warmth still hugged the inside of the car, even though she'd left the windows down a little to clear out the cigarette smoke. The wind squealed over the window tops as she found the pack in her purse on the seat next to the large, brown folder. She lit another cigarette, inhaled slowly, gratefully, and turned the key in the ignition. The engine burst into life. The clock on the dashboard showed 11:30.

She threw the gear into drive and headed out of the cemetery and onto the road, taking another long drag from the cigarette. She'd arranged to meet an old college friend, Vicky Holden, for lunch in Lander. Just the person to help her find Sacajawea's memoirs, which were somewhere on the reservation. She pushed down the accelerator. She

23

didn't want to be late.

⟫ 3 ⟪

Vicky Holden watched the small woman lifting herself out of the blue SAAB on the other side of Main Street. The long, straight blond hair parted in the middle, blowing in the wind, the pinched, anxious face, the way she gripped some kind of brown package as she crossed the street, shoulders hunched inside the white coat, a tan bag swinging at her side. She wondered if she would have recognized Laura Simmons had they passed in a crowd.

The call had come yesterday—a call out of the blue—and at the sound of Laura's voice, the memories had flashed through her mind, like an old, grainy movie in fast forward. She and Laura struggling through statistics class together, meeting for lunch in the glass-brick CU-Denver cafeteria, crying through commencement. They'd stayed in touch after Laura went back east to work on her doctorate in history and she'd entered law school. Phone calls now and then, a few quick lunches whenever Laura was in town. But after Vicky had moved to Lander, close to the reservation, to open a one-woman law office, the calls had become less frequent. She'd heard Laura had taken a position in the history department at CU in Boulder.

Vicky slid out of the booth and was halfway to the door when it flew open. A gust of cold air swept over the café, rippling the red-checkered tablecloths and paper napkins. Laura closed the door and smoothed back her hair with one hand, the other still gripping what Vicky could see was a large folder.

"Laura," Vicky said, walking over. And then she saw it—a large, purple bruise traveling like a shadow over Laura Simmons's right cheekbone. She tried not to stare as she held out her hand. Laura's hand felt as cold as an ingot inside the smoothness of the leather glove. "We have a table over here." Vicky nodded toward the booths along the plate-glass windows.

"God, I'm glad I found you," Laura said when they were seated across from each other. She had left the white coat draped over her shoulders, which made her seem even smaller, like a child lost in a tent of fabric. She wore a silky mauve blouse that folded loosely around her pale throat.

"It's good to see you, Laura," Vicky heard herself saying, trying not to let her eyes rest on the bruise. She'd forgotten how much she missed some of the friends she'd made at the university, after she'd left Ben and gone to Denver thirteen years ago—a lifetime ago. The women like Laura, whose eyes didn't reflect "Indian" every time they'd looked at her. She didn't have many friends on the reservation anymore. The girls who had gone to college hadn't returned. And the others—girls like herself who'd gotten married out of high school—well, she no longer had much in common with them. She tried to push away the feeling nagging at her lately: she didn't belong anywhere. Not among her people, not in Denver.

A guffaw of laughter erupted from the cowboys in an adjoining booth, and Vicky forced her attention to the waitress who had wandered over and was scratching Laura's order on a small pad: Caesar salad, hot tea. She ordered the same.

The waitress moved away and Laura said, "I still can't believe you came back here." She gestured toward the squat, flat-faced buildings beyond the window, the two pickups and the twenty-year-old Chevy grinding down Main Street. "You had a great career at that Denver law firm."

Vicky laughed. Wes Nelson, the firm's managing partner, had said almost the same thing when he'd called last week and offered her a new position. "Seventy-hour weeks making rich corporations a whole lot richer," she said. "Is that your idea of a great career?"

It will be different, Wes Nelson's voice sounded in her head. *Indian land issues, natural resources, artifacts. A chance to help the tribes. We need you, Vicky.* She pushed the voice away. "What brings you here, Laura? You sounded anxious on the phone. Is there any trouble?"

"Trouble?" Laura gave a tight, mirthless laugh. "I think I'm finally free of trouble." She waited until the waitress had set down twin plates of Caesar salad, two mugs of steaming water, and a couple of tea bags. Then she unfolded her napkin, smoothed it in her lap, and began unwrapping one of the bags.

26

"I'm working on the definitive biography of Sacajawea. Actually, it's the work of another CU professor, who started it twenty years ago."

She swished the bag into the mug in front of her a moment before taking a long sip. Light glinted in her pale, gray eyes. "It's the opportunity of a lifetime, Vicky, and it dropped into my lap. An old woman came to my office last summer and said she was Charlotte Allen's mother. Well"—a glance at the ceiling—"I'd never heard of anyone named Charlotte Allen. And get this," Laura went on, leaning closer, "I almost sent her away! I thought the woman was looking for directions to somebody's office, and I don't consider myself a traffic cop. But for some reason, thanks to whatever spirits exist, I let her in."

Laura lifted the flap on the folder next to her and withdrew a thick stack of papers, which she laid on the table. "This is Charlotte Allen's biography of Sacajawea," she said. "Her mother asked me to finish it and see that it's published." She shrugged. "A memorial, I suppose."

"What happened to her daughter?" Vicky asked.

"Charlotte Allen was a wilderness freak." Laura took a bite of her salad and chewed thoughtfully a moment. "Well, that wasn't exactly the way her mother put it, but she was one of those women who like to take long hikes in the mountains." She pushed a piece of lettuce around her plate, her attention caught by an intervening thought. "Like Sacajawea, I suppose. Only Charlotte Allen set off on a long hike and didn't come back. She got lost up around Sacajawea Ridge twenty years ago. They never found her body. Maybe you heard about it?"

Vicky shook her head and took a bite of her own salad. Twenty years ago her life had revolved around Ben. A contortionist's life, bending herself to Ben's comings and goings, his moods. If a white woman had gotten lost in the mountains, she had no memory of it. People were always getting lost in the mountains.

"Do you have any idea how many biographies have been written about Sacajawea?" Laura went on. "Why, I came very close to asking the woman to leave. I'm up for tenure next year, Vicky. I have to publish something significant or my career is finished. I told the woman I had no interest in trying to publish another biography of Sacajawea."

Suddenly Laura pushed her plate to one side. Most of the salad remained. She leaned across the table, the gray eyes darkening with intensity. A vein pulsed at the outer edge of the purple bruise. "That's when the woman told me her daughter had discovered Sacajawea's memoirs."

Vicky held a gulp of warm tea in her mouth a moment, then swallowed. She'd grown up with stories about the old Shoshone woman who had claimed to be Sacajawea. Stories about the medal Meriwether Lewis had given her, which was buried with her son, Baptiste. The important papers she always carried to prove that she was somebody, which were buried with her adopted son, Bazil. And

28

stories about how Bazil's grave had been exhumed in the 1920s. The papers were found, but they had turned to dust. She had never heard any stories about Sacajawea's memoirs.

Laura dug into the folder again and pulled out a red leather notebook. "Charlotte Allen was a meticulous researcher," she said, waving the notebook over the table. "She kept a journal of her research, a record of her sources and where she located them, the names of Sacajawea's descendants she'd interviewed. Her mother found the journal wedged in the spare well in the trunk of Charlotte's car after she disappeared."

Laura opened the notebook at the place where a bookmark protruded and began to read out loud, with the precise diction of a lecturer: "Sarah Trumbull Irwin, wife of the agent, Dr. James Irwin, spent many hours with Sacajawea. She recorded in a notebook everything Sacajawea said about the part she had played in the expedition. Mrs. Irwin placed the notebook at the agency in Fort Washakie, which was destroyed by fire in 1885. It has always been assumed that Sacajawea's memoirs were lost."

She closed the journal. "The memoirs survived, Vicky," Laura said, her voice rising in excitement. "Do you have any idea what this means?"

"I can imagine." A piece of the past, Vicky thought, something that would explain what had really happened.

Laura was shaking her head, as if the meaning was too important, too precious, for anyone to grasp fully. "It will settle a hundred years of arguments about what happened to Sacajawea after the expedition. It will prove that she lived out her life with her people and told her stories when she was a very old woman."

Vicky pushed her own plate aside. Another shout, like a hurrah, went up from the cowboys, mingling with the clatter of plates, the swish of the door opening and closing. She took a sip of the tea, lukewarm now. "I've never heard that the memoirs survived, Laura. Where do you think they are?"

Laura studied the red notebook in her hands. "The Shoshones have kept the memoirs a secret. A man Charlotte called Toussaint knows where they are," she said. "Can you help me find him?"

The name had a familiar ring, Vicky thought. Something she'd read? Some story she'd heard? "Toussaint," she said, trying the sound of it. "Wasn't he . . ."

"The French trader Sacajawea was married to," Laura said quickly. "Toussaint Charbonneau. The man Charlotte met must be a descendant."

Vicky remembered now. Once in a while the elders had mentioned the name. *He was a hard, brutal man. He beat her. Captain Clark had to interfere. And after they got back from the Pacific, Toussaint whipped her in front of his Ute wife.*

"I've never heard of anyone on the res by that name," Vicky said.

Laura pressed back against the seat and began lifting and closing the cover of the journal. Open, shut. Open, shut. "Charlotte did some research in the Shoshone cultural center. Maybe she found a document that led her to Toussaint. Or maybe one of the elders she interviewed . . ." She leaned forward again, allowing the white coat to drop behind her. The pale light filtering past the window burnished the mauve silk blouse. "Would you introduce me to them? Assure them that I intend to write the truth? Sacajawea was a great woman, Vicky. Her story must be told."

"The Shoshones may not agree."

"That Sacajawea was a great woman?" Laura's head snapped forward, gray eyes wide in bewilderment.

"That her story should be told."

"You can't be serious."

Vicky took another sip of tea, pulling from her memory the voices of the elders. *The white people came and fastened themselves to our land.* She said, "Lewis and Clark thought they were exploring the wilderness, where no one had gone before, but everywhere they went, they found Indian trails. After the expedition, everything changed for Indian people."

Laura beckoned the waitress. She waited until the woman had refilled the mugs with boiling water, fished a couple more tea bags from her apron pocket, and turned way. Then she said, "Okay, a hundred years ago Shoshones thought Sacajawea betrayed her people. But for Godsakes, Vicky, this is now."

"Traditions live on," Vicky said. "Sacajawea stepped ahead of the men; she did something outstanding. She acted like a chief and made her husband look like a fool." *You goin' off to Denver to make yourself into a* ho:xyu' wu:ne'n. The grandmothers' voices in her head now. *You think you're better'n Ben?*

"Toussaint Charbonneau was a fool." Laura swished a new tea bag into her cup. Steam wrapped around her thin fingers like a glove. "The Lewis and Clark journals make that very clear. Sacajawea was smarter and cleverer. She knew what to do in emergencies. She was the one who saved the expedition's scientific instruments when they washed into the Missouri River, not Toussaint." She hesitated, as if a new idea had overtaken her. "Maybe that's why he beat her," she said, almost to herself.

Vicky closed her eyes against the image. The young Indian woman, an infant on her back, the husband's raised fists. Did nothing change? Was the past always part of the present? She looked at the woman on the other side of the table. "What makes you so certain someone named Toussaint has the memoirs?"

Laura opened the journal again and flipped rapidly through the pages. "Here's what Charlotte wrote on November sixteenth, the day she disappeared. 'Toussaint called this morning. The elders have agreed to allow me to use Sacajawea's memoirs. He'll bring them this evening. We're going to dinner to celebrate. This is the most important day of my life.'"

A glance up. "The day I hold the memoirs in my hand will be the most important in my life," Laura said, then began paging backward through the journal. "Here are the names of the elders Charlotte interviewed. One of them may know Toussaint. Mary Whiteman."

"She's been dead almost twenty years."

A stricken look came into the other woman's expression. The bruise seemed to darken. "James Silver."

Vicky shook her head. "I'm sorry."

"Florence Rain."

"She was buried a month ago."

Laura dropped back against the booth, the journal limp in her hand. "I should've come to the reservation last summer when I got the manuscript. I should've finished the biography by now. What am I going to do?"

"Perhaps you could talk to Florence's daughter—Theresa Redwing."

"Her daughter." Laura repeated the words and stared blankly across the café. "I could have talked to Florence herself last summer. So much is lost with each generation." After a moment she brought her eyes back. "Could you arrange an interview?"

Vicky tipped her mug back and forth, watching the thin brown liquid roll up the sides. She regretted making the suggestion, and yet—Laura was so determined, so desperate. "Sacajawea was Shoshone," she began, searching for a way to explain how the past had melded into the present. "I'm Arapaho.

Our people were enemies in the Old Time. We share the reservation because the government thought it was a good idea. We try to make it work, but that doesn't mean we love each other. I very much doubt I could arrange anything with a Shoshone grandmother."

Pinpricks of panic flared in the other woman's eyes, and Vicky hurried on: "There's someone who can help you. John O'Malley, the pastor at St. Francis Mission."

"A priest?"

"And an historian, Laura. You'll speak the same language. All the elders trust him. I was planning to stop by the mission this afternoon to talk to him about something else. Why don't you come along? I'll introduce you."

Laura's shoulders relaxed. "I feel a lot better," she said.

"Do you?" Vicky held the other woman's gaze. "Why didn't you come here in the summer? What's going on?"

"You know, lectures, meetings, the usual . . ." Laura shrugged.

"Is this usual?" Vicky gestured toward the other woman's cheekbone.

A thin hand flew to the bruise and covered it. "I walked into a door some time ago."

"I'm on the board of the Eagle Shelter for victims of domestic abuse," Vicky said. "We see a lot of women who walk into doors."

"I wouldn't expect you to understand." Laura

gathered her coat, plunging both arms into the sleeves. A cuff brushed against her mug, sending it wobbling across the table. "Let's go see that mission priest."

"I used to walk into doors myself." Vicky reached out to steady the mug.

Laura froze, coat bunched around her shoulders, collar tucked inside. "You never told me that's the reason you left your husband."

Vicky stopped herself from saying that she and Ben were trying to work things out again. She turned toward the window and stared at the passing traffic a moment, the two businessmen with down jackets pulled over their suits moving along the sidewalk, heads thrust into the wind. The loud clack of dishes, a laugh somewhere, filled the quiet.

"I haven't told anyone either," Laura said finally. "I'm a professor, for Godsakes, and Toby's on the English faculty. You've probably heard of him. Toby Becker? He wrote *Time Gifts*."

Vicky shook her head.

"He's a great writer, I give him that. At least his male characters are sensitive and rational and . . ." She hesitated. "Not brutal."

"How long did the beatings last?"

Laura's jaw was working silently. "I was in love with him," she said finally, as if that fact answered the question. "He was the most brilliant, handsome, and charming man I've ever been involved with. Tall and muscular, with thick, curly brown hair and eyes as blue as the sky. He's almost perfect." She swa-

35

lowed and glanced away. "After the last time—two weeks ago—I moved back into my old apartment. It was hard, Vicky. People can change. I kept hoping Toby would change."

Vicky nodded. How often had some woman sat in her office, rubbing a black eye, dabbing at a bruised face, saying, I *don't want a divorce, Vicky. He's gonna change*. Just this morning, Alva Running Bull had told her the same thing. Lester was gonna change. And she, herself, hoping Ben had changed, wondering . . .

"He doesn't want to let me go," Laura said, her voice flat. "He's been calling ever since I left, sometimes four and five times a night. I think he was following me before I came here."

"Did you get a restraining order?" Vicky heard the false note of confidence in her own voice, as if a restraining order ever stopped a batterer.

"A restraining order?" Laura said, her tone sharp with incredulity. "I don't want anyone to know. What would people think? I decided to take off for a couple weeks, come here and finish the biography. One of my colleagues is covering my classes. No one thought anything about my leaving now. They know I've been trying to work on the biography. I've taken a room at the Mountain House."

"Did you tell anyone where you're staying?" Vicky asked, making an effort to conceal the uneasiness coming over her.

"The department chair," Laura said haltingly. "I had to tell him, in case he had to get ahold of me about next semester's schedule. I asked him not to tell anyone else." She shrugged, as if to brush away her own uneasiness. "By the time I get back to Boulder, Toby will have found someone else, I'm sure, probably one of the grad students who used to call the apartment all the time."

Laura stacked the manuscript and journal back into the folder, then closed the flap. "How did you do it?" she asked.

"Do what?" Vicky had slid across the booth, her black bag in one hand, and was about to get to her feet.

"Get away from the man who made you walk into doors."

Vicky didn't say anything. She felt like a reluctant witness in the courtroom, composing some kind of acceptable explanation.

"Don't tell me you've gone back to him!" Laura said, incredulity edging her voice.

"We have two grown kids, Lucas and Susan," Vicky began, groping for the words, the logic behind the decision. *The kids need a family, Vicky.* "They're in Los Angeles, but if Ben and I are together—if things are better—they'll move back. We're Arapaho, Laura. We want our family close by." Explaining. Explaining. She sounded like the women in her office, the women at the Eagle Shelter. She was *not* one of them.

"Well, we're both like Sacajawea, aren't we," Laura said after a moment. It was a statement.

"What do you mean?"

37

"We have our reasons for staying. Sacajawea stayed with Toussaint."

"She was an Indian woman who lived two hundred years ago. She didn't have any choice."

"Oh, you're wrong, Vicky. She could have left him when the expedition reached the Shoshones. Her own brother, Cameahwait, was the chief. He would have protected her. But she stayed until. . ." Laura paused. Suddenly she picked up her folder and bag and rose from the booth. "Shouldn't we go over to the mission?"

Vicky got to her feet and faced her friend. "Until what?"

"Until Toussaint nearly killed her."

⇛ 4 ⇚

Flecks of moisture spattered the windshield as FatherJohn drove the old Toyota pickup west across the reservation under a sky of satiny gray. Seventeen-Mile Road stretched ahead, a ribbon of asphalt that ran into the hazy clouds falling down the slopes of the Wind River Mountains. It was trying to snow. The music of *Idomeneo* rose from the tape player beside him—sounds of loss and impossible vows and hopeful journeys. He pushed the off button, leaving only the sound of the tires crunching gravel as he turned into the parking lot in front of the senior citizens' center. He passed the pickups angled at the curb, stopped a few feet from the front door, and checked his watch. Almost nine-thirty. Thirty minutes late.

Howard Elkman, one of the Arapaho elders, had called yesterday. A gravelly voice: Could he come by for a talk? About nine tomorrow? Father John had been half expecting the call. The moccasin telegraph was probably loaded down with news of the skeleton buried by the river, and an article had run in yesterday's *Gazette*. The elders would be concerned.

He didn't know any more about the skeleton than he had when he found it. He'd met two Wind River police officers at the site, and by the time he'd left, there had been a crowd milling about: a couple of other officers, Art Banner, the police chief, and Ted Gianelli, the local FBI agent. An unexplained death on the reservation fell under the agent's jurisdiction. He'd called Gianelli yesterday, after Howard had called. Nothing yet, the agent had said. "Let you know soon's we get the lab reports."

Now he hurried up the sidewalk and gave the front door a hard pull. There was a warm, moist fog of stale coffee and cigarette smoke inside the meeting hall. Elders and grandmothers were scattered about the tables, metal pitchers and mugs arrayed in front of them. A window on the far wall framed an expanse of snow-tipped plains and buttes and gray sky.

"Hey, Father." Howard Elkman rose from the table across the hall, waving both arms. He had the rough-edged voice of the outdoors. Roger Bancroft and Elton Knows-His-Horse were seated across from him. Father John started over.

"Please sit down, Grandfather," he said, taking Howard's arm and easing him back onto the metal chair. Then he shook his hand. Howard's grip was strong and confident. He was probably in his eighties, Father John guessed, with white hair that hung in two thick braids down the front of his red wool shirt and the hooded eyes of a man used to staring into the far distances.

Father John reached across the table and shook hands with the other elders. Also in their eighties, most likely, but it was hard to tell. A lifetime spent outdoors could age a man, and at the same time make him seem fit and strong. Like Howard, they had the wiry build of cowboys who could mount a pony on the run, and there was a nervous, contained energy in the way they sat, square-shouldered with heads tilted back. Steam curled from the mugs encircled by the rough, brown hands. Elton peered at him over the top of rimless glasses.

"Sorry I'm late," he said.

"You runnin' on Indian time now, Father?" There was amusement in Howard's tone.

"When in Rome . . ." Father John tossed his cowboy hat and jacket on a vacant chair. He was thinking that Indian time made a lot of sense. Things didn't take place until everyone was ready, and he hadn't been ready for the meeting until now. His phone had started ringing at eight o'clock—at least ten calls: Was he leaving St. Francis? Why did he have to go? Yes, to the first question. He'd ignored the other. He hadn't found the answer.

He sat down next to Howard, who had picked up the metal pitcher and poured steaming coffee into a mug, which he shoved along the table toward him. "This'll curl your toes," he said.

Father John took a sip. The coffee was bitter, but hot, and he still felt chilled by the November cold. The elder talked on—winter was coming, gonna be lotta snow and cold this year, bones already aching. The other men joined in—Roger saying he was gonna get the roof fixed so he could stay home, Elton telling him he'd better get his old truck fixed so he could go places. Preliminaries, Father John knew. A polite prelude to stating the reason they'd asked him here.

After a few minutes—Father John had drained half of the mug—Howard fixed his gaze on the men across the table, as if he'd suddenly spotted a couple of warriors riding over the crest of a hill. "We wanted to ask you about that skeleton your dog dug up," he said.

Father John understood. If the skeleton was an ancestor, it shouldn't have been disturbed. The elders were traditionals: *ne'3 ne:teyou' u:wut*. They clung to the Indian religion and the old ways. Still, he often looked out over the congregation on Sunday mornings and found the three men in a back pew, heads bent in prayer. "You gotta pray all the time," Howard told him once. "You can't slack off."

"I doubt it's an ancestor," he said, hoping to allay their fears.

"You know for sure?" Roger leaned toward him.

He had to admit that he didn't. It was his own theory. Something about the bones had seemed so—new. "Ted Gianelli's in charge of the investigation," he said. "He'll have a report soon. I trust him."

"Well, you're a white man." Roger again. " 'Course you trust him."

"We want those bones back so we can bury 'em and give 'em the right blessings so the Creator'll take good care of 'em." Elton stared over the glasses riding partway down his nose. "We don't want 'em desecrated and left to rot on some shelf."

"I'm sure Gianelli will release them as soon as he makes an identification," Father John said.

"Hold on." Howard raised his hand. "We don't want nobody poking and hacking at the bones trying to identify them. You can't identify an ancestor."

Roger slammed down his mug. Drops of coffee splashed over his brown hand and dotted the cuff of his light blue Western shirt. "The fed's never gonna release 'em. Soon's white people get a hold of Indian bones, they wanna study 'em. They don't like it much when we start jumpin' up and down, demanding to get the bones back. So I figure some bones show up, they're gonna say they come from modern times. That way the tribe won't cause trouble, and they can do their studies."

Howard scooted his chair toward him. "We been talking," he said. "We want you to get the skeleton back with the people, where it belongs."

Father John drew in a long breath. "Look," he began, searching for the words. What they expected was impossible; he could only let them down. Yet they trusted him. He wondered if his superior, his fellow Jesuits, would ever really trust him again. He said, "The fed has his job to do. He has to let the lab determine if the skeleton's ancient or from the present time. Nothing I could say will change that."

The elders were quiet. Father John realized the conversations around them had died back. The air was thick with tension. "You explain to the agent what we say," Howard said finally.

"I'll do my best." Father John got to his feet and grabbed his jacket and hat.

"You leavin' the res, Father?" Howard asked.

"Not before I talk to Gianelli."

"I mean next week. We don't like the news we been hearing on the telegraph." The other men were nodding in unison.

"I don't like it much either."

"Then why you goin'?"

Here it was, the question that had been running through his head ever since the provincial had called. "I've been here almost eight years," he started to explain, then gave it up. It was complicated. "My boss has found a new pastor for St. Francis. He'll be here any day." The man's belongings had already arrived, several neatly taped cartons that he'd put in the extra bedroom upstairs.

"Kevin McBride's the new man's name." Father John hurried on. And they would accept him, he was thinking. Just as they had accepted *him*. An alcoholic trying to recover, fresh from treatment, with the thirst still upon him.

"Another Irishman?" Howard's eyebrows rose in mock incredulity that the powers that be could impose such a penance upon them. He shot a glance at the men across the table. "You hear anything about the people askin' for a new pastor? Maybe it's time we had a talk with the boss."

Father John tasted the backwash of coffee in his throat. A call from the elders and the provincial would pull him out of St. Francis tomorrow. Forming attachments wasn't part of his job description. He was to remain free and independent, a solitary man ready to go anywhere, at any time, with no backward glances. "I'll be here until Tuesday of next week," he said hurriedly, an awkward attempt, he knew, to forestall any telephone calls. He had ten more days here and he wanted every moment of time he had left. "I'll call you as soon as I talk to Gianelli."

He could feel the elders' eyes on him as he started across the hall, shrugging into his jacket as he went, squaring the cowboy hat on his head, nodding to the upturned faces of the other elders. Still watching as he let himself out the door.

It was snowing lightly, and Seventeen Mile Road

disappeared into the clouds bunching up over the plains. The Toyota felt like the inside of an icebox. Father John jiggled the heater knob, trying to coax more than the occasional promise of warmth from the vents. He'd replaced Mozart with Puccini—*La Bohème*—as if the tender, melodious music could compensate for the cold.

He banked around a curve, tires skittering on the asphalt. As he slowed for the turn into St Francis Mission, the roar of an engine, like a truck grinding up a mountain, cut through "Che gelida manina." Suddenly a motorcycle swung in front of him, bike and rider a perfectly harmonious unit. He stepped hard on the brake pedal, sending the pickup bucking toward the barrow ditch. Dead stalks of thistles and sunflowers scratched against the door as he fought to keep the tires on the asphalt. The motorcycle disappeared in the mission grounds.

≫· 5 ·≪

Father John followed the tracks in the thin snow on Circle Drive. Past the yellow stucco administration building, past the church with the white steeple riding in the clouds, past the old school building that was now the Arapaho Museum. He pulled up in front of the two-story, redbrick residence, next to a black Harley-Davidson, moisture glistening on the chrome.

The rider, encased in black leather with a black

45

helmet encircling his head, was in the process of swinging one leg over the bike. He jumped to his feet, then began rolling his shoulders, boots planted a couple of feet apart, arms stretched outward, like a large, grounded bird trying to take to the sky. Father John got out of the pickup and walked over. "Can I help you?" he asked.

The biker dropped his arms, then reached up and pulled off the helmet. Snow peppered the dark hair flattened about his head. "You wouldn't know where I can find Father O'Malley, would you?" He cradled the helmet under one arm.

"You found him."

The other man bounded forward, right hand extended, his gaze traveling over Father John: the cowboy hat and jacket, the blue jeans, the boots. "Kevin McBride," he said. "I wasn't expecting a cowboy."

"I wasn't expecting a biker." His replacement, Father John realized, the new pastor of St. Francis Mission, probably still in his thirties—ten years younger than he was—with a doctorate in anthropology. Kevin McBride stood close to six feet and had the look of a man used to regular workouts in a gym, although it occurred to Father John that the leather jacket and trousers could give a false impression of well-defined muscles. He had the laughing blue eyes and open, handsome face of the Irish. A familiar face, Father John thought. The man might have been one of his own relatives, or a neighbor back in Boston. His smile revealed a row of perfect white teeth.

"Just got here from the East," Kevin McBride was saying. His gaze shifted to the bike, and he stepped over, drawn by the machine, and began running his glove over the shiny black fender. "Rode this beauty all the way from New York. Just me and the road and the wind in my face. Man, what a sensation. Got to the middle of Nebraska before a blizzard grounded me, so I spent a couple days on a farm. Nice house. A bit like a bed-and-breakfast with lunch and dinner thrown in. Had a chance to interview the family about life on a modern-day farm."

He glanced away, smiling at the memory, and Father John wondered if everyone Kevin McBride encountered was an opportunity for anthropological scrutiny.

The other priest removed his gloves and began flicking the snow from the front of his leather jacket. "Looks like I got here ahead of another blizzard." His eyes were still roaming around the buildings circling the grounds and, beyond, the plains lost in snow and clouds. "It must get lonely here."

"No more than other places," Father John said. Less than some, he thought. As he followed the other priest up the walk, boots snapping against the snow, he assured him that his things had arrived safely and were in an upstairs bedroom. "Elena probably has lunch ready," he said.

"Elena?" Father Kevin turned around, curiosity flashing in the blue eyes.

"The housekeeper," Father John said. Did the

man think he kept a concubine? "She's been here thirty years or more. Does the cooking, looks after the house." He walked up the steps to the stoop and opened the door, ushering the other priest inside. "Truth is, she pretty much runs things around here."

The odor of simmering chicken floated from the kitchen at the end of the hallway. There were the sounds of water cascading out of a faucet and pipes groaning beneath the floorboards, so familiar, he thought, that he would probably hear them after he'd left. He hung the other priest's leather jacket over the coat tree and draped his own beside it, then tossed his cowboy hat onto the bench next to the helmet.

Elena appeared in the doorway to the kitchen, wiping her hands on the white apron draped from her neck. She stood just over five feet tall, part Arapaho, part Cheyenne, with the cushioned build of a woman who had borne and nursed eight children. The kitchen light glinted in the gray curls tightened around her head. Her face was in shadows.

"Meet the new priest," Father John said. He'd meant to say pastor.

Father Kevin was already striding down the hallway. "Kevin McBride," he said, taking her hand. "You must be Elena."

The housekeeper stared up at him as if she were trying to place him in some category: trustworthy, not trustworthy. Then she moved backward, managing to pull her hand free.

"I got some chicken sandwiches," she said, peering past the new priest toward Father John.

They sat across from each other at the oak table. Father John washed down bites of sandwich with gulps of Elena's fresh coffee as Kevin went on about the ride from New York, gliding along the highways nose to nose with the best sports cars, the most determined semis. Elena moved between the stove and the refrigerator, preparing chili for dinner. The moist kitchen air was now thick with the smell of onions and seared hamburger and hot chilis.

Two things he'd always known he would do, the other priest said. Well, three if you counted riding a Harley. Yes, he'd always wanted to ride a Harley. He munched thoughtfully on a bite of sandwich for a minute. And he'd known he would be a priest and an anthropologist. He was always interested in ancient people. A bit like historians, huh? He gave a long glance in Father John's direction. You had to love the past to be a historian, wasn't that true?

It was true. Father John had nodded and taken another sip of coffee. Kevin hurried on. He intended to make the most of his stay here. Six years? He wasn't sure he'd be around that long. As a matter of fact, he doubted it. He'd probably return to teaching before that. But there was a book in this assignment. Oh, yes, indeed. He intended to interview as many of the old Arapahos as possible. See how the Arapaho traditions have been transposed into the present. He had a new, state-of-the-art tape recorder that could pick up a pin dropping across a large hall. So small no one realized it was there. Never inhibited an interview.

"What about you, John?" The other priest lifted up his mug and held it in front of his mouth. "You do any writing on the history of the Arapahos?"

Father John laughed. He couldn't imagine when he might have found the time. There wasn't enough time to answer the letters stacked on his desk.

Suddenly the other priest swung toward Elena, as if he'd just realized she was there. "Were you born on the reservation?" he said to the woman's back.

The housekeeper turned and looked at Father John. "I expect so," she said tentatively. It was impolite to ask personal questions.

"Wonderful." Father Kevin gave a series of nods, as if he'd just confirmed an unexpected gift. "A primary source right here under the roof. I'll want to learn all about your life. Everything you can remember. And don't worry. This house is much too large for you to take care of alone." His gaze took in the kitchen and the hallway. "First thing I'm going to do is hire someone to help you."

He pushed back from the table and announced that he intended to unpack his boxes, make sure the tape recorder and computer had arrived in good condition. Then he was going to stroll about the mission. "Might as well get familiar with my domain," he said, a glint of mischief in his eyes.

What's he talking about?" Elena plopped down in

the vacant chair. The sounds of the other priest's footsteps on the stairs echoed down the hallway.

"He'll probably make some changes," Father John said. "He's the new pastor." The words sounded strange, unreal, like a new phrase interjected into an old melody. He wished he disliked the man: it would be easier. But he didn't dislike Kevin McBride. There was something infectious about the man's energy and enthusiasm. He'd have to learn the ways of the Arapaho, but they would teach him, just as they'd taught *him*. The new pastor was going to work out just fine. Father John felt as if a stone had been laid on his heart. *Not my will. Thy will be done.*

"I don't want no help around here." Elena shoved Kevin's plate and mug to one side. "I don't want nobody messin' in my kitchen and gettin' the laundry all tangled up. I do just fine by myself, thank you very much. The house looks good, don't it?" A rising note of panic had come into her voice.

Father John drained the last of his coffee and got to his feet. He leaned over and patted the woman's shoulder. "Don't worry," he said. "Father Kevin hasn't seen the accounts yet. He won't be hiring anybody else."

In his study, Father John punched in the telephone number for the local FBI office in Lander. An answering machine came on the line, and he hung up. Gianelli was probably still at lunch. He decided to drive over and catch the agent as soon as he got back to the office.

❯❯· 6 ·❮❮

ather John parked in front of the two-story, red-brick building that rose into the snow swirling over Lander's main street. He switched off the tape player and hummed "Ch'ella mi creda" as he jaywalked across the street, dodging a truck. He opened the metal-framed glass door, nearly colliding with Ted Gianelli.

"I was just on my way upstairs to call you." The agent waved a slim folder. Dressed in dark slacks, starched white shirt, and paisley tie, he might have been an insurance salesman or a realtor, except for the black harness that held a holstered revolver next to his ribs. He stood just under six feet, with thick black hair, intense eyes accustomed to tracking whatever was going on around him, and the relaxed yet alert stance of the outside linebacker he'd once been with the Patriots.

"Let's go to the office," he said, starting up the stairs braced against the wall on the left. Father John followed. A familiar melody, "0 mio bambino caro," drifted through the open door off the second-floor hallway. Waving the folder like a baton, Gianelli conducted the music as they walked down the hall and into the cube-shaped office. A stereo cabinet took up most of one wall. Still conducting, he dropped into the chair behind the oblong desk and pointed a remote at the cabinet. The aria faded into the background.

"Soprano?" he asked.

This was a game they played—opera trivia. If they'd kept score over the last couple of years, Father John figured he would have won hands down, but Gianelli never gave up. The man loved competition almost as much as he loved opera.

Father John took the chair at the corner of the desk. He was on firm ground with Puccini. "You might have me," he said, shaking his head deliberately. "Could it be Renata Tebaldi?"

"Oh, you're good, John." The agent pounded his fist on the desk. "Damn good. But you can't know everything about opera. You're not even Italian." He opened the folder and lifted out a densely printed sheet of paper. "I take it you're here about the buried skeleton."

"I met with some of the elders today," Father John said. "They're worried it's one of the ancestors."

"Oh, boy." Gianelli dropped the sheet and tipped his chair back toward the window that gave out over snow blowing across the flat roofs on the other side of the street. Raising his hand, he loosened the knot of his tie. Wisps of black hair poked around the white cuffs of his shirt. "I was afraid of this. Tribes all over the country are raising a ruckus whenever bones are found on what they call their ancestral homelands, which could be anywhere. They're stopping scientific investigations into ancient peoples on this continent."

"Can you blame them?"

"Please, John." Gianelli ran a finger inside his

collar. "Spare me the 'how would you like it if they dissected your grandmother and paraded George Washington's remains through the reservation?' routine." He picked up the sheet and started reading. "Shape of skull consistent with Caucasian female. Small supraorbital brow ridge and mastoid processes. Pelvic bones show no evidence of postpartum pits or a preauricular sulcus. Age, mid-twenties to mid-thirties. Permanent dentition, including three molars, in occlusion. Basioccipital suture is fused, medial clavicles are fused, almost no fusion of endocranial sutures. Hiking boots at site manufactured between 1974 and 1979." He raised his eyes, as if to emphasize the point, then looked back at the sheet. "Levi rivets from blue jeans, same time frame."

The agent slipped the sheet into the folder. "This is no ancestor. You found the body of a woman who was buried twenty, twenty-five years ago."

"How did she die?"

"I'm getting to that." Gianelli removed another printed sheet. "Probable cause of death, perimortem fracture of the right temporal, with edges of a portion of the fracture bent. Also incomplete fracture of right zygomatic bone." He glanced up. "That's the cheekbone." Reading again: "One horizontal fracture in the cranial vault radiating from point of impact above left ear. Another strike to the left supraorbital and left zygomatic bone. Jaw fracture. Parry fractures of both arms and multiple rib fractures. Death consistent with traumatic fall or"—

he paused—"homicide." He dropped the sheet. "It's homicide, John. People who fall down don't end up in shallow graves down by the river."

Father John didn't say anything. Outside the window, the snow was falling steadily. The music of *Manon Lescaut* softly enveloped the office: "In quelle trine morbide." He said, "When will you have an ID?"

Gianelli's fingers tapped out a rhythm against the sheet. "You want the truth? Maybe never. These kinds of cases are the hardest to solve. We're running a check on people reported missing in the late seventies, but the woman could be from anywhere. It'll take a while to find possible matches. Even if we get lucky and come up with a lead, we may never track down the perpetrator after so much time. So you see . . ."

"She's not a top priority." Father John finished the sentence.

"I didn't say that. She's been dead a long time."

"I'm sure her family wants to know what happened to her."

"You don't have to tell me my job." Gianelli glanced away, then brought his eyes back. "Look, I've got four daughters. You think I like the idea of a world where this could happen to one of them? I'm going to do my best to solve this, John, but it might not be enough."

Father John got to his feet. "I'll let the elders know about the report. They'll still want the woman to have a proper burial, even if she isn't an ancestor or one of the people. Frankly, so do 1. If you get the ID in the next ten days, give me a call." He put on his cowboy hat and started for the door.

"Next ten days? What're you talking about?" Gianelli walked around the desk, blocking his way.

"Doesn't the moccasin telegraph reach Lander?"

"Yeah, all the time. I hear everything those Indians think I oughta know. If they don't want me to know it, I don't hear it. You going on vacation?"

"I'm going to Marquette University to finish up a doctorate and teach history." Father John had an odd sense that he was talking about someone else, someone he didn't even know. "The new pastor's already here."

"What?" Gianelli looked stunned, as if a tailback had just turned the corner on him. "They can't send you away. The people need you here, John. I need you to run interference from time to time. You tell that to whoever's in charge."

"The provincial."

"Yeah, you tell him."

"I've already mentioned it." Father John walked around the man and opened the door. "It didn't do any good," he said as he stepped into the hallway.

The snow was heavier as Father John drove north through Lander. It clung to the asphalt unfurling ahead and blew through the branches of the ponderosas. He crossed the reservation under a steel-gray sky and turned into the mission. As he came around Circle Drive, he saw Vicky's Bronco parked in front of the Arapaho Museum next to a blue SAAB that he didn't recognize, but visitors were always dropping by the museum. He felt his spirits lift. It had been two months since he'd seen Vicky. She hadn't called, and there had been no legitimate reason to call her. He parked next to the Bronco and hurried up the steps.

⋙· 7 ·⋘

A murmur of conversation drifted through the silence of the old school building, bouncing against the glass-fronted cases with Arapaho artifacts: painted parfleches, beaded moccasins, deerskin dresses, an Arapaho ledger book.

He followed the voices down the corridor to the library in what had once been a classroom. Vicky was at one of the rectangular tables that had replaced the ink-hole desks. Across from her, huddling inside a white coat, a small, blond woman with the blanched complexion of someone who spent too much time under fluorescent lights. A large brown folder lay on the table in front of her. Standing by a stack of cartons next to the row of metal shelves was Lindy Meadows, the Arapaho woman Vicky had helped him talk into taking the job as museum curator.

"John. We've been waiting for you." Vicky glanced up. The slim brown hands were clasped on the table, fingers laced together. The ceiling light shone in her black hair, which fell loosely around the collar of her blue blouse. There was a faint blush in her cheeks, a hint of red in her lips. Her eyes narrowed with intensity the way they always did when she had something important on her mind. It surprised him. There was so little he had forgotten about her.

"My friend Laura Simmons." A nod toward the blond woman across the table. "Laura teaches Western history at the University of Colorado. Lindy and I were just telling her about you."

"I wouldn't believe any of it," he said, shaking the blond woman's hand. He realized with a start that the dark bruise on the woman's cheek was the size of a fist.

"I'd say the museum speaks well enough for you, Father." She gave him a nervous smile and turned away from his gaze.

Vicky went on, explaining that her friend was here to research a biography of Sacajawea.

"How can we help you?" Father John swung a chair over and sat down at the end of the table.

"I've been telling her about our collections." Lindy thumped one of the cartons, as if she were leading a spelling drill. She might have come with the building, he thought, one of the teachers a hundred years ago, dressed in a white blouse and navy skirt, black hair pulled into a knot at the back of her head. She had the dark complexion and eyes of the Arapaho, and the businesslike manner. He hadn't worried about the museum since she'd taken over.

She gave the cartons another thump. She was still shelving and cataloging documents. Some oral histories here, she knew. Letters from Arapaho elders in the early 1900s that might refer to Sacajawea. No guarantees, but she'd try to locate them.

"I'd be very grateful." Laura kept her face tilted sideways. The bruise might have been a shadow. "You never know where an important document might turn up." A hint of anticipation and excitement worked into her voice.

Father John smiled. He'd almost forgotten the surge of joy at the smallest possibility of finding something new in the past. This was why he'd fought for the museum—gone to the mat with the provincial—to help the Arapahos preserve their own past so that scholars like Laura Simmons could understand what had really happened.

"There's something else." Vicky turned toward him. "There could be some evidence on the res that proves that the old woman who died here was the real Sacajawea."

Father John didn't say anything for a moment. He'd heard the stories about such evidence as long as he'd been here—the Jefferson Medal given to Sacajawea, which the old woman supposedly gave to her son, Baptiste. He'd never heard that any evidence had been found. "Sometimes"—he hesitated, then plunged on—"there's a powerful will to believe." He'd seen it many times among his colleagues—the insistence that one theory or another must be true, regardless of contradictory evidence.

"What do you believe, John?" Vicky met his gaze. She was always testing him, he knew. Was he really for the people? Or just another white man pretending that the truth of the past was important? The room was quiet, the other women watching him, too. He said, "When I came here I agreed with historians that Sacajawea died in 1812. William Clark himself believed she'd died."

"And now?" Vicky persisted. He might have been a defendant and she the prosecutor.

Now, he thought, now there were the stories, passed down among both the Shoshones and the Arapahos, stories told by a woman buried in the Shoshone cemetery. He said, "The woman here knew things about the expedition that only someone who'd been part of it could have known."

"Exactly." Laura seemed to jump in her chair. Her hands fluttered in the air. "My colleagues—our colleagues"—she lifted her chin—"refuse to give oral histories the same importance as documentary evidence. Well, I intend to present them with a document they can't ignore. Sacajawea's own memoirs." The words seemed to hang in the silence a moment. "The memoirs are on the reservation somewhere," she said.

Lindy spoke up: "If it's true, it would be an incredible find."

An incredible find indeed, Father John thought. One of the most important in American history—an Indian woman's own account of the great American expedition. "What makes you think they're here?"

Laura's expression dissolved into what passed for a smile. She sat back, drew in a breath, then began explaining. Another historian—Charlotte Allen—had discovered the memoirs twenty years ago. Someone named Toussaint knows where they are.

"Toussaint?" he said. "I've never met anyone by that name."

"Theresa Redwing may know who he is," Vicky said. "Her mother was one of the elders who gave Charlotte Allen permission to publish the memoirs. Laura's hoping the Shoshones will extend her the same courtesy." She leaned toward him. "Would you ask Theresa to talk to her? You can explain the importance of writing the truth about the past."

"You sound like a historian," Father John said.

Vicky laughed, a soft, rippling sound. A relaxed look of familiarity came into her eyes. "Maybe I've been around historians too long."

"I don't know Theresa Redwing very well." He'd met the woman at celebrations and powwows. She was a respected Shoshone elder, but she wasn't one of his parishioners.

"The elders trust you," Vicky persisted.

Father John glanced at the blond woman. A friend, Vicky had said. She didn't have many friends, it seemed. Woman Alone, the grandmothers called her. *He sei ci nihi.* A few relatives scattered about the res, two kids in Los Angeles, an ex-husband . . . He pushed the thought away. Laura Simmons was her friend, and Vicky had asked him to help. He had always found it difficult to turn her down.

"I'll stop by and have a talk with Theresa," he said to Laura.

61

The woman gave him a thin smile, a crack in the pale face. Then she began rummaging in the folder. She plucked out a legal-size notepad and pen, scribbled something, and tore off three triangles of paper. She handed them around. "You can reach me at this number," she said. "The Mountain House in Lander."

Then she was on her feet, pulling on the white coat, fingering the buttons, nodding at the curator. "You'll call me the minute you locate the letters?" she asked, gripping the folder and fixing her tan bag over one shoulder.

Lindy promised. A day or two, and she should have them.

"Still some time to visit the Shoshone cultural center," Laura said, inspecting the gold watch on her wrist. "You never know, Sacajawea's memoirs could be on a shelf somewhere."

The remark brought another jolt of memory. There was always hope—Father John knew it well—that other historians had missed something important, something in plain view on a shelf somewhere.

"I'll call you, Vicky." Laura was at the door now, and in a moment she was gone, leaving only the shush of her footsteps fading in the hallway, the whack of the front door trembling through the floorboards.

Vicky turned to him. "There's something I'd like to talk to you about."

"I can put on a pot of coffee in the office," he said.

⇝ 8 ⇜

"What about the skeleton?" Vicky glanced up at him as they walked along Circle Drive, cutting fresh tracks in the membrane of snow on the asphalt. The wind sprinkled white flecks in her hair. She was wearing a long, black coat that she held closed with one hand. Her briefcase swung from the other, and the strap of the familiar black bag was fixed over one shoulder. She moved with an easy naturalness into the space ahead, displacing the emptiness. "Any chance it's ancient?"

"The elders think so," Father John said. "They asked me to check with Gianelli." This wasn't what she wanted to talk to him about. She could have brought up the skeleton back at the museum.

Vicky stopped and threw her head back. She gave a little shiver of cold. "The elders asked you?" Then, as if she would have liked to recall the words, she said, "See how they respect you, John? You're the one they trust to find the truth." She started walking again, and he stayed in step, not knowing what to say. The elders had turned to him, a white man. They should have asked her.

Vicky linked her arm in his. "Of course they'd call you. They trust you, John, and you and Gianelli are friends." She was quiet as they passed the church, the alley leading to Eagle Hall and the guest house. "I wish they'd called me," she said finally.

"I'm sorry, Vicky." He could feel the light pressure of her hand through the sleeve of his wool jacket.

"It's not your fault you're the one they trust," she said as they walked up the icy steps in front of the administration building. He held the heavy wooden door and waited for her to step inside, acutely aware of the place on his arm where her hand had rested.

He followed her into his office on the right and flipped the switch, displacing the gray afternoon with a tungsten bright light that flooded over the desk and the two chairs arranged along one wall. Vicky sank into one of the chairs. He could feel her eyes on him as he picked up the glass coffeepot from the little metal stand next to the door. He went in search of water from the sink down the hall.

"I came back home to help my people," she said when he returned. Her coat was arranged around the chair behind her. "How naive and stupid it sounds. Indian lawyer wants to help her people! I'm just a woman who had the temerity to put herself forward. Divorce her husband and become a lawyer, like a man. My people don't know which category to put me in—wife, mother, lawyer. I don't really belong anywhere."

Father John took off his jacket, hooked it on the coat tree, and sat at the edge of the desk, facing her. "It takes time, Vicky. Old traditions are slow to change."

She lifted one hand and brushed back a small strand of hair that had fallen over her forehead. "What does Gianelli say?" she asked, bringing the subject back to the skeleton. A kind of uncertainty showed in her eyes.

He said, "A Caucasian woman, somewhere between the mid-twenties and mid-thirties. She was buried twenty to twenty-five years ago."

Vicky stared at him, eyes opened wide in astonishment. "Charlotte Allen disappeared on the reservation twenty years ago."

In the quiet, the sound of dripping coffee. "What happened to her?" Father John said after a moment.

"She was hiking in the mountains. Her body was never found. Maybe she wasn't lost in the mountains after all. Maybe she'd gone walking along the river, fell down, knocked herself unconscious—"

"The woman was murdered, Vicky. Her skull was fractured. She had a broken jaw and cheekbone, broken ribs and arms, consistent with a—"

"Beating." Vicky finished the sentence. Some of the color had drained from her face.

"What does Laura know about Charlotte Allen?"

"Not much." Vicky was shaking her head. "Charlotte's mother gave her the unfinished manuscript, as well as the journal Charlotte kept while she was here."

Father John reached back and picked up the phone. "We'd better let Gianelli know," he said, tapping out the number.

An answering machine clicked on at the other end. "You have reached the Central Wyoming offices of the Federal Bureau of Investigation." He told the machine that he had some information on the identity of the skeleton, then replaced the receiver.

Vicky had poured two mugs of coffee, set one beside him on the desk, and was cradling the other in both hands as she dropped back into her chair. "What about Laura?" she asked. "She's here to do the same research that Charlotte Allen was doing. She could be in danger."

Father John leaned over and laid a hand lightly on her arm a moment. He could feel the tenseness in her muscles beneath the silky fabric of her blouse. "Look, Vicky, let's not jump to conclusions. We don't even know that Charlotte Allen was buried in that grave." He heard his own voice, calm, logical. "Even if it turns out to be her, there's no reason to suppose that whatever happened twenty years ago had anything to do with the research."

"You don't understand, John," Vicky said. "Indian people believe the real Sacajawea is buried here, but historians have argued the matter for decades. Some of them have probably staked their professional reputations on the theory that Sacajawea died years earlier. What if someone killed Charlotte Allen to stop her from publishing the truth?"

"A lot of what-ifs, Vicky." An image of the slight, pale woman in the museum flashed in his mind: the joy in her expression at the possibility of finding something no one else knew, like the joy of an explorer coming into a place no one else had ever seen. "Gianelli will follow up on this," he said. "As soon as I hear anything, I'll call you. There's no sense in alarming Laura."

"You're probably right." Vicky shifted in her chair. "I'm worried about Alva Running Bull," she said after a moment. "I'd already drawn up the divorce papers when she and Lester started coming to you for counseling. Now she's told me to tear up the papers."

This was what she'd wanted to talk to him about. Father John picked up his mug, walked around the desk, and sat down, aware of a distance opening between them. Usually they were on the same team. He didn't like playing on opposing teams. "Alva and Lester want to make their marriage work," he began. "Divorce court isn't exactly the place where that can happen."

"He beats her. She has to leave him. Even Sacajawea left."

"Alva and Lester are both in counseling, and Lester's agreed to go to an anger management group. There's a good program in Riverton. People can change, Vicky. The grace of God can work in all of us, if we give it a chance."

"Can you imagine what it's like?" Vicky went on, as if she hadn't heard. "The man you live with every day, sleep with every night? The man you love? Can you imagine what it's like?"

"You took Ben back." It startled him, the way he'd flung the words at her, like an accusation erupting out of his own uncertainty.

Immediately he regretted stepping across the invisible line drawn around her personal life. He waited for her to rise from the chair, take her coat, and walk out of the office. If she did, he knew he would never see her again.

She remained seated, sipping thoughtfully at the coffee, her gaze somewhere on the bookshelves behind him. Silence filled the space between them. He had the feeling that often came to him in a counseling session, in the confessional, when someone was about to reveal something they had never revealed before. The moment passed. She gave him a familiar, determined look. "We're not talking about Ben and me. We're talking about Alva. Lester will kill her one day."

Father John squeezed the bridge of his nose. Dear God. Don't let it be.

"I've given Alva the telephone number of the Eagle Shelter," Vicky said. "If Lester goes on another rampage, she could be too scared or too ashamed to call. Will you encourage her to call the shelter if anything happens?"

"Of course."

Vicky set her mug on the desk and pulled her coat around her shoulders as she got to her feet, a hint of reluctance in the motion, he thought. And then he thought he was only imagining it because he didn't want their time together to end. He didn't want her to leave.

"Will you talk to Alva before you leave?" she asked. He had to readjust his thoughts to bring the reality into focus. *He* was the one leaving. "You are going away, aren't you?"

"So they tell me," he said, a steady, matter-of-fact tone. He had to look away from the regret in her eyes. It was good he was going, he told himself. It would be good to teach and study again, to fill his mind with other things, he told himself.

"When do you leave?"

He brought his gaze back to hers. "Next Tuesday. The new pastor has already arrived."

"You mean the Harley?" The hint of amusement flashed in Vicky's eyes.

"The Harley," he said.

She glanced away. "So that's it, then."

Her words gave him a sense of uneasiness. Had she been holding on to some vague hope that things might be different? He dismissed the notion. She was back with Ben. "My boss has decreed it so." He got up and walked her across the office and into the corridor. Then he remembered she'd parked in front of the museum. "I'll walk you to the Bronco," he said, turning back for his jacket.

"No," she called after him, her tone almost cheerful. "I can find my way." The sound of the door opening and closing reverberated through the thick walls.

He stepped over to the window. She was hurrying along Circle Drive, a slim figure in black, a shadow moving through the snow. He sat back at the desk and dialed Howard Elkman's number.

"Hello?" The gravelly voice on the other end.

He told the elder about the report on the skeleton.

69

"You sure the fed's telling the truth?" Howard asked.

Father John said he was sure.

There was a long pause, then: "I'll tell the other boys."

Father John had just hung up when the phone started ringing.

"Father O'Malley," he said into the receiver.

"Okay, Detective O'Malley. What do you know about the identity of the bones?" It was Gianelli.

⇒ 9 ⇐

The odor of seared meat and the sound of grease popping against metal filled the living room. Vicky closed the front door, tossed her briefcase on the sofa, and shrugged out of her coat, which she laid next to the briefcase. In the kitchen, she found Ben at the stove, a fork poised over two bloodred steaks in the frying pan. He gave her a sideways glance. "Dinner's about to be served," he said.

Vicky stood motionless at the counter that divided the kitchen from the small dining alcove. The scene was surreal, nonsensical—*ho:ho:ke:*—like a crazy dream where none of the fragments fit together. Ben Holden in the denim shirt and blue jeans and cowboy boots he wore on the Arapaho ranch, descended from warriors and Arapaho chiefs—this was the man standing in her kitchen cooking dinner. "I don't believe my eyes," she said.

Ben flipped the steaks before setting the fork on the counter and slipping an arm around her waist. He pulled her toward him. "Told you if you came back to me, I'd make dinner for you." He leaned over and kissed her neck, her cheeks, and finally her lips. His mouth was soft on hers, and she found herself struggling against the familiar rush of warmth and the urge to melt into his touch that burst through all bounds of reason, of what was sensible and orderly and right, and left her not knowing who she was or what she wanted.

She ignored the questions in his eyes as she stepped back, freeing herself. She said, "I've brought some work home to finish tonight."

Ben turned back to the steaks, disappointment outlined in the hunch of his shoulders beneath the denim shirt. "Lawyers have to eat like everybody else, don't they?"

Vicky slid two plates out of the cabinet. Then she gathered knives and forks and napkins from a drawer and carried the stack into the dining room. The phone on the counter started ringing as she set the table. She reached over and picked up the receiver just as Ben was about to grab it. "Hello," she said, sensing his eyes burning into her.

"Ben there?" The woman's voice was tentative and uncertain.

Vicky gripped the receiver hard a moment, feeling shaky at the confirmation of the old fears. Then she handed it across the counter. "One of your girlfriends," she said.

Turning toward the kitchen, Ben cupped the receiver between his neck and shoulder. "Who's this?" A long pause.

"I told you, I'll talk to you later." He wheeled around and dropped the receiver into the cradle. "One of my girlfriends? Is that what you think?"

Vicky went back to arranging the table. Knife here, fork there. Napkins folded with corners meeting precisely. Suddenly Ben was next to her. "I want an answer, Vicky," he said, taking her arm.

She moved along the table, disengaging herself. "What am I supposed to think? A woman calls you here. My secretary tells me her friend has been asking about you at the Highway Lounge."

"Who?"

"It doesn't matter."

The quiet exploded between them. After a moment he said, "What do you want of me? Do I have to swear never to talk to another woman? I deal with women all the time." He nodded toward the phone. "That was Cerise at the ranch."

"There's a woman working at the ranch?" Vicky didn't try to hide her skepticism.

"The bookkeeper, Vicky. The goddamn bookkeeper. She was calling about this month's statements. Do I have to explain every time I talk to another woman?"

Vicky blinked and looked away. In the sliding-glass doors that led to the patio outside, she could see the faintest trace of two figures—a man, a woman, and the dark space of the table between them. She had the sensation of floating backward through time. Another house, other explanations, other women. Only the glib justifications that cast her as the doubting, mistrustful wife were the same. She had known then—and she knew now: if she wanted her family together, if she wanted Susan and Lucas close by, this was the way it would be. She was no different from Alva Running Bull, willing to look away from the bleak reality hurtling toward her like an eighteen-wheeler coming down the highway. The realization gave her a sickening feeling.

She locked eyes with him again. "Can we eat?"

"Not until this is settled."

"It's settled."

He reached along the table and ran his fingers gently over her cheek, pushing back a strand of hair. "No more jealous outbursts?"

She managed a nod. Blinking hard at the tears starting behind her eyes, she sank onto the nearest chair and waited while Ben brought the steaks, a bowl of salad, and a loaf of French bread to the table.

He took the chair across from her. "Alva Running Bull come see you today?" he asked, holding out the plate of steaks, waiting while she lifted one onto her own plate.

The question caught her by surprise. Her clients, the problems they brought to the office—they were confidential. She never discussed them. Even an inadvertent slip could set the moccasin telegraph humming. Before she could say anything, Ben said,

"Lester drove out to the ranch today to see me. The man doesn't want a divorce. Neither does his wife."

Vicky had been about to take a bite of steak. She set the fork down. "That's completely inappropriate."

"You could discourage her."

"I can't discuss this."

Ben sliced a piece of meat and brought it to his mouth. After a moment he said, "Divorce is ugly business. Look what happened to us. All those years apart when we should've been a family. Kids growing up with your folks instead of with us, going off to Los Angeles, away from their own people. Whole family's scattered, just because you wanted to go down to Denver and become a—" He stopped.

"What, Ben? A white woman?" Vicky pushed her plate away. She was no longer hungry. She had never wanted to leave the reservation, had never dreamed that one day she would find the courage to walk away.

"Lester's not a bad sort," Ben went on.

"He's going to kill her." Vicky could feel her heart thumping against her ribs. She hated the man across from her at that moment for making her violate her own rules, a part of herself.

"You're exaggerating." He bit off a chunk of bread and began chewing it. A second passed, another. "He hits her once in a while." He raised both hands. "I'm not saying it's right. He shouldn't do that. But he's a good man, and they've got three kids. He's going to counseling. You could talk to Alva, tell her not to make the same mistake you made."

Vicky pushed herself to her feet, fighting to catch the breath stuck in her throat like a sharp bone she could neither swallow nor spit up. "You're saying the divorce was my fault?"

"I would've never left you." Ben threw his napkin onto the half-empty plate and stood up.

"You ran around on me. You got drunk and slapped me and pushed me down. You hit me with your fists."

"Do we have to keep going over this?"

"We've never gone over it. It's still between us."

"Well, I've spent the last two months trying to make things right. The kids'll never move back, Vicky, until they've got a family again. We should be setting a wedding date, not going on about the past. What do you want me to say? I'm sorry. I've said it a thousand times. I was drunk when I hit you."

"Does that make it okay? Should I forgive you?"

"You should forget."

"The way you have."

Ben brought one fist down hard on the table, rattling the fork against the plate. Vicky flinched and stepped back, her heart pounding in her ears.

"We both have to forget and move on," he said. His breath came in short gasps, his chest rising and falling in a rapid rhythm beneath the denim shirt. He tightened his lips into a thin line and stared at the sliding-glass doors a moment. Bringing his eyes back, he said, "I'm trying, Vicky. I want us to be a family again, the way we used to be."

"Sometimes, Ben," Vicky began, reaching for the words, struggling against the tremor in her voice, "I think it's too late, too much has happened between us. Sometimes I think there's nothing else for us."

"No, Vicky. Don't say that." He walked around the table and took her hand. Then he ran his fingers along her arm, across her shoulder, and under her chin, turning her face toward him. In the warmth of his body close to hers, the memories started to blur, melting into a half-forgotten longing and the sharp pain of her own loneliness.

"We belong together," he said, "and don't you ever for get it."

⋙ 10 ⋘

The Bingo Palace sat back from the highway, a low white structure with the look of a truncated shopping mall. The violet shadows of late afternoon spread over the parking lot that wrapped around the building. Father John slowed between rows of pickups and twenty-year-old sedans. He found a vacant space and got out, taking a minute to work the kinks out of his legs.

He'd spent the morning showing Father Kevin around the mission, giving him a tour through the files: the programs and classes, the meeting schedule. He'd also handed him the financial records—a long list of bills to be paid that would gradually work themselves off the list as donations floated in. Then they'd gone to the senior citizens' center, Kevin following on the Harley, the motorcycle roaring over Puccini. Father John introduced the other priest to the elders and grandmothers. When he left, Kevin was sitting with three elders, the miniature silver tape player in the middle of the table.

Father John had driven north on Highway 132 and stopped at Theresa Redwing's. A dark-eyed young woman had answered the door. It was Grandmother's bingo day. He'd find Theresa at the Palace.

Now he made his way past the parked vehicles to the entrance. Inside, a cloud of smoke hung over the large hall with tables arranged in front of the stage at the far end. People were scattered along one side of the tables, peering at the cards flattened in front of them. The caller sat on stage, his attention on a framed-glass box with small, white balls tumbling inside. Numbers lit up the bingo board behind him. "Under B, fourteen." The voice boomed into the microphone. "B, one four." Hands flew over the cards, quickly daubing the number.

"Wanna play, Father?" A middle-aged woman walked over, disbelief and confusion in the dark face. "Next game's a blackout. Pays real good. Mission could use the money." That was true. St. Francis could always use an infusion of funds. "I'm looking for Theresa Redwing," he said.

The woman nodded toward the gray-haired woman seated at the front table. "Always sits over there in her lucky place."

Father John waited until the blackout game had ended before making his way along the rows of tables.

"Gonna take a little break, folks." The microphone screeched back on itself. "Stand up, stretch, get yourselves a cup of good, hot coffee." People were already getting to their feet, chairs scraping the floor. Father John slid into the chair next to Theresa Redwing.

"These old eyes must be gettin' worse." The woman blinked at him through thick lenses that made her pupils seem blurred and outsized. "That you, Father John, or am I seein' ghosts? Here, let me pinch you." She reached out and pulled at his jacket sleeve.

He laughed. "I'm here, Theresa."

"Get yourself a card, then. You got the luck of the Irish."

"And it's all bad."

"So I hear." The woman kept her eyes on his. "Moccasin telegraph says you're leaving these parts."

"They want me to teach history again."

She nodded, as if it made perfect sense, his going. "You like history, don't you?"

"I like it here. History matters here."

Theresa Redwing pulled a tissue from the sleeve of her gray sweater and wiped at her nose a moment. "You hear about that history professor on the res asking a lot of questions?" For a moment he

78

wondered if she was referring to the new priest. "She was up at the cultural center yesterday afternoon, wanting to know about my ancestor Sacajawea. The director give me a call soon's she left."

He started to explain that Laura Simmons was working on a biography that another historian had begun, then stopped. The old woman already knew, by the indulgent look she was bestowing on him.

"I remember that other historian comin' 'round about twenty years ago, askin' my mother a lot of questions," she said.

"Now Laura Simmons would like to talk to you, Grandmother," he said.

"About the old stories?"

He nodded. "She believes Charlotte Allen found someone who may have Sacajawea's memoirs written in a notebook—someone named Toussaint."

Theresa Redwing sat motionless, her eyes on some point across the room. "Never heard of nobody by that name." Looking back, she said, "Why ain't they enough, Father, the old stories? Why do them white historians always gotta have something written down? The people kept Sacajawea's stories, but the historians don't care about them. They say those old people that remembered the stories didn't know what they was talkin' about. Now this Laura Simmons comes along wanting written memoirs? What difference? Memoirs wouldn't tell nothin' that the old stories don't tell."

It was true, all true, Father John thought. Historians wanted written records. Laura Simmons hadn't said anything about wanting the Shoshone stories. He drew in a long breath. "Could she come to see you, Grandmother? You could help her understand."

The woman studied her hands a long moment. "Since you're askin', Father, you tell her to call me up, and we can set up a time. But I gotta warn you, my granddaughter—her name's Hope Stockwell— has been asking for the old stories. She's working on her dissertation at the university in Laramie. She's gonna be one of them historians."

The young woman with serious eyes who had sent him to the Bingo Palace. Father John leaned back against his chair. She had seemed so young. But she was getting her doctorate. He would be in classes with kids while he finished his own doctorate.

"Hope's gonna get all the stories and records she wants," Theresa was saying, her eyes following the caller now making his way up the steps to the stage. "She come down from Sacajawea. Folks around here know she's gonna write the truth."

Father John was quiet a moment. "Are you saying the memoirs exist, Grandmother?"

"Lots of us descendants around, Father. We don't tell everything we know. Somebody might've been keeping the memoirs till the right one come along to tell the story. Hope's gonna be the one."

A shriek burst through the microphone and people began wandering back to the tables, settling into the chairs, realigning the cards. An air of expectancy and concentration settled over the hall. Father John thanked the old woman and made his way past the tables to the door.

The Toyota's headlights cast a cone of yellow into the darkness settling over the open spaces as Father John drove toward the mission, past the lights blinking in the windows of the occasional house along Seventeen Mile Road. He replayed the old woman's words in his mind. If the memoirs did exist, they would go to Hope Stockwell, a descendant of Sacajawea. It was as it should be.

And yet—he felt a stab of disappointment. Vicky had asked him to help a friend. A last favor, and he'd failed. Theresa had agreed to see Laura, it was true, but he doubted the old woman would help her. Whatever she knew about Toussaint or the memoirs, she would tell her granddaughter. Which meant that Charlotte Allen's biography would remain unfinished.

He slowed for the turn in to the mission grounds, waiting until an oncoming pickup had shot past. So many things unfinished, he thought. The programs he'd hoped to start: a social club for teenagers, a day-care center, cultural classes. And who would coach the Eagles baseball team next spring? The days had always stretched ahead into some indeterminate time when, he'd known, he would have to leave. But not yet. He needed more time. *Most priests would be glad to get out of there.* The provincial's voice again.

Well, he wasn't most priests. His replacement was already here, settled in, making the rounds, getting to know the people. But *he* was also here. He hadn't even started to pack. He resolved to have another talk with the provincial.

Father John saw the Harley leaning on the kickstand, chrome glinting under the street lamp in front of the residence. He parked in front of the administration building, took the steps two at a time, and pulled open the heavy door. Light from outdoors slanted off the portraits lining the corridor: past pastors at St. Francis Mission, staring out of wire-rimmed glasses, obedient and non-questioning, solemn in their rectitude. Had it been easier in the past, he wondered, to keep the vows?

His desk looked as if he'd just walked away. Folders and papers, stacks of messages, unopened envelopes spilling over the surface. So many things unfinished. He tossed his jacket and hat onto a side chair, sank into the cracked leather of his own chair, and drew the phone past a pile of papers. He called Vicky's office. The secretary's taped voice: "Vicky Holden's office. Please leave a message." He hit the disconnect button and tapped out her home number, surprised that he remembered it. He seldom used it.

Another answering machine, Vicky's voice this time. "Leave your name and number . . ."

"John," he said. "I've seen Theresa. Call me." As he replaced the receiver, he heard a shuffling noise on the stoop, the sound of the door opening, then the clack of footsteps in the corridor. He looked up.

Elena stood in the doorway, crushing a black purse against the front of her blue coat, anger flashing in the round face. "I quit," she said. Then she turned back into the shadowy corridor.

Father John was on his feet. He caught the housekeeper at the front door. "Wait a minute, Elena." He had a sense of what was going on. "Come in and sit down." He took her arm and led her back into the office to a side chair. Tossing his jacket and hat onto the floor, he sat down beside her. "Talk to me," he said.

The woman threw both hands into the air. The black purse slipped off her lap and sank onto his jacket. "How's he expect me to get my work done? Grocery shopping, cleaning, the laundry. And all the cooking, and you know I gotta fry some good-tasting Indian bread once in a while. How am I s'pose to get it done with his asking questions all the time? 'Sit down, Elena,' he says. 'Tell me about today's Arapaho courtship practices.' Courtship practices! What's the man goin' on about?"

"I'll talk to Father Kevin," Father John said.

"Well, you're leavin', so I'm leavin'." She gave him a look weighted with determination.

"You can't leave. The mission will fall apart without you."

"You got that right, Father." The old woman swallowed back a smile.

"Look, Elena, go home and think about it." He reached out and took one of her hands in his. "And please come back."

She started out of the chair, and he picked up her purse and handed it to her. "There isn't any dinner. I didn't get time."

"We won't starve to death."

"There's some hamburger in the fridge," she said.

He walked her to the door and returned to his desk. This wasn't right. Nothing was going the way he'd assumed it would. Everything was changing, rearranging itself in ways he hadn't imagined. Only the thirst was the same, coming on him when he least expected it, when it was the last thing he needed. He wanted a drink, that was the whole of the matter. He could taste the whiskey sliding down his throat, sense the initial control and clarity it would bring, and the joy. One drink was all he needed—

He laughed out loud at the notion, and the sound of his own voice came back to him in the quiet of the old building. He needed the entire bottle. There had never been enough whiskey to quench the thirst and ease the loneliness. *Lord, give me courage. Let me not start drinking today. Let this not be the day.*

He got up and poured a mug of the thick, black coffee stagnating at the bottom of the glass pot— coffee he'd made this morning. It was still warm, but it had passed beyond bitter to something bland and tasteless.

He sat back down and punched in the provincial's number. A man's voice, sharp and annoyed, picked up. He could picture the priest at the other end: a young Jesuit roused from a good book, a favorite television sitcom. He gave his name and asked to speak to the provincial. And then he was on hold, canned music playing in his ear.

"We have office hours, John." Bill Rutherford's voice interrupted the music. They went back a long way, he and the provincial, to their days in the seminary together. "This better be an emergency."

"Look, Bill," he began. "Things aren't working out here. I'm not ready to leave."

"What do you mean, not working out? Kevin's there, isn't he?"

"He's here."

"Good. I've made all the arrangements for you at Marquette. Everything's set. The history department's looking forward to welcoming you. Your airline ticket's in the mail."

"I want to finish my work here," Father John began. And then, the same litany of reasons: new programs to start, the church to refurbish, finances to tend to—

The provincial cut in. "We've already had this discussion. There's no sense in going over it. I believe it's time for you to leave for your own spiritual welfare. You're in the way of temptation there."

The way of temptation. Father John stared at the shadows out in the corridor, trying to formulate the logical argument. There was no logic in his desire to stay. Logic was on the provincial's side. It was time for him to return to his former life. He pushed the logic away. "I need more time here," he said.

A sigh of exasperation floated through the line.

"You're making this difficult, John. Change is in your own best interests. You'll see it's true when you're back."

Father John slammed down the receiver. *If I go back.*

The phone started ringing. He was about to answer, then decided against it. It was probably the provincial again. Still ringing as he walked around the desk and retrieved his jacket and hat from the floor. Still ringing. He reached over and picked up the receiver. "Father O'Malley," he said. Still here at St. Francis. Still a priest.

"John, I was afraid I'd missed you." It was Vicky's voice. He stepped around the desk and sat down, combing his fingers through his hair, forcing his mind onto what he'd called her about. Then he related what Theresa Redwing had said. She'd agreed to see Laura. He wasn't sure it would do any good. He told her about Hope Stockwell.

Vicky didn't say anything for a moment. He could hear the disappointment in the sound of her breathing. Finally she said, "Laura wasn't counting on anyone else looking for the same evidence, especially not a Shoshone doctoral student." She took a long breath and thanked him. He waited for her to say good-bye. "Are you all right?"

"Sure." He tightened his grip on the receiver. "Why do you ask?"

"Oh, I don't know. Just something in your voice."

"I'm fine."

In the background was the muffled whack of a

door closing, the sound of a man's voice. "I'd better go," she said quickly, and hung up.

He found the new pastor in his room upstairs at the residence, hunched over his computer. "Elena just quit," he said.

Father Kevin tapped at the keys, his eyes locked on the black lines forming and reforming across the white screen. "What're you talking about?"

"She doesn't like being interviewed."

"Oh?" Kevin swung around. "That's the reason she quit? Good heavens. This is serious, John."

"You're right about that. She takes care of everything around here."

"I mean, the woman's a walking file of incredible information. She remembers everything she's ever heard. All the old stories. Imagine! Her great-grandparents lived on the plains, roaming about, pitching villages along the streams. They passed down a lot of valuable stuff that Elena's carrying around in her head. She knows how her people adapted the old ways. It has to be recorded, John, or it'll be lost."

"It won't be lost. Elena's told her own children. She's probably told her grandchildren."

The other priest was shaking his head. "It's not the same, John. You're a historian. You know it's not the same as written records." He hesitated and glanced back at the computer screen. "I've been pushing too hard, haven't I?"

Father John didn't say anything.

"I'll call her right away. What's her number?"

Father John gave him the number. Kevin jumped up and brushed past him, heading out into the hallway. Father John followed him downstairs, where the other priest picked up the phone on the table in the entry and started dialing.

In the kitchen, Father John stared into the refrigerator, looking for a package of hamburger. It had been a while since he'd done any cooking. How hard could it be? The cajoling sound of Kevin's voice drifted from the entry. Elena would be back tomorrow, he knew. He set the hamburger on the counter and began rummaging through one of the cabinets for a frying pan. He was a good man, this new pastor. St. Francis would be in good hands. The mission would go on without John O'Malley. That was what mattered, didn't it? That was all that really mattered.

⇒· 11 ·⇐

There is no fraud in the statement which I am making to you. Fraud is not with the Indians in matters of this kind. They do not put up a story just to have it startling and out of place. What the early Indians say relative to their old stories is true and can be accepted.
— James McAdams,
  great-grandson of Sacajawea

Laura stared at the statement a moment, then set the page on the table next to the gray carton with SACAJAWEA in bold black letters on one side. Somewhere in the depths of the old house that served as the Shoshone cultural center, a furnace cranked and rattled, sending a stream of hot air through the second-floor library. A pale afternoon sky shone through the oblong windows; the fluorescent light danced on the plank floors. Two doors led to other rooms, where the records themselves were shelved.

With the exception of the director, a plump, middle-aged Shoshone woman who had introduced herself as Phyllis Manley ("And how may I help you?"), Laura was alone. The director sat at the small desk inside the door, stapling stacks of papers. *Whoosh. Kerplunk. Whoosh. Kerplunk.*

Laura shuffled through the other pages spread in front of her, like cards in a game of solitaire. Oral histories given eighty, ninety years ago by Shoshones and pioneers who had sat with Sacajawea years before and listened to her stories. She picked up one of the pages:

She said she was traveling with a large body of people in which army officers were in charge. The people became very hungry and killed some of their horses and even some of the dogs for food. —Grandma Herford

On the trip to the big waters, there was a war party against the soldiers. Sacajawea drew out her blanket and by signs she made with the blanket, the Indians knew she was friendly, and the soldiers were not molested. —James McAdams

She also mentioned many narrow escapes from

drowning in making the trip through the rapids and falls of the Snake River and the Columbia. —Finn G. Burnett

She said she had guided Clark to the Clark's fork of the Yellowstone River, where they had great difficulty in finding timber large enough to build canoes. They decided at last to make two small canoes and connect them together. With this craft they voyaged down the river. —Finn G. Burnett

Her first husband was a Frenchman. She called him Schab-a-no. He was pretty rough in his treatment of her, and she ran away after he whipped her. —James McAdams

Laura closed her eyes a moment. The images of Sacajawea blazed in her mind: a young woman, the fringed, deerskin dress, the moccasins, the black hair clipped in back, the bundle on her back, disappearing ahead, always ahead, into the wilderness.

The sound of the stapler biting into a stack of paper filled the quiet. Laura sighed. There was nothing new in the files. No sign of an old notebook—the kind in which the agent's wife would have recorded Sacajawea's memoirs. And the director had assured her she'd never heard that the memoirs had escaped the agency fire, and there was no one on the reservation named Toussaint. She was running into brick walls. Without the memoirs, she could never finish the biography.

Laura picked up her bag and went outside for a cigarette. She huddled for warmth under the eaves at the front door, cursing herself for leaving her coat on the chair. Billows of clouds rolled overhead, forming and reforming against a sky that was dull and flat in the fading daylight. The air was cold and the mixture of ice and smoke stung her throat. She let her gaze roam over the tribal compound at Fort Washakie—a collection of modern brick buildings and century-old, white-frame bungalows that housed the tribal offices, the Wind River Police Department, the BIA agency. Next to the agency was the vacant site where Sacajawea's small log cabin had stood: one room above, one room below, a shed attached to the side. They had found her one morning, dead in her shakedown of buffalo robes.

Laura stubbed out the cigarette and flipped it into a tangle of scrub brush. The sense of desperation seemed less acute. She'd confirmed that the memoirs were *not* at the cultural center. That was valuable. And she knew where they were, had known from the moment she'd arrived. Wrapped in brown paper or in a parfleche, stashed in a trunk, forgotten in a closet in one of the little houses scattered about the reservation. She would find them. Lindy Meadows was checking the old letters at the Arapaho Museum. Who knew what information might be in them? And on Thursday, she'd talk to Theresa Redwing.

She'd made the appointment last night, after Vicky had called to tell her that Theresa would see her. The woman's granddaughter would be there. That could be a problem. Laura hadn't counted on a Shoshone graduate student writing a dissertation on Sacajawea. Still, if Theresa knew who Toussaint was . . . That was all that mattered. She could convince the man that the memoirs should be in the hands of a professional historian, not a graduate student. They should be part of Sacajawea's definitive biography.

Hugging herself against the cold, Laura went back inside and climbed the stairs to the library. A man about six feet tall was leaning over the director's desk, his voice low and confidential, as if he were telling an off-color story. He must have come in through the back door. His sheepskin coat hung open over a white shirt and blue jeans; a white Stetson dangled from one hand. He slapped the hat against his thigh and gave out a laugh that rumbled across the plank floor. Phyllis Manley tilted her face upward, eyes shining, a ripple of laughter joining his.

Laura recognized the man: Robert Crow Wolf, Shoshone, historian at the University of Wyoming. She'd heard a paper he'd delivered two years ago at the Western History Association, something about the cultural impact of trading posts on the Plains Indians. She'd been impressed by the depth of his research, the new insights into old material. She walked over.

"I'm going to need everything you have on the early agriculture on the res," he told the director.

Phyllis Manley started to lift herself out of her chair. "It'll a take a while to pull out the files."

"Better get to it." He waved the Stetson, as if he

were shooing a stray calf into the corral. The director was smiling as she stepped backward, then disappeared through one of the doors to the archives.

"Robert Crow Wolf," Laura said.

The man swung around. Everything about him spoke of a warrior's strength and alertness, from the broad shoulders to the way he planted his boots on the floor, his dark eyes traveling over her. His hair was black, parted in the middle and combed back from a dark, sculptured face with a firmly set jaw and full lips that parted in a half smile of appreciation. She was suddenly conscious of being a woman in the presence of an assured and handsome man. "Laura Simmons, University of Colorado, I believe." He stepped forward and gripped her palm against the roughness of his suede glove. The odor of coffee and aftershave floated between them. "What brings you here?"

"I'm working on a biography of Sacajawea," Laura explained.

The Indian threw back his head and gave a snort of laughter. "Another one?" He ushered her over to the chair she'd left a few moments ago, one hand on her elbow. She had the sense that she had his full attention. "Tell me," he said, pulling out a chair and sitting down beside her, "what could you possibly write that hasn't already been written?"

Laura flinched. She could expect Crow Wolf's reaction from all her colleagues unless she found the memoirs. "I believe there's evidence that has never been published," she said, hearing the tenseness in her voice.

The man shrugged. "You're not the first historian to come here looking for new evidence." He leaned close. The odor of coffee was strong on his breath. "You after the papers that were buried with Bazil? Fact is, they disintegrated. Poof!" The gloved hands clapped together. "Nothing but ashes in the wind. How about the Jefferson Medal Clark supposedly gave to Sacajawea?" He smiled; the white teeth gleamed in his brown face and flecks of light danced in the black eyes.

"The medal would suffice." Laura forced a lightness into her tone. Careful, she thought. She'd already said too much. If Robert Crow Wolf had any idea that the evidence was Sacajawea's memoirs, he would find them himself and publish them first. She said, "I'm completing the biography that another historian, Charlotte Allen, started. I've edited the manuscript and I've been rechecking the sources she listed in the journal she kept while she was on the reservation."

"You don't say." The Indian let his gaze roam over the stacks of papers arranged on the table, as if one of them might be the manuscript. A look of disappointment came into the black eyes. "This Charlotte Allen"—the name rolled slowly off his tongue, as if he were trying to place it with a face— "gave you her work?"

"Her mother asked me to complete the biography," Laura said. "Charlotte disappeared twenty years ago while she was hiking near Sacajawea Ridge. Perhaps you met her?"

"Twenty years ago I was in grad school in Berkeley." He glanced around at the director, and Laura realized the woman had materialized from the archives and was standing at the table behind them, a large cardboard box in her arms. "You meet an historian named Charlotte Allen about twenty years ago?"

A pink blush came into the woman's cheeks, like that of a schoolgirl who'd found herself under the scrutiny of the most popular boy in the class. Phyllis bumped against the table and lowered the box. AGRICULTURAL FILES was printed on the side. "I'm afraid that was before my time." She shivered and threw a glance at the window and the light slipping into grayness beyond. "Imagine getting lost in the mountains in the winter."

"Happens all the time." Robert Crow Wolf turned back to Laura. "How can I help a fellow historian?"

Laura felt herself beginning to relax. The man had his own projects; she was being silly to think he would want to take hers. "Would you happen to know someone named Toussaint?" she asked.

The Indian's eyes went to the window a moment, then he turned in his chair and faced the director. "Phyllis, see if you can get old Willie Silver on the phone."

"He must be related to James Silver," Laura said in a voice thin with excitement. Charlotte had interviewed James Silver.

"One and only son of," Crow Wolf said.

As the director started for the desk, he brought his gaze back to Laura. She felt a stab of pleasure at the acute masculine power in the man's black eyes. "Old Willie might be able to help you out," he said. "He's a proud descendant of Toussaint and Sacajawea." There was a faint tap-tap noise as the director dialed the number.

"I envy you, you know," Robert Crow Wolf went on. "Researching a mystery like Sacajawea, and I'm stuck with delivering a paper next month on how the Indians took to farming."

"Willie's on the line." Phyllis held up the phone, stretching the knotted cord over the desk.

Crow Wolf got up, took the receiver, and sat on the edge of the desk. "Willie, old boy. How the hell are you?" There was a half second of silence. Crow Wolf rolled his eyes to the ceiling. Finally he said, "Got a nice lady here wants to talk to you. Teacher down in Colorado writing a book about your famous ancestor." Another silence. "No, not Jim Bridger. Since when you related to that old trader? The lady here wants to talk to you about Toussaint. You gonna be around tomorrow? Earlier the better? Got ya, old boy."

Crow Wolf replaced the receiver. Leaning back onto the desk, he found a Post-it pad and a pen among the stacks of stapled pages and began writing something down. Then he tore off the top page and, handing it to Laura, said, "Here's the directions to Willie's ranch up on Sacajawea Ridge. I suggest you get out there before noon, while he's still sober." He tapped the pen against the tiny pad. "You've got me interested in this project of yours, Laura. I'll see if I can convince some of the other elders that you're an honest white woman and they oughta talk to you. Where you staying?"

She gave him the address of the Mountain House. She had the distinct feeling that her luck was about to change.

Laura worked through the rest of the afternoon, reading the oral histories again, story after story told by an old woman about the scarcity of food when the expedition crossed the Rocky Mountains; the roots she had dug to help feed the soldiers; the rough waters that had tossed the boats about at the mouth of the Columbia; and the fish that had washed out of the ocean which was, she said, as long as from the door of her log cabin to the hitching rack outside. Laura studied each story, searching for some clue, some small piece of information that could have sent Charlotte Allen to the man she'd called Toussaint. At one point she realized that Robert Crow Wolf had left, and she and the director were alone. Darkness was lapping at the window.

She returned the oral histories to the carton, then gathered up her notepad and bag and slipped into her coat. She thanked the director on the way out.

Highway 287 shone white in the headlights ahead as Laura drove south across the reservation. Except for the few stars twinkling overhead and the smudge of moonlight, the sky was black. After several miles, the lights of Lander flashed on the horizon. Another couple of miles and the neon lights of convenience stores and gas stations were passing outside her window. She turned into a fast-food drive-in and ordered a hamburger, then continued east into a neighborhood of houses from another era, a quieter, less stressful time, she thought. At a white Victorian on the corner, she slowed into the driveway and parked next to the garage in back. Clinging to the brick wall was an outside stairway that led to the rooms perched above, like an afterthought.

Tense with cold, she hurried up the stairs, holding the hamburger bag in one hand, fumbling in her purse for the key with the other. Her fingers curled around the cold metal, and she jammed the key into the lock and pushed open the door.

The instant she found the switch, the light from a faux Tiffany fixture flooded the round table near the window. Charlotte Allen's manuscript sat in a neat stack, just as she had left it. In the shadows beyond the table stood an upholstered chair and a dresser with a television perched on top. Most of the room was taken up by a double bed, the flowered comforter trailing onto the worn green carpet. Against the far wall, next to the door that led to the bathroom, was a closet-sized kitchen.

She dropped the hamburger on the table and tossed her coat and purse onto the bed. After she'd retrieved a soda from the miniature refrigerator, she turned on the TV and sat down at the table, angling the chair so that she had a straight view of the nightly news. A feeling of sadness hit her like a blast of cold air as she opened the bag and took a bite of the hamburger. Was this the way it would be? She, always alone?

She forced herself to concentrate on what the beautiful blond newscaster, cloned from a hundred others, was saying. The FBI was close to an identity of the skeleton found last week near St. Francis Mission on the Wind River Reservation. According to a spokesman, the skeleton was not ancient, as was originally suggested by tribal elders. Lab reports confirmed that the skeleton was a Caucasian female around thirty years old who was buried about twenty years ago. The death had been ruled a homicide.

Laura set the hamburger down, staring at the screen, all of her senses on alert. A familiar feeling washed over her—the feeling that often came when she was doing research and had picked up strands of information that suddenly came together. Charlotte Allen was in her early thirties; she'd disappeared twenty years ago. Could it possibly be?

She shrugged the notion away. Charlotte had disappeared in the mountains, miles from St. Francis Mission. It couldn't be Charlotte.

Laura was about to take another bite of the lukewarm meat when the footsteps sounded on the stairs—a slow, steady ascent. She sat motionless, wondering if the sound came from the television. There was a loud, firm knocking. She mentally ticked off the people who knew she was here. Only a few. She wasn't expecting any of them.

The knocking came again, impatient now, crashing over the television noise. Laura got to her feet and pushed back the flimsy white curtain at the window. On the stairway landing was the large, shadowy figure of a man.

She stepped over to the door and slid the chain into the channel. Leaning into the tiny crack at the frame, she called, "Who's there? What do you want?"

⇛ 12 ⇚

Let me in, sweetheart." The voice came like a painful memory floating uninvited into her consciousness. "I'm turning into the iceman out here."

Laura slid the chain free. Her hand trembled. Her legs felt weak and unattached as she opened the door and watched Toby Becker stride in, boots stomping the carpet, shoulders rolling, so that tiny snow crystals flew into her face like sand blowing in the wind. He had on blue jeans and the bulky red ski jacket he always wore to campus on cold days. The tips of his brown curly hair fanned over the thick collar as if it were a pillow.

"How did you find me?" she managed. She knew the answer. She'd told the department chair where she was staying.

"Did you really think you could get away from

me?" Toby threw her the indulgent smile that he bestowed whenever she'd disappointed him. She knew his face by heart: the hint of amusement behind the dark eyes, the flare of nostrils in the long, perfectly shaped nose, the way his mouth began to move before he spoke.

"Just like you, Laura, to land in a place like this. Efficient and cheap." His gaze flitted from the shabby bedspread to the dresser and television with a formation of airplanes floating across the screen. The announcer's voice droned above the roar of engines. He took off the ski jacket and threw it onto the bed next to her coat. His muscles rippled through the fabric of his navy-blue shirt, and a wisp of brown hair poked into the V of his opened collar.

"Hardly worthy of you, sweetheart," he said. "You deserve a penthouse overlooking Central Park, roses in the foyer, a roaring fire in the fireplace, and champagne chilled on a marble table. You deserve the world, Laura. You're beautiful."

Laura braced herself against the door. "Why are you here, Toby?"

"I'm dying without you, sweetheart." As he started toward her she slid along the door, wincing as the knob dug into her spine. He stopped. "Can you try to imagine for one moment, one moment, Laura, how miserable I've been? I've lost my appetite, can't sleep. I'm an automaton up there in front of my classes, mouthing words. I don't even know what I'm teaching."

He wagged a finger at her, as if she were a student

who'd missed the main point of a lecture. "I haven't been able to write, Laura. Not one word on my new novel. I thought you understood it's my most important work yet." The finger moving, moving. "You're responsible."

Laura fought against the impulse to apologize, assure him that he was a great writer. He must finish the novel. The role she usually played in a scene they had enacted—how many times in the last year?

She stepped past him and clicked off the television. In the mirror she caught his image, hands dangling helplessly at his sides. If he touched her, she feared she would be lost. "It was always about you, Toby," she managed.

"It's about us. We belong together, Laura. You're the sun in my sky, the air I breathe. I need you. Give me another chance. Give us another chance."

Laura turned slowly. "I gave us enough chances."

"It'll be different this time." Light reflecting through the faux Tiffany shade gave his face the soft, languorous look she'd seen when she'd turned to him in the middle of the night. "I'm seeing a therapist," he said. "I've had some real break-throughs. I understand where the rage comes from. Mother, the enabler, and Dad, that SOB. Don't you see? I've simply displaced the rage onto you. Now that I understand, I'll be able to control it."

Suddenly he dropped to his knees. "Please, Laura."

"What are you doing?" She had to stifle a laugh. He looked like a clown, walking toward her on his knees.

"Begging you, Laura. Come back to me." He wrapped his arms around her legs and started to lift her into the air. "I adore you. I need you."

"Stop it, Toby." She pushed at his head. The thick softness of his hair flowed through her fingers; his breath was warm against her thigh. She jerked herself free.

"We'll stay together, you and I." He was still on his knees. "Walk to classes, write, make dinner, go to bed. You and I, Laura, just like before."

"It's over between us, Toby." Laura could hear the waviness in her voice. Her breath burned in her chest. "I'm going on with my life and my own work. I have a meeting tomorrow with a man who may be able to get me the critical evidence I need. I intend to finish the biography"—she shot a glance at the manuscript on the table—"and get tenure next year."

"Oh, yes. Pocahontas." He gave a snort that flared out his nostrils.

"Sacajawea."

"Yes, yes, I meant Sacajawea." He shrugged. "You can work on the biography while I write my novel."

"We tried that. Somehow, my time was spent making it possible for you to write." She stopped herself from saying, And entertaining your friends, typing your notes, typing your endless drafts.

"Surely you don't mean the biography takes precedence over our being together." He lifted his hand and gave a dismissive wave toward the manuscript.

"Please leave, Toby." She stepped past him and

opened the door.

He got to his feet, his eyes hard on hers now, as if he were trying to decipher the meaning of his dismissal. Then he grabbed the jacket from the bed. "You think I don't have anything better to do than drive all the way up here to see you?" His tone rose to an angry pitch. "I should be working on my novel, not groveling to some ungrateful bit—" He tightened his lips over the word. Still keeping his gaze on her, he walked past and out the door.

As he started down the steps he turned back. "You're still my woman, Laura, and you know it. I'm not going away. I'll be here as long as it takes for you to come to your senses."

Laura felt shaky, slightly nauseated, when she crawled into bed. She'd watched the black BMW back out of the driveway and dart out of sight past the Victorian, weak with a sense of emptiness. People could change. Vicky had taken her ex-husband back after all these years, and Toby was seeing a therapist. He'd driven all the way to Wyoming to beg for another chance. He was filled with remorse. What more could she ask?

She snatched pieces of sleep from the night, floating through a jumble of dreams. She was treading through a mountain wilderness, snow blowing through the ponderosas, the dark-haired woman walking ahead, always ahead. Suddenly the woman stopped and turned back. *Who are you to come for my story?*

104

Laura sat up in bed, her heart banging hard. She felt cold with perspiration. What was she doing here? So far from home and her own life—a life she could share with Toby. Chasing after a phantom, a spirit. After all, it was another scholar who had discovered the memoirs.

But that scholar was dead, she told herself, and the biography was hers to finish. She would be the one who would first publish the memoirs. Her reputation would be firmly established. Everything was going just as she'd hoped. She was making contacts on the reservation, and sooner or later she'd find Toussaint.

Laura settled back against the rough sheets. From outside came the sounds of voices and car doors slamming. She tried to ignore the fear moving like a shadow at the edge of her consciousness. Toby was gone now. Everything would be fine.

He would be back. She couldn't get the nagging voice out of her head. He knew where she was staying.

≫ 13 ≪

Laura sped through the northern reaches of the reservation, gobbling up the miles, the foothills flashing by outside her window. The sun angled overhead, compressed between puffs of clouds. At the junction of 287 and 26, she veered west, closing in on the mountains. She felt as if she were floating in space, Toby part of the unsettling dreams, nearly forgotten in the bright morning light. He had left, she kept reminding herself. Surely it would be final now, the breakup. Surely he'd go back to Boulder and forget about her.

Ahead on the left was a wide dirt road, just as Robert Crow Wolf's directions indicated. She swung onto the road and started climbing around the mountain slope, the ponderosa branches dancing in the wind outside her window. As she came around a curve she saw the gray ranch house, the sloping roof outlined against the sky. She turned through the opened gate of a barbed-wire fence and stopped near the front stoop.

As she lifted herself out a large, round-shouldered man in blue jeans and fringed brown leather jacket came around the corner of the house. Somewhere in his sixties, she guessed, with a reddish complexion and tufts of gray hair that dropped beneath the rim of a black cowboy hat.

"Hello," she called. The wind brought her words back to her. "I'm looking for Willie Silver."

He came forward, milky dark eyes taking her in. "You must be that professor lady Crow Wolf called about."

"Laura Simmons." She thrust out her hand and went to meet him. A gust whipped the front of her coat back and sent a chill running through her.

"Come on in," he said, shaking her hand. She flinched at the tightness of his grip. He ushered her to the front door and into a narrow living room with a sofa, a couple of chairs, and a table scattered about, as if they'd been dropped from overhead. Newspapers, food-crusted plates, and beer cans toppled over the tops and trailed onto the floor.

"Excuse the mess," the man said. "My woman took it into her head to go off somewhere a week ago." He cleared a stack of newspapers from an upholstered chair, the cushion stained and ragged at the edges. "She'll be back. They always come back. Have a seat."

Laura perched on the edge of the cushion, keeping her bag in her lap. "I understand you're a descendant of Sacajawea," she said in a firm, businesslike voice. He was different—rougher—than the men she was used to. An outdoorsman with squint lines fanning from hooded eyes and bulky, chapped hands.

"Yeah, that's me." Willie Silver straddled the sofa armrest. "Come down from Baptiste himself, natural son of Sacajawea and Toussaint Charbonneau. Bazil, he was her nephew, born to her sister. She might've adopted him, but that didn't make him her natural son, like Baptiste."

"Bazil took care of her in her last years." Laura heard the lecturing note in her tone. "The 1880 census identified her as Bazil's mother."

The Indian flapped a hand at the air, as if he were swatting away a pesky fly. "Baptiste was out hunting when they made that census, gettin' food for the people. He was a helluva guide, too, like his old man. Guided people all over the mountains, some of 'em real important, like that so-called explorer

Frémont. Couldn't explore his ass without Baptiste."

Laura shifted in her chair. "Mr. Silver," she began.

"Willie."

"I've been asked to complete a biography of Sacajawea."

"You gonna tell the truth?"

"I don't understand."

"The truth about Toussaint, her old man. None of them history books—" He hesitated. The dark eyes narrowed, deepening the creases in his forehead. "Don't be lookin' so surprised. I read about my own ancestors. Them books don't tell the truth. Toussaint was one helluva guy. Made his way from Montreal across the plains, learned to speak Indian, lived by his wits. Trading with all them tribes up north, guiding folks about. Old Lewis and Clark never would've made it west without Toussaint."

"I'm afraid there's no evidence to support that theory." Laura felt a spasm of irritation.

"Hell there ain't. He was one helluva man."

"He was a wife beater."

"Yeah, well, maybe his woman needed some discipline once in a while for her own good."

"Listen, Willie," Laura began again, struggling to keep the irritation out of her voice. "Twenty years ago an historian named Charlotte Allen came here to research Sacajawea. Did you know her?"

"That's a long time ago. Been a lot of women around since then." The man's gaze flitted around the room. A vein pulsed in his temple. "If I remember right," he went on, "she got lost up here on the ridge. She'd been goin' around the res, trying to get folks to talk to her. Lots of folks don't trust white people much." He winked, as if to make sure she understood he wasn't one of them.

Laura opened her bag, drew out the red journal, and began flipping through the pages. "Let me read you what Charlotte wrote. 'Toussaint came today. He told me the most incredible news. His great-grandfather rescued Sacajawea's memoirs from the agency fire. They've been in the family ever since.' "

She glanced up. "Can you help me find the memoirs?"

"You thinkin' I'm that Toussaint she wrote about?" Willie Silver swung out a scuffed boot and kicked at the sofa. His boot made a muffled, pounding noise.

"Are the memoirs in your family?" Laura could hear her heart beating. She was close, close.

"They'd be valuable, right?"

Laura didn't respond for a moment. "I'm certain my publisher would compensate you," she said. She was thinking that she didn't even have a publisher yet.

"I sure wanna help a pretty professor lady like you." The man kicked at the sofa again. "I'll ask around the family, see what I can come up with. I'll get back to you. Where you staying?"

Laura told him. Then she rose to her feet and started for the door, limp from the rush of excitement. She was so close to the memoirs, she could almost feel the weight of the old notebook in her hand. She was about to let herself out when the man set his hand on her shoulder.

"What's it worth to you?"

She spun around. "I told you, my publisher—"

"I mean you, lady." An array of smells engulfed her—sweat and stale cigarettes and the inside of barns.

She braced herself against the edge of the door. "Bring me the memoirs, Willie, and we'll discuss it."

The man reared back and gave a bark of laughter that dissolved into a choking noise. A second passed before he caught his breath. "Oh, you can bet I'll get you them memoirs, sweetheart. You come back tomorrow, and I'll have 'em. That's a promise."

Laura gripped the steering wheel to stop the wave of nausea flowing over her as she drove out of the mountains. Robert Crow Wolf had tried to warn her: I *suggest you get out there before noon, while he's still sober.* She should have guessed what Willie Silver would be like. And yet . . . Charlotte had trusted Toussaint, believed in him. Notes of excitement and expectation ran through every mention of him in the journal. If Willie were the man Charlotte had called Toussaint, how had he changed so much?

And then a new idea hit her. Suppose Charlotte had been so blinded by the idea of the memoirs she'd overlooked the man? What arrangement had she made with him? What had she agreed to do for

110

the memoirs? Suddenly she understood Charlotte's longing to go off into the wilderness by herself. *I have to clear the fog in my head,* she had told her mother. The memoirs were valuable, all right. They commanded a high price.

She regretted telling Willie Silver where she was staying. She could have arranged to call him back. She hadn't been thinking straight. My God, she thought. She was like Charlotte. All she cared about were the memoirs.

The apartment looked vacant and lonely, black windows staring down on the driveway, light flaring yellow over the door. Laura pulled in close and made her way up the stairs, her fingers brushing the soft leather of the journal as she drew the key from her bag. For a moment she wished Toby were there, that things were different—the way they had been at first. She would tell him about Willie Silver: the thinning gray hair, the way he sat on the armrest because there wasn't another clear spot. They would have a good laugh. Toby's obligatory laugh. While she talked he would have been working out the perfect opening sentence of a paragraph.

She reached the landing and stopped. A white sheet of paper fluttered from the piece of tape stuck on the door. She yanked the paper free. The manager's loops and curlicues flowed over the page: *Lindy Meadows called from Arapaho Museum. Found letters you want.*

Laura jammed the key into the lock and tried the

knob. It held fast: she'd just locked the door. She must have left it unlocked when she left this morning. And then she saw the tiny scratches, the workings of a knife between the door and the jamb. She tried the key again and stepped inside , taking in the small room awash in shadows. It looked the same—bedspread tidy, makeup bag on the dresser next to the television. But there was something different, like an invisible presence floating toward her. She turned on the lamp, then walked over and flung open the door to the bathroom. Empty. She whirled about and checked the closet. An extra pair of jeans, a couple of blouses, a black skirt, just hanging as she had left them.

Laura set her bag on the bed and walked back across the room. Surely the manager would have used a key. But the manager hadn't come in; she'd left the message on the door. Laura heard the sounds of her own breathing in the quiet. Toby had returned. What was he looking for?

She moved to the table, lifted the flap on the folder, and pulled out Charlotte Allen's manuscript. And then she knew. The manuscript was like an extension of herself, an extra arm or leg, the shapes and variations of color familiar. The blue Post-its that she used to mark various sections protruded from the pages at odd angles; the paper clips were in the wrong place. Toby had gone through the manuscript.

Frantically she began checking the pages. Sacajawea's childhood among the Shoshones. The capture by the Minnetarees. The forced marriage to Toussaint. The birth of Baptiste. The chapters on the expedition, the long years of wandering the plains, the final years with her people. All in order.

She stacked the pages carefully. It didn't make sense. Toby could have read the manuscript months ago. He'd never shown any interest in her work. Someone else had broken in and gone through the pages. She felt a wave of relief that the manuscript was still here, still intact. She'd left a copy in Boulder, but a copy wasn't the same as the original, with Charlotte Allen's handwriting in the margins. Whoever was here wasn't interested in the manuscript itself, only in its contents.

And yet the manuscript didn't contain anything that wasn't already known. Suddenly it hit her. It was the journal that contained new information, the journal that mentioned the existence of Sacajawea's memoirs. Someone had come for Charlotte Allen's journal, which she had taken with her.

She had to think. She hadn't made a copy of the journal. She could take it somewhere and copy it, but it wouldn't matter. The original was important. The original couldn't be altered. After the biography was published, other historians would want to see the original record of Charlotte Allen's research.

She replaced the manuscript, then withdrew the journal from her bag and set it in the folder. She knew exactly where she had to take the documents to keep them safe while she was here.

❯❯ 14 ❮❮

There were the faint odors of desperation and transience that mixed with the smells of beef stew simmering on the stove at the Eagle Shelter, Vicky thought. The kitchen was like a hundred kitchens on the reservation Cabinets and Formica countertops, cartoons on the refrigerator, gauzy curtains drooping in the window, an archway leading to the living room.

She took a drink from the mug of coffee that Myra Bushy, the director, had handed across the table, and tried to concentrate on what the woman was saying. There were three guests now, two women and a three-month-old boy. With the tightly curled gray hair, the pink-framed glasses bisecting the placid face, the director might have been a grandmother, gossiping about visiting relatives. Was she really talking about the blasted dreams, the upended lives?

A woman darted past the archway, a specter in blue jeans and T-shirt, long black hair falling around her shoulders, arms crooked around a package of diapers, head turned. Vicky flinched at the memory: she herself, sidling into a store, tilting her face, hoping no one would notice the bruises lengthening on her cheek. The old sense of shame burned in her cheeks. It was as real as the chrome-legged, Formica-topped table someone had donated to the shelter.

Vicky realized that Myra Bushy had extracted a form from the manila envelope on the table and was explaining the financial situation, the reason she'd asked Vicky to come by this morning. "We can expect funds from the county and the tribes." She glanced over the top of her pink-framed glasses. "Thanks to your efforts, Vicky."

Vicky shrugged. She had filed the proper forms for nonprofit status, set up the corporation and board of directors, written grants. Any paralegal could have done the same.

"Fact is, we need more money." An unsettled note invaded the other woman's voice. "Always more expenses than we were counting on. Things like towels and soaps." She nodded toward the archway. "Janet there"—her voice lowered to a whisper—"had to get out fast. Not even enough time to grab a diaper for the baby. Naturally I had to go out and buy more diapers and formula."

The director straightened herself against the back of the chair. "I was thinking we could sponsor a powwow and run an article in the *Gazette* asking for donations."

Vicky sighed. Temporary solutions. A few thousand dollars, some cast-off household items. And in the next few months another powwow, another call for donated goods. What the shelter needed was a dependable income. "There are organizations that support women's shelters," she began. "I can apply for other grants."

Myra Bushy's dark eyes glinted. "Oh, Vicky, you

don't know how I've stayed awake nights, worrying about the women and their babies. We been open two weeks, and we've had six residents. The other shelters are always full. You can't have women and kids sleeping on the floor. They gotta have someplace comfortable, where they can feel safe for a while."

The woman kept her eyes on the window curtains, breathing in the warm air blown from the floor vent. "We gotta do the best we can for them here, even if most of 'em go back."

Vicky finished the coffee and set the mug on the table. *We* go back, she thought. It should be a simple matter, breaking away from a batterer, but it was so complicated. It had to do with family and home and a sense of belonging someplace in the world. It had to do with fear, an odd kind of fear that masqueraded as love. Thirteen years, and she'd gone back to Ben. How could she expect anyone else to walk away? Alva Running Bull? Laura Simmons? How bad did it have to be before a woman left? How deep the shame? *She stayed until he almost killed her.* That wasn't true, she thought. The stories said Toussaint had whipped Sacajawea in front of his young, Ute wife. Sacajawea had left because of the shame.

She said, "Has Alva Running Bull called the shelter?"

The director shook her head; a puzzled look crept into her expression. "I heard she was gonna divorce Lester."

"She's changed her mind." Vicky unhinged her bag from the back of the chair and got to her feet. "Please ask her to call me if she comes."

"She'd probably be callin' you anyway."

"I don't think so," Vicky said. "She'll be too ashamed."

In her office, Vicky flipped through the messages Laola, her secretary, had piled on the desk. No calls from Laura. She'd been trying to reach her since yesterday, wondering how the research was going, whether she'd talked to Theresa Redwing yet. Surely if Laura had located Tonssaint, she would have called. Vicky rummaged through her bag for the piece of paper with Laura's number on it, then dialed the Mountain House.

A woman answered. No, Laura Simmons wasn't in at the moment. Could she take a message? Vicky gave her name again and said she was a friend of Laura's. "Ask her to call me," she said.

There were three messages from Ben. A message from Jack Old. His son had been picked up as a DUI last night. And Mary Heat wanted to sue the guy who had rear-ended her pickup on Seventeen Mile Road. Another call from Wes Nelson in Denver. Anxious for her decision.

Vicky closed her eyes. She'd been putting off the decision, appalled at the thought of moving back to Denver, appalled at the idea of staying. The days and months stretched ahead, a parade of DUIs and petty lawsuits and nonprofit boards like the one at

117

the shelter, and what difference did any of it really make? How in the name of heaven did it help her people?

Wes offered the chance to make a real difference. And yet, and yet . . . this was home. This was where she wanted to belong. She tossed the messages to one side and opened the folder containing Jake Longman's lease. The man would be here in five minutes to pick up the final copy. She tried to push away the idea that had taken hold of her lately: John O'Malley was leaving. She could leave, too. She wondered how she would ever get away from Ben this time.

≫ 15 ≪

Father John hung his vestments in the sacristy and set the chalice and Mass prayer books in the cabinets, acutely aware of last things. The last days at St. Francis, the last Masses and meetings, and, the day after tomorrow, the last Sunday Mass.

The morning quiet had already settled over the church. From outside came the sounds of motors and of tires munching the snow. The elders and grandmothers who drove across the reservation to early-morning Mass—the old faithfuls, he called them—heading home. He switched off the light and made his way across the altar, genuflecting in front of the tipi-shaped tabernacle. Then down the aisle, checking the pews for anything left behind. He let himself out into the icy air. A pale pink light was spreading across the sky as he walked to the residence.

"Pancakes?" Father John said, taking in the sweet aroma in the kitchen. He pulled out a chair and sat down at the table across from Father Kevin. Elena stood at the stove, her back to them. "How come this Irishman gets pancakes when you've been feeding me oatmeal for the last eight years?"

The housekeeper turned and set a plate of saucer-size pancakes on the table. "You like oatmeal. Father Kevin likes pancakes." She stepped back, then set down two mugs of coffee. "I'll have your oatmeal in a minute."

Kevin pushed the plate toward him. "Help yourself," he said. Then he glanced at the housekeeper. "Thank you, my dear woman. You've brought sunshine into my dreary life."

"Don't give me your blarney." Elena ran a spoon around the large bowl cradled in her arms.

"No need for any oatmeal this morning, Elena." Father John helped himself to several pancakes, which he drenched in syrup. He felt almost grateful to the man across from him. "I see you two have reached a truce."

"Truce?" Elena's head swirled sideways. "If that's what you wanna call it. Father Kevin's not gonna ask me any more darn-fool questions, and I'm gonna get my work done."

"That's right," Kevin said. "No more questions. Besides, I had a good interview with Betty Crooner yesterday."

"What did she say, that old woman?"

"Told me how the Arapahos and Shoshones learned how to farm."

"Hah! Her people are Sioux. Didn't marry up with the Arapahos till the thirties. What's she know? You asked the wrong woman, but I'm not talkin' anymore."

"I understand, Elena." Father Kevin took a bite of pancake, his eyes fastened on the woman.

"My grandfather learned all about farming." A plop on the griddle, a little sizzling noise. "How to plow and sow the seed and run the irrigation lines. Real hard work, and they weren't used to it, none of them warriors. They liked riding out and getting buffalo. They were hunting experts. Could show some of the hunters around today a thing or two."

Kevin said, "I asked Mary how they had managed to keep the values they lived by as warriors—you know, honor, courage, and generosity—when they became farmers."

"Good, I'm glad you pestered her and not me." Elena scooped up a stack of hot pancakes and dropped them onto the plate. Father John reached for another one. " 'Course that old woman only knows what she's heard from folks that was here. My grandfather told me they felt like warriors some days, out there in the fields. Especially when they was herding cattle and working with horses. Weren't nobody better at horses than Arapaho warriors."

Father John took a long draw from his mug, washing down another forkful of pancake with the hot coffee, and waited for the rest of it.

"So ranching was in keeping with the warrior way of life," the other priest said, a musing tone.

"That's nothin' but one of your questions. You're not foolin' me." The housekeeper pivoted around, hands set on her hips. "I tol' you, I'm not telling you any more. Besides, ranching was a lot like the hunt, so the warriors were still ridin' out, like they always did. Made it easier to hold on to the old ways. And they were still gettin' meat for the people." She turned back to the stove. "Sure glad I wasn't the one you were bothering with all your questions."

Father John finished off his coffee and got to his feet. "Thank you both for the delicious breakfast and enlightening conversation," he said. He retraced his steps down the hallway and shrugged into his jacket. Then he let himself out and started for the administration building. A black truck was parked in front.

Lester Running Bull sat upright in one of the side chairs, hands curled over the ends of the armrests, strands of blue-black hair showing beneath a red baseball cap. He looked like a marathoner, Father John thought, poised at the starting line, muscles tensed to bolt out of the office at the sound of the gun. Alva was in the other chair, a small woman with a thin, narrow face shadowed under a row of black bangs. They had been in his office thirty minutes, the tension between them as palpable as a swollen tumor.

121

Father John had swung his own chair around the desk, past the packed cartons. He'd been packing the last two days: the books and opera tapes he carted from assignment to assignment, old letters, notes to himself, past sermons—the detritus of his life. He sat facing the couple. He preferred a circle for counseling sessions, but this was like a knife-sharp triangle.

"We're gonna be just fine," Alva said, a barely perceptible note of fear running through her voice. "I'm real sure of it, now that we're comin' for counseling."

Father John said, "What else would you like Lester to do?"

Alva blinked several times, as if she were trying to round up the herd of thoughts stampeding through her head. Finally she drew in a long breath and turned slowly toward her husband, who sat stone-faced, his eyes trained across the room. "I don't know," she began, halting, biting at her lower lip. "He's been real good to me now."

Father John turned to Lester. "What would you like Alva to do?" he asked.

A second passed. Quiet filtered around them, and Father John let it remain. Epiphanies came into the quiet. Finally Lester said, "She oughta quit makin' a big deal out of everything. Everybody fights once in a while. Can't expect to get along all the time. I don't see why she was thinkin' of leaving me. She's got no cause to do that."

The woman began rummaging through a floppy,

ruglike bag. She found a tissue, which she ran along the ridges of her cheeks. "I told you, I'm not leavin' you, Lester. Vicky tore up those divorce papers."

Lester let out a snort of laughter. " 'Bout time Ben Holden got some control over that wife of his."

"You know they're not married anymore." A look of perplexity came to Alva's eyes.

"They're gonna be."

"How's the anger management group going?" Father John said, changing the subject.

"Just fine, Father." Lester shifted uneasily in his chair. "You don't have to worry about nothin'." He shot a sideways glance at his wife. "Come on, let's go."

"I didn't see you last week," Father John persisted.

"What?" Lester's eyes narrowed.

"At the AA meeting."

"Oh, yeah." The man gave a little shrug. "Well, I got me some things to do, you know. Can't be runnin' to meetings all the time." Another glance at his wife. "We're done here." He stood up and motioned Alva to her feet, nudging her upward with a fleshy hand. Then he pulled their jackets off the coat tree and handed her one.

"Will you be at next week's meeting?" Father John asked. He would not be there, he realized.

"Yeah, sure." Steering his wife out the door now.

Alva threw a glance over her shoulder. "We'll be back, Father."

"Father Kevin will be here," he heard himself

saying as the couple disappeared into the corridor. He'd heard the new pastor moving about the other office; he'd be taking over this office soon.

After the front door had thudded shut, Father John went back to packing the books on the bookshelf behind the desk. His thoughts were on Alva and Lester. *He's going to kill her,* Vicky had said. And yet, when Alva first came to see him three weeks before, she'd said two things, almost in the same breath: she loved Lester and she was going to divorce him. He'd suggested the woman bring her husband the next time, and they had both come several times since. Lester had agreed to go to anger therapy; he'd agreed to attend AA. People can change, Father John told himself, with God's grace. He cleared the top shelf and started on another row of books, setting them carefully into a large carton. He'd been packing for almost two days now, but there was still another shelf to clear, the file cabinet to go through, a couple desk drawers left un-touched. The phone had rung almost nonstop and people had been stopping by—a stream of traffic pulling around Circle Drive, a steady hum of motors.

Late Wednesday, he'd seen the blue SAAB go by. When he'd walked back to the residence, the car was still in front of the museum. It had given him a stab of satisfaction. Lindy must have found the old letters, and Laura had come to look through them for any mention of Sacajawea.

And yesterday and today, Howard Elkman's

brown truck had lumbered past his office. He'd expected the elder to appear in the doorway, but he hadn't come in. When Father John glanced outside, he'd seen the truck in front of the museum. The museum would be here, after he was gone, and he was glad about that.

He'd just started filling another box when the phone jangled. Another parishioner wanting him to come to supper, he thought. Another elder asking him to come for a last visit. There wasn't enough time. The airline ticket had arrived in yesterday's mail, a white envelope stiff with the heavy paper inside. Tuesday, five A.M., Riverton to Denver. Eight-thirteen P.M., Denver to Milwaukee. A one-way ticket.

He stepped around the cartons and picked up the receiver. "Father O'Malley," he said.

"This is Theresa, Father." The voice crackled over the line. "That friend of yours, the historian? She said she'd come over yesterday. She didn't show up."

"I'm sorry, Grandmother," he said. It was strange. Laura had seemed anxious to talk to the woman. He stepped over to the window, stretching the cord over the top of the desk. The blue SAAB wasn't at the museum today, and he hadn't seen it yesterday. "I'll see if I can reach her and get back to you," he said. He hit the disconnect and shuffled through the piles of papers on his desk, finally locating the paper triangle that Laura had given him. He pushed in the numbers.

A woman's voice, little more than a whisper, as if

she'd just awakened, floated over the line: "Mountain House."

He asked for Laura Simmons.

"Sorry, not in." A hint of enthusiasm came into the voice now. "You can leave another message."

"Another message?"

"Yeah, I don't mind. I just run 'em up to her room and put 'em on the door. She gets quite a few."

He gave his name and number, thanked her, and hung up, an uneasy feeling coming over him, like a slow chill. He tried to examine it logically. There was no reason to feel uneasy. Laura Simmons had probably gotten lost in some archives Thursday and forgotten about the appointment with Theresa Redwing. It could happen. He'd often lost the sense of time when he was caught up in research.

He finished filling the last carton and smoothed a strip of brown tape over the flaps. The gray afternoon light seeped through the window; it would be dark soon. The phone started ringing again, but before he could work his way past the cartons, it stopped. The sound of Kevin's voice broke through the quiet, followed by hurried footsteps. The other priest leaned around the doorjamb, his face half-obscured in the shadows of the corridor. "The FBI's calling," he said.

Father John lifted the receiver.

"John? What's going on?" Gianelli sounded tense and distracted. "I've been trying to reach you all afternoon. Line's always busy."

Father John ignored the comment. "What's

happened?"

"Thought you'd like to know. Your tip paid off. We have a positive ID on the skeleton. Checked the dental records for Charlotte Allen. A perfect match. The FBI closed the case when her car was found up by Sacajawea Ridge. All the evidence indicated she took herself on a long hike, got lost, and couldn't find her way back. Now we know Charlotte Allen was murdered. Somebody parked her car up there to make it look like she'd gone hiking. Just what I need." The agent let out a raspy sigh. "Another homicide to solve around here, and this one twenty years old."

Father John was quiet a moment, Theresa's voice sounding in his head. *Your friend didn't show up, Father.* And Vicky's: *Laura's doing the same kind of research as Charlotte did, John. She could be in danger.*

He thanked the agent, pressed the disconnect lever, and punched in Vicky's number.

≫· 16 ·≪

The square bungalow that Vicky had called home for the past four years sat behind a row of leafless trees, a dark block sliced by shadows. Lately Ben had gotten there before her. Lights twinkled in the windows, the faintest music floated outside. He'd even started dinner. But he'd called this afternoon to say he had to go over the books at the ranch. She wasn't disappointed. She had a briefcase full of work—depositions to read, a will to draft, the endless, dull minutiae of her practice.

She parked in the driveway and made her way across the yard, moist and soft with melted snow, like tangled wild grasses along the river banks. She let herself in and found the light switch. A well of light filled the center of the small living room and lapped at the sofa and chairs and small tables, the desk and bookcases arranged around the white walls. A red light blinked on the answering machine on her desk.

She dropped her coat and briefcase on the sofa and started for the kitchen, pushing the message button on her way. A woman's voice followed: "Better not come by tonight, honey. My ex is on a tear. He might show up. Call me tomorrow." Vicky stood motionless, staring into the refrigerator, the door handle cold in her hand. She pulled out a bottle of water, slammed the door, and walked back into the living room.

The next message had already started. The deep tones of a man's voice now. "Vicky, Wes Nelson. You must be busy up there in the boondocks. No luck reaching you at the office. Hope you get this message." Vicky sank onto the chair next to the desk and took a sip of water. Her throat felt tight with fury. She forced herself to concentrate on what the voice was saying. The firm needed her expertise and sensitivity to tribal cultures. They had some complicated cases involving natural resources on reservations in New Mexico and Arizona. Probably go all the way to the Supreme Court. She could be a part of it, make a difference for her people. She was too good a lawyer to waste her time. He was waiting for her call.

"What's this?"

Vicky felt her heart pounding. She swiveled around. Ben stood in the dining alcove, framed in the darkness of the kitchen, fists bunched at his sides. He must have used the back door.

"Just business," Vicky said, pulling herself to her feet. Her legs were shaky, her heart still kicking.

"You're thinking about going back to Denver."

"I don't know." Vicky forced herself to hold her place, wedged against the desk.

"You don't know? You don't know?" Ben walked over to the sofa and swept her briefcase to the floor with his fist. Then he turned toward her. "What's going on, Vicky? I thought we had a future here. I thought we were working on something."

"The managing partner. . ." She hesitated, powerless against the heat in his eyes. She stumbled on. "There's an opening in the firm. He's offered me the chance to work on some important cases for different tribes. The cases could set precedents and help our people."

"What's that got to do with you? You're helping our people enough."

"I do divorces and custody battles. I sue people over unpaid bills. I write wills. I represent drunks in county court, and none of it helps Indian people. I've been offered the chance to practice the kind of

129

law that can make a difference."

Ben came toward her, arms outstretched, concern working into his expression now. The new Ben, the man she had gone back to, the man she had to be wary of. "You don't have to do any of it," he said in a low voice. "We'll get married again, make it official. We'll live out at the ranch. You can say good-bye to all the hard work and worry. The kids'll come back to the res, and we'll be a family again."

Vicky blinked at the images flashing into her mind. She hardly recognized herself—cooking for the celebrations, looking in on the elders, wondering when Ben would come home, who he was with, if he was sober.

The silence thudded between them. After a long moment Vicky heard her own voice: "There was a message for you. A woman called to tell you not to come by tonight."

His expression dissolved from comprehension to annoyance. He sucked in a long breath. "She doesn't mean anything to me, Vicky. You know that."

"What about the woman at the Highway Lounge who keeps asking my secretary about you?" Vicky pushed on.

"So I stop at the lounge for a beer once in a while. What's the big deal?"

"You're an alcoholic, Ben."

"I can control it now. It's not a problem." His eyes grew more watchful, defying her to say otherwise.

The phone started to ring, and Vicky reached for the receiver.

"Let it ring," Ben said. "We have to settle things here."

"It's already settled." Vicky glanced nervously at the phone. It could be one of the kids, Aunt Rose, Grandmother Ninni, someone who needed her. "Everything broke apart thirteen years ago, Ben. We can't put it back together."

The ringing stopped, giving way to the click of the answering machine. "Vicky, John O'Malley. I've been trying to reach you."

She picked up the receiver. "I'm here."

"Good." The familiar voice gave her a sense of calm. "I've just talked to Gianelli. He has a positive ID on the skeleton. It's Charlotte Allen."

The receiver felt heavy and inert in her hand. She was only half aware of the man watching her from across the room. "Does Laura know?"

"I doubt it."

"I've been trying to call Laura since Wednesday," Vicky said. "She hasn't been around."

The line went quiet a moment. "Listen, Vicky, Theresa Redwing just called. Laura had arranged to see her yesterday. She never came."

"I'll try her again," Vicky said. Then: "Thank you, John." She dropped the receiver and lifted her briefcase from the floor. Inside she found the scrap of paper with Laura's telephone number. Grabbing the receiver again, she dialed the Mountain House.

"This isn't about other women or my having a beer now and then." Ben's voice cut through the buzz of a phone ringing on the other side of town.

131

"This is about you and the fact you've got the hots for that priest."

"Don't be ridiculous." The buzzing was interminable. *Pick up, somebody.*

"You think O'Malley's gonna chuck the priesthood for you." Ben threw his head back and gave a hard shout of laughter. "Oh, I got it now. It's a real clear picture."

Still the buzzing noise sounding into a vacuum. Vicky dropped the receiver. Stepping around him, she scooped her coat and bag from the sofa and started for the door. He grabbed her arm, the force of it jerking her partway off her feet. "You're going to meet him, aren't you?"

"I'm going over to a friend's place. She's in danger. Something could already have happened to her."

"You're lying."

"I have to go," Vicky said, pulling her arm free.

⇒ 17 ⇐

The white Victorian house, a collection of gables and turrets, brooded over a side street on the western edge of town. Light shone through the oblong windows, illuminating the wide wooden door, the columned porch, and the dried stalks poking from the brick planters on either side of the steps. Vicky drove down the driveway along the side and stopped in the turnaround that separated the house from the garage. Laura's blue SAAB wasn't there. Above the garage was a second story with windows that mimicked those in the house. A pale light flickered over the front door.

"Laura?" Vicky called, hurrying up the outside stairs. The wind had come up, carrying the unmistakable smell of snow. An array of small sheets of paper flapped from strips of tape on the front door. Vicky saw her name on several messages: Wednes-day, Thursday, today. There was another message today from John O'Malley, and two yesterday from Theresa Redwing. She rapped on the door, then tried the knob. It turned in her hand.

She stepped inside and pushed the light switch. A lamp over the table stuttered into life, flowing over a space that resembled a cheap motel room, trashed by the last occupant. Yellow legal-size sheets of paper were strewn over the table. Blankets and sheets were crumpled on the bed; the dresser drawers gaped open. A pencil of light escaped from beneath the door on the far wall.

Vicky made her way across the room, numb with apprehension. She shoved the door open. White enamel came at her—sink, toilet, tub with a pink curtain stacked at one end. Standing out in relief against the white tile floor, like rose petals scattered about, were blotches of blood. Laura was not there.

Struggling to keep her thoughts rational, Vicky walked over to the nightstand. She stopped herself from lifting the receiver. Whoever had been here may have used the phone. She started for the door, taking in the room again—the pages torn from a notebook still on the table. No sign of the brown folder, no sign of Charlotte Allen's manuscript and red leather journal.

"Everything okay up there?" A woman shouted from the foot of the stairs.

Vicky hurried down, her hands shaking on the railing. "Are you the landlady?"

"Claire Shultz. I manage the place." The woman had short, dark hair that framed a narrow face with large, anxious eyes. A gray jacket hung around her shoulders like a cape, sleeves flapping in the wind.

"We have to call the police."

The manager stood riveted in place, eyes darting to the top of the stairs and back. Suddenly she turned and crossed the cement paving to the house. Vicky followed her into a boxcar-shaped kitchen with an arrow of light shining over the stove. The phone was wedged on the counter between two pots of purple African violets. She dialed 911 and waited, the buzzing noise accompanying the sound of her own breathing. When the operator picked up, she gave her name and explained that a woman, a professor named Laura Simmons, was missing from the Mountain House and that her room had been ransacked. There was blood in the bathroom. Claire Shultz gasped.

Vicky hit the disconnect button and—on automatic now, holding her breath—tapped the number for St. Francis Mission. One ring, two, and then the familiar voice. "Father O'Malley."

"Something terrible's happened to Laura." She blurted out the words.

"Where are you?"

"At the Mountain House."

"I'm on my way."

She set the receiver in place and faced the manager. Struggling for the steady voice of the courtroom, she said, "Did you see anyone going to Laura's apartment?"

"This is a respectable apartment complex." Claire Shultz was wringing her hands, a blank look of disbelief and shock in her expression. "Miss Simmons said she was a college professor."

"Did you see anything?"

The woman's eyes fluttered, and she reached back and gripped the edge of the counter, swallowing once, twice. "I told you, this is a respectable place. Since Miss Simmons didn't say anything about being married, I didn't like her having men coming around. I don't approve of liaisons"—her tongue stumbled over the word—"between unmarried men and women. St. Paul to the Hebrews, chapter thirteen, verse four, says—"

Vicky interrupted, "What men? Did you see them?"

"Well"—Claire Shultz made a little clicking noise with her tongue—"I heard the cars comin' and goin' down the driveway. And I saw the man here last Tuesday night. Same man come around about an hour ago."

"What did he look like?"

"Big shoulders, lots of dark, curly hair, wild like one of them old hippies you see around the coffee shops." *He's very handsome, Vicky, with thick, curly brown hair. My* God, Vicky thought. The man Laura had just broken up with. The man who'd been calling and following her—stalking her—had followed her here. Vicky felt her heart take a jump.

There was the sound of an engine cutting off outside, then the crackle of a police radio. Blue and red lights fluttered through the window behind the manager. Vicky pushed open the door and hurried across the cement apron. A tall, blue-uniformed police officer who looked about thirty was levering himself out of a white police car, a studied expression on his pale face. The radio sputtered behind him.

"You the woman made the call?" he said, approaching her as if he had all the time in the world, as if Laura were not missing and there was no blood on the white tile floor.

Vicky gave him her name and said she was an attorney. Then she told him what she'd found, that her friend was missing. Glancing at the woman huddled near the back door, she said, "This is Claire Shultz, the manager."

"Wait here." The officer turned and started up the stairs, boots pounding on the wood steps.

Vicky hugged her coat around her. The wind was sharp, chilling her to the bone. Headlights trailed down the driveway as another police car pulled in behind the first. The doors swung open and two detectives lifted themselves out and walked over. Vicky recognized the tall man with the slight build, the hunched shoulders, and hollow space in his chest beneath the lapels of a tweed topcoat. Bob Eberhart. She had worked with him on numerous cases; anytime an Indian got into trouble in town, she got the call. A fair man, Eberhart. He treated Indians the same way he treated everybody else.

"What's going on, Vicky?" he said, walking over.

She began explaining: a friend from Colorado, a professor named Laura Simmons, was gone. There were signs of a struggle. She tilted her head toward the second story of the garage.

"Stick around a couple of minutes." Eberhart threw out the request as he and his partner started up the stairs. In a few minutes he was back, a small notepad clutched in one hand, pen in the other. "You say the missing lady's a friend of yours?"

Vicky nodded. The first police officer had come down the stairs with the other detective, two broad-shouldered men flanking Eberhart, blocking out the faint light in the kitchen window. They kept their eyes fixed on her and she went on: "Laura's car isn't here, and I've been trying to reach her since Wednesday."

"Well, I taped her messages on the door." The manager had walked timidly forward and was standing off by herself, leaning into the conversation. "I figured she'd come back sooner or later."

Vicky stared at the woman. What had she been thinking? The messages had accumulated for two days; why hadn't she notified someone? She'd told the woman she was Laura's friend. She could have called her.

Looking back at Eberhart, she said, "Mrs. Schultz said a man was here earlier. It could be Laura's ex-boyfriend."

Eberhart shifted his gaze to the middle-aged woman. "You see the man?"

The manager nodded slowly. "Three nights ago he come around."

"You saw him again tonight?"

"Yes," she said haltingly. "A fine-looking man, I'd say." She raised one hand. "Please understand I don't approve of single women inviting men into their apartments. This is a very respectable, Christian establishment—"

"Yes, I'm sure. Could you identify him?" Eberhart's voice was insistent, honing in.

"Oh, no. I make it a firm policy never to get involved in my guests' private lives."

That was the truth, Vicky thought. She hadn't even bothered to notice that a tenant was missing.

"We've got the messages," Eberhart said, nodding toward the other detective. "Looks like three from you, Vicky. One from your friend Father O'Malley. We'll check out the others." He took in a quick gulp of air. "What kind of car your friend drive?"

Vicky told him: a blue SAAB, she wasn't sure of the year. Not new. Then she said, "Her ex-boyfriend's Toby Becker, an English professor at the University of Colorado. Laura had just broken

138

things off with him, and he followed her here. He's battered her in the past."

Eberhart's expression remained the same. She knew he'd taken a bullet in the chest once. Nothing else could jolt him. He wrote something on the pad, then, peering at the manager: "You see what he was driving?"

"I believe so," the woman said. "One of them sports cars. A black BMW, I'm pretty sure."

"There's something else, Bob," Vicky went on. "Laura had a manuscript of the biography she's working on and a red leather journal. They're not in the room."

"They could be with her."

Vicky flinched at the image of Laura, beaten, bleeding, clinging to the brown folder with the precious documents, forced down the stairs and into her car.

She said, "Laura was trying to find a man on the res who has an important document that she needed for the biography."

"A man on the res? Give me a break, Vicky. You got a name?" Eberhart kept his eyes on her, pen stopped over the notepad.

"Toussaint."

"First name? Last name?" The pen tapped impatiently.

"I don't know." She told him about Charlotte Allen. There could be a connection.

It sounded preposterous, she thought, as flimsy as the last traces of snow dissolving in the wind. A man who may not even exist, breaking into Laura's apartment, attacking her, forcing her to go with him.

Eberhart drew back the front of the topcoat and—slowly, slowly—tucked the notebook and pen in the inside pocket. His eyes mirrored her own doubt. The man who'd been here was Toby Becker. The manager had seen him.

"It's possible Laura and this Becker fellow had an altercation. He could've taken her to one of the hospitals," he said, motioning toward the uniformed officer, who snapped to attention and walked over to his car. The officer perched on the driver's seat, boots still planted on the driveway, and lifted a small black microphone to his mouth. Radio static burst over the hush of his voice. In a moment he walked back. "No record, sir, of Laura Simmons at any hospitals. She might've gone to a private doctor."

"She doesn't know anyone here," Vicky said, urgency cutting through her voice. "You've got to find her, Bob. She's hurt."

"Well, we'll get Becker's plate number," Eberhart said. "If he's left the area, he could be heading back to Colorado. State patrol will pick him up before he reaches the border. We'll have a talk with the neighbors and other tenants. Try not to jump to conclusions till we sort it out. I'll let you know the minute we know anything."

Out of the corner of her eye, Vicky caught sight of the tall figure coming up the driveway, the long strides, the easy, confident posture. She went to meet him. "Oh, God, I'm glad to see you," she said.

"What happened?" Father John set his hand on her arm.

She told him about the room, the blood. She told him that Laura was missing.

She waited while John O'Malley explained to the detective that Laura had been at the Arapaho Museum late Wednesday afternoon, but she hadn't kept an appointment with Theresa Redwing on Thursday.

When he had finished, Vicky said, "Can we go somewhere?"

He could have killed her."

"Start at the beginning," Father John said.

Vicky sat across from him at the little round table, hands wrapped around a coffee mug, the black coat draped across her shoulders, her neck and face like polished copper in the overhead light. They were the only patrons in the coffee shop. From behind the counter, where the proprietor was wiping down an aluminum coffeemaker, came the late night sounds of running water and clinking glass. The neon light had gone black outside.

Vicky shifted against the red Naugahyde chair, a hint of reluctance mingling with the fury in her eyes. The man's name was Toby Becker, she was saying. A brilliant writer, according to Laura, who just happened to be a batterer. She'd finally left him and was trying to reclaim her own life and finish her work. There was redemption in work. Did he understand?

Father John nodded slowly, his eyes on hers. He

had lost himself in work. It was the choice he had made, the vow he had taken.

"Toby followed her here," Vicky said. "It must have been Toby the landlady saw Tuesday night. He was determined to get her back. He wouldn't leave her alone. She could have been staying somewhere else for a couple of days to avoid him. When she came back to the Mountain House this evening, he could have been waiting. It's the most dangerous time for a woman, John, when the batterer figures out that the relationship is really over. Whatever happened, she took the manuscript and journal. They're not in the apartment."

"The police will find him. Laura's probably with him. She could be hurt, but she may be okay."

Vicky tilted her head back and stared at some point above his head. She was crying silently, the moisture glistening on her cheeks. He shifted sideways, pulled the handkerchief from the back pocket of his blue jeans, and handed it to her, feeling lost and helpless.

"Nothing ever works out the way you want it to, does it?" She was dabbing at the moisture. "Someone always wants to change you, wants you to be someone different, for them."

Was she talking about Laura, he wondered, or about herself? Is that what Ben asked of her—to be someone other than who she was?

Suddenly he realized she could be talking about him. That he should be someone different. For her. Was that what she was saying?

142

He shoved the idea away. He was imagining things, hearing a melody that played only in his head. She was with Ben now.

"I'm thinking about moving to Denver," she said, her expression blank with acceptance. "My old firm has an opening. It's the chance to handle the kind of cases I'd hoped to take on for my own people."

He felt as if she'd thrown her coffee in his face. He had assumed she would always be here; that later, when he was gone, he would think of her here. "It takes time, Vicky," he heard himself saying, as if she were the white person, he the Arapaho, explaining how things were on the reservation. "They're still getting used to you. A woman and a lawyer. You've broken the mold." And then he understood what she'd been saying: her own people wanted her to be someone else.

She gave him a mirthless smile. "Exactly what I told Laura about Sacajawea. She'd stepped out, become like a chief, went ahead of the men. Not the way of an Indian woman. That was two hundred years ago, John. I'm not sure things have changed."

"Somehow I don't see Ben living in Denver."

She laughed at this. "Riding a horse down the Sixteenth Street Mall? Rounding up a herd of cattle in the suburbs?" She pushed her mug to one side. "I didn't ask him."

Father John didn't say anything for a moment. Finally he told her that he was sorry it hadn't worked out for her.

"You can't reclaim the past, John," she said,

slowly pushing her chair back and getting up. "I mean, you can't live there anymore."

The words burned through the turmoil in his own mind. The academic world, the student-crowded halls, the lectures and papers and endless round of meetings. How could he live there again? He threw a couple dollars on the table and followed her outside.

The air was heavy and cold with the expectation of snow. The wind whipped along the sidewalk and blew the skirt of her coat against his blue jeans as he walked her back to the Bronco, the *click-click* of their footsteps echoing off the brick-and-glass walls that lined the sidewalk. She seemed small beside him.

He held the door and waited as she settled herself behind the wheel of the Bronco. She said, "I'll go see Eberhart first thing in the morning."

"Call me as soon as you hear anything," he said, closing the door.

Snow clouds obliterated the stars and moon as Father John curved east on 789, cutting through Hudson, then north onto the reservation, *Idomeneo* filling the cab—the strange realism of Mozart. Father John's thoughts careened from Laura to Vicky. They were friends. Vicky would be awake all night, consumed with worry. She'd be at Eberhart's first thing in the morning. She wouldn't rest until she'd found her friend, the pale, blond woman clutching a brown folder.

She'd taken the folder with her, Vicky had said. He tapped one fist against the wheel, something gnawing at him, something not right—the rationality imposed on an irrational act, an attack on a woman. How in heaven's name did Laura have time to grab the folder? And why did she want it with her?

Unless, unless—tapping the wheel in rhythm to the music now, ordering his thoughts. Laura didn't want to lose the manuscript and journal. She was trying to keep them safe. But if she had been worried about them, wouldn't she have put them somewhere else?

That was it, he thought, giving the wheel a hard jab. A logical explanation for the documents not being in the apartment. Laura hadn't grabbed them during the attack. She'd taken them somewhere else before Toby Becker had arrived.

And then the logic collapsed, like the farthest reaches of the headlights in the darkness. Why would Laura want to protect the manuscript and journal from a former boyfriend?

Suddenly he saw the problem—a false proposition. It wasn't Toby Becker from whom Laura had wanted to keep the documents. It was someone else, and Father John had a pretty good idea where she might have taken them.

⇒ 18 ⇐

Father John left the Toyota in front of the residence a few feet from the Harley and walked through the splash of light to the museum. On Wednesday, Laura's blue SAAB had been parked in front. Obviously Lindy had found the letters and called Laura. She would have seen at once that a museum devoted to the Arapahos was a safe place to store documents on the Shoshones. No one would look for them there.

He let himself in with the master key. Thin slivers of light fell across the entry and ran into the shadowy corridor, which he followed to the library. He turned on the fluorescent ceiling light. The pile of cartons along the wall had dwindled, and new boxes lined shelves that had been vacant a few days ago. Wedged on a middle shelf was a large gray box marked ORAL HISTORIES AND LETTERS, 1900-1910.

He tilted back the lid. The brown folder was almost obscured by the overstuffed folders in the front. He lifted it out and carried it over to the table. Inside he found the manuscript and the red leather journal.

On the top sheet of the manuscript, in large print, was the title: *Sacajawea: The Hidden Life*. Below, in smaller print: By *Charlotte Allen, Ph.D.* He couldn't read the entire manuscript—four hundred brittle pages. It would take all night. He started scanning the chapters, hunting for the gist of the story, the way he'd scanned hundreds of documents in the past when he was researching some question in history.

April 7, 1805: the great adventure begins. The Corps of Discovery under the command of Captains Meriwether Lewis and William Clark sets forth from the Mandan villages. Thirty-one men, a woman, an infant. The woman digs roots and wild vegetables, gathers berries as they cross the mountains. She cares for her infant. *Toussaint was very brutal with her.*

The woman maintains her presence of mind in a squall and saves the expedition's important scientific instruments after they are washed into the Missouri.

The woman is sick, and Captain Clark fears she will die. *The thoughtlessness of the husband; he didn't take care of her.*

She holds her infant close in a flash flood. She weeps with joy at the sight of her brother, Chief Cameahwait, when the expedition reaches the Shoshones. She adopts her deceased sister's son, Bazil, whom she leaves in the village.

On and on the expedition goes, through the Bitterroots and down the Snake and the Columbia to the Pacific. A winter camp is established seventeen miles inland. The men go on to the ocean and see a whale that has washed onto the beach. *The Indian woman was very importunate to be permitted to go, and was therefore indulged; she observed that she had traveled a long way with us to see the great waters, and that now that monstrous fish was also to be seen, she thought it very hard she could not be permitted to see either.* Clark arranges for Sacajawea to go to the ocean.

Spring, 1806: the expedition starts the return trip. The familiar hardships—heavy snows, scarcity of meat and timber, the ever-present mountains. *I see the way.* Clark follows two routes that Sacajawea points out. They return to the Mandans. *Sacajawea has borne with a patience truly admirable the fatigues of so long a route encumbered with the charge of an infant, who is even now only nineteen months old.* "My little dancing boy," Clark calls him.

August 20, 1806: letter from Clark to Toussaint: If you wish to live with the white people, and will come to me, I will give you a piece of land . . .

1810-1811: the family is in St. Louis, but the old trader doesn't take to civilization.

And it is here, Father John realizes, that the stories diverge. He scanned the written records:

March 1811: Toussaint and his Shoshone wife travel back up the Missouri to Indian country.

December 1812: an entry in the ledger at Fort Manuel: *Toussaint's Shoshone wife died of putrid fever today . . . the best woman in the fort.*

The oral histories of the Shoshones were next; Father John lingered over them: It is Toussaint's other Shoshone wife who dies at Fort Manuel. Sacajawea and Baptiste remain in St. Louis. The trader returns for them, and the family moves onto the plains, where he takes another wife, a beautiful, young Ute woman. Sacajawea no longer pleases him. *He whipped her in front of his Ute wife.*

Sacajawea flees south to the Comanches, a new land, a new life. She remains until—Charlotte Allen is speculating now, Father John realizes—the news travels across the plains that the old trader is dead. Sacajawea goes north to her people and is reunited with her sons.

Father John restacked the manuscript and leaned back in the chair, stretching his cramped legs, watching the prism of light—reds, blues, yellows—in the black windowpane. The old building was absolutely still, frozen in the past, in a time when everything was new—the reservation, St. Francis Mission, the roads the Arapahos and Shoshones would travel. Sacajawea had come home to her people then. She had told her stories; her spirit was in the stories.

Stories that contradicted the written records. Without the memoirs, he knew, the biography was inconclusive, a rehash of material already published. He could sense the desperation permeating the manuscript. The same desperation he had sensed in Laura Simmons, and Laura had been searching for the memoirs when she disappeared. Just like Charlotte Allen.

He placed the manuscript back in the folder and began thumbing through the journal. The writing was small and precise, the careful notes of an indefatigable scholar detailing each step of research. Records from the cultural center, interviews with the four oldest descendants, an entry for each day: *Drove to the senior citizen center. Talked to the elders.* There was no mention of Toussaint until two weeks before the final entry. *Toussaint has been a great help to me.*

Father John read quickly through the other entries.

A great secret! Toussaint told me that the memoirs

escaped the fire! His own great-grandfather rushed into the burning building and grabbed everything he could. The memoirs have been with the family since. Toussaint has made me promise not to tell anyone. I am the only one outside the family who knows about the memoirs . . .

Toussaint says the family is reluctant to speak of their famous ancestor. They are like Sacajawea herself. She was modest and unassuming. She lived quietly . . .

Toussaint will plead my case with the family elders. He will swear that I am of good heart . . .

Good news! This is the most wonderful day of my life. The elders have given me permission to use the memoirs. Toussaint will bring them tonight.

Father John laid the journal in the folder next to the manuscript and rubbed at the headache tracing his temples, struggling to make sense of the notations. If Toussaint had been a great help, why hadn't Charlotte Allen mentioned him earlier? Why did she call him Toussaint? Was that his name, or was she trying to conceal his identity? What had she been hiding? It didn't make sense. She had trusted the man. She was planning to meet him the day she died.

The day she died, he thought, the headache starting to pulse now. Suppose it was Toussaint who had beaten her to death, then buried her body by the river and taken her car out to Sacajawea Ridge? And suppose she had kept her promise? She'd told no one about the memoirs. But she was an historian and she'd made a written record. Toussaint probably had no idea it existed.

Until Laura Simmons had appeared on the res with Charlotte Allen's manuscript and journal, looking for the memoirs. But it wasn't the manuscript that Toussaint cared about. Toussaint had to have the journal—the evidence that linked him to the murdered Charlotte Allen. That explained why he'd come after Laura and ransacked her room.

The headache was pounding, a siren in his head. What had Toussaint done to Laura?

He returned the folder to its hiding place. Retracing his steps through the empty corridor, he let himself out and locked the front door. As he walked back to the residence he heard the scratching sound of a wild animal in the darkness beyond the perimeter of lights. Before he talked to Gianelli, he wanted to test his theory on Vicky, search for the flaws in the clear brilliance of her mind. He'd call her first thing tomorrow.

≫ 19 ≪

The red-brick building that housed the Lander Police Department exuded a bleak, impersonal authority in a neighborhood of bungalows and fenced backyards with swing sets and red wagons abandoned for the winter. Vicky adjusted the strap of her black bag over one shoulder as she let herself into the heat-dried air of the entry. Bob Eberhart stood in the glass-enclosed cubicle on the right, waving a sheaf of papers at a uniformed officer, lips moving in a fury of noiseless words. He looked up and gestured toward the door next to the cubicle.

A low buzz sounded, like that of a persistent hornet, as the door swung open. "Just called your office," Eberhart said over the shoulder of his blue shirt as he started down the narrow hallway, papers gripped next to the black strap of his holster. Vicky walked beside him past a succession of closed doors with names printed in black letters on the pebbly glass. The pale green walls gave back faint odors of perspiration and stale smoke.

The detective pushed open the door at the far end and waited as she stepped into the closet-sized office so tidy it might have been vacant. The last time she had been there, she could hardly push her way through the clutter. Now the top of the desk was perfectly clear, except for the folder lined up with the front edge.

"Any word on Laura?" she said, dropping into the side chair. Her voice was hoarse with anxiety and fatigue.

"Sorry." The detective took the swivel chair behind the desk. "Checked with the Boulder police last night, had them go to her apartment. No sign of her. Landlady said she hadn't returned."

"And her SAAB?"

"No enchilada." Eberhart picked up a pencil and began tapping the edge of the desk. "State patrol did pick up her boyfriend outside Rawlins, turns out."

Vicky scooted forward; she felt her heart begin to accelerate. This was good news.

The detective held up the pencil, a traffic cop raising his stick to stop the rush of traffic. "Don't get your hopes up. Becker was hightailing it to Colorado, like we thought. Patrol brought him back. Just finished a little question-and-answer session with him and his lawyer over at the county jail."

"Where's Laura?"

"He was alone, Vicky. No sign of any struggle in his car. No blood."

A phone was ringing down the hall somewhere, a muffled distant jangle, like a memory. The scenario she'd worked out last night when she'd found herself awake, staring into the blackness, was wrong. Toby hadn't forced Laura to go with him.

"What did he do with her?"

"He admits he went to her apartment last night." The detective tilted his head back and peered at her down the long, sharpened angles of his face. "He claims that when he saw the mess, he took off."

"He didn't report it? Something terrible could have happened to Laura, and he didn't bother to pick up a phone and call the police?"

Eberhart was shaking his head. "The man says he and Laura Simmons had a few misunderstandings in the past."

Vicky cut in: "He beat her up."

"Well, he called it misunderstandings, and he was afraid if he reported her missing, with the room ransacked and all, we might think he had something to do with it. So he says he got out of there."

"He's lying." Vicky gripped the armrests against

the impulse to propel herself out of the chair and start pacing. She could think better, marshal her thoughts, when she was moving. She paced at home, in the office, in the courtroom. There was no room to pace here.

"You know that for sure?"

"He's a batterer, Bob," Vicky said. "Laura was trying to leave him. He was stalking her. He wouldn't let her go. You know that's the most dangerous time for a woman, when she tries to break away. He came here Tuesday night. He could have come back the next night."

"Okay, let's say that's what happened. Becker bludgeoned her and took her somewhere. Why did he return to the apartment last night?"

The detective leaned back until the top of the swivel chair scraped against the wall. He laced thin fingers over the blue shirt. "The man says Laura rebuffed him, crushed his ego, as he put it, on Tuesday. So he drove back to Colorado. Says he was there two days before deciding to give it another try. He drove back yesterday. According to him, he's been on the highway most of the time Laura's been missing. A friend he poured out his troubles to will vouch for him, he says. Laura Simmons's department chair, as it turns out. He's one of her acquaintances we've got a call into right now."

"He'll cover for Becker, Bob. He's the one who must have told Becker where Laura was. The chairman knew where she was staying." She locked eyes with the man on the other side of the desk.

"You're going to let Becker go, aren't you?"

"What choice do I have? This is a man with no priors. He's gotten two speeding tickets in the last fifteen years."

Vicky got to her feet and moved to the window. One, two, three steps. She stopped and turned back. "Laura never reported the assaults. She must have been too ashamed."

The detective tossed the pencil down on the file folder. It made a soft thud. "Look, Vicky, I want to find your friend. I want to know what happened in that apartment. Gianelli's in on the case. He's got that twenty-year-old homicide of another Colorado professor who came here to research Sacajawea. Could be a big coincidence, one professor murdered, another missing, but we can't ignore the similarities. Right now we don't have any evidence that Toby Becker had anything to do with whatever happened to Laura Simmons."

Vicky stepped back and leaned over the desk, flattening both hands on the smooth surface. "He knows where Laura is. I want to talk to him."

"Highly irregular, Vicky. You know that." He unfolded his lanky frame and stood up, gripping the edge of the desk. "Besides, he's probably been released by now."

Vicky picked up her black bag and started for the door. "Maybe I can catch him before he leaves."

The detective's footsteps made a *slap-slap* sound on the vinyl floor behind her as she hurried down the hall. She opened the door to the entry and glanced back. "Don't worry, Bob," she said. "I won't compromise your investigation. I'm Laura's friend, that's all."

Vicky saw the two men emerge through the double-glassed entrance to the squat, red-bricked Fremont County Jail as she turned into the parking lot. They stood on the sidewalk, the taller man snapping up a bulky red jacket, eyes surveying the rows of vehicles. The tousled brown hair, the striking features, the insouciant air—Laura had described Toby Becker to a T. The man in the gray topcoat and pressed gray trousers raising a gloved finger in the air, was Mark Hensler, local attorney. She'd clashed with him in the courtroom a number of times.

Suddenly the attorney stepped off the curb and headed toward a white 4x4. Becker turned in the opposite direction, walking in a relaxed, confident stride toward the black BMW at the end of the row. Vicky slid the Bronco into the vacant space next to the sports car and jumped out.

"Toby," she called as the man pointed an opener toward the BMW and smiled, satisfied at the clicking noise.

"Do I know you?" He glanced up.

"I'm a friend of Laura's."

She moved around the hood as he snapped open the door, placing it between them, and started to drop inside. "Anything you want to say, you can say to my lawyer."

"I'm very worried about her. I'm sure you must

be, too."

Slowly he lifted himself upright and rested both arms on the top of the door, allowing his eyes to take her in. She could sense the strength of the man, not unlike the strength that was in Ben. "Of course I'm worried," he said.

Not worried enough to have reported her missing, Vicky thought. She said, "I went to see Laura last night." Her voice was firm. "I'm the one who called the police."

Toby Becker gave a low whistle as if he'd just assured himself that she could not be trusted. "Well, you can talk to my lawyer. I don't know anything about what happened to Laura." He started to get back inside, and Vicky took hold of the door. The metallic cold penetrated her glove. "Did you and Laura argue when you came to see her Tuesday night? Did she tell you she never wanted to see you again?"

"None of your business," he said. He stood up again and drew in a breath, his nostrils collapsing into thin, disapproving lines, his blue eyes darkening into black stones. "Laura and I have had our misunderstandings over the past year, and she's told me it was all over, but she always came back. This breakup was no more permanent than the others. Laura's very emotional. She gets upset about nothing." He leaned over the door toward her. "I find high-spirited women very interesting, however. Just begging to be tamed."

"Did you hit her again, Becker? Did you tear up

her notepad and throw the pages around, ransack the room?"

"Now, why would I do that? I don't give a robin's shit for some biography of Pocahontas. Unlike Laura, I'm not willing to spend my life editing somebody else's work. I create my own work. I'm a novelist."

"The Sacajawea biography is important to Laura."

"Brilliant deduction. Much more important than I am or the novel I took valuable time from to come running after her. That was my mistake. Let me explain what happened when I saw Laura Tuesday night. She was all aquiver about meeting some man who could get her some great historical document. Well, I figure she found him, and he roughed her up. Or maybe she threw one of her tantrums and trashed the place herself and went off someplace to sulk. I don't know, and frankly I don't care."

He started to pull the door in, but Vicky grabbed the edge. "Wait a minute. Who was the man?"

"I didn't ask, sweetheart. I drove all day to grovel, which is what she likes. Oh, she gets her jollies watching me grovel. And all she can talk about is some guy who's going to get her critical evidence. Critical evidence." A falsetto voice now. "And I'm supposed to believe that's all she wanted? I refer any further questions to my attorney." He yanked the door free from her hand and slid in behind the wheel.

Vicky stepped back as the BMW's engine burst

into life and the car shot backward, peppering her with miniscule specks of dust and ice before swinging onto the street. She walked to the Bronco, slid inside, and turned the ignition. The engine hummed and vibrated around her; cold air pushed through the vents. Eberhart was right. There was no evidence. Anyone could have come to the apartment and attacked Laura. Toby Becker could be telling the truth.

She drew in a long breath, threw the transmission into reverse, and began backing out, her thoughts switching gears now. Maybe her instincts had been right to begin with. Maybe Laura's research had put her in danger. She could have found the man who had the memoirs. She could have found Toussaint.

Vicky wheeled out onto the street and headed north to the reservation.

≫ 20 ≪

It was mid-morning before Father John got to the work he wanted to finish before he left—bills to pay, letters to answer, phone calls to return. Boxes were accumulating in the office; he still had another couple of drawers to pack. The phone had started ringing the moment he'd come in—parishioners asking if the farewell feast was still on after Mass tomorrow, if he was still leaving. Yes, he'd said absentmindedly, his thoughts on Laura Simmons.

He'd called Gianelli about the journal and

manuscript. The agent would be by later to pick them up. Father John hadn't explained his theory. Not yet. Last night, in the quiet of the library, it had seemed perfectly logical. This morning it seemed like more and more of a stretch. He wanted to talk to Vicky first. He'd tried her office and left a message.

The phone had rung again before he could call Lindy at the museum. It was the director, a tense, worried note in her voice. She'd seen the police notes in the morning's paper. She'd asked question after question; he'd done his best to explain about the journal and manuscript without alarming her. "The FBI agent's on his way over," he said. "Try not to worry. They're safe until he gets here."

"I'm not worried about them," she'd said. "What about Laura Simmons?"

"The police will find her." He told her again not to worry, the words hollow in his ears.

Four or five pickups—Howard Elkman's old brown Chevy was one of them—had passed outside the window while they'd talked, and he'd asked the director what was going on. She'd found some old letters the elders were interested in, she'd explained.

Now Father John arranged a stack of bills by dates—the oldest to be paid first. The most recent, sometime in the future, God willing. He was about to write out a check when Kevin walked in and dropped the *Gazette* on the desk, an index finger on the police notes near the bottom of the first page.

"The emergency you went out on last night?" the other priest asked.

160

He nodded. He'd passed Kevin on his way out and told him there was some kind of emergency in Lander. A perplexed look had come into the man's face. Lander? How big is our parish? He'd taken a minute to explain that a CU professor here to do research on the reservation could be in trouble.

"I assume this professor was interviewing people."

"I assume so."

"She was interviewing people, and now she's missing?" There was stunned disbelief in the man's voice.

"There's an ex-boyfriend in the picture."

"Oh, I see," Kevin said, as if he didn't see at all. He shrugged and disappeared into the corridor, his footsteps fading on the hard floor.

Father John went back to the bills, aware of the sounds of rustling paper, a chair scraping the floor in the other office—impatient sounds. Kevin had been going over the finances, and Father John guessed the new pastor had just grasped the thin financial ledge on which St. Francis tottered along. He wrote the check and was stuffing it into an envelope when the front door squealed open. The footsteps were quick and tense. He got to his feet just as Vicky appeared in the doorway, one hand poised to knock. Her hair fell loosely over the collar of her black coat, which gave her a relaxed look that belied the anxiety in her eyes.

"Any word on Laura?" Father John knew the answer even as he asked. He walked around the desk and sat back against the edge at her eye level.

Vicky shook her head, and then she explained: the state patrol had found Toby Becker; Eberhart had questioned him and let him go. She'd caught up with the man in the jail parking lot. "He admits he saw Laura Tuesday night, but he claims she was fine when he left."

"Do you believe him?"

Vicky walked past him to the window, then to the desk, then the window again, winding her way among the packed boxes. After a moment she said, "I don't know what to believe, John. Laura was trying to break off with him. She was afraid of him. But he says they'd been through this before, and she always came back. Maybe this time he knew she meant it, and he . . ."

She turned and stared outside a moment. Looking back, she said, "There's no evidence against him, no signs of blood in his car. He's a cocky, self-obsessed bastard, but he could be telling the truth."

It was then that he told her where Laura had hidden the manuscript and journal. And he told her about his theory.

She was quiet several seconds—pacing, pacing. Finally she dropped against the edge of the desk next to him. "It makes sense," she said. "Toussaint— whoever he is—must have heard that Laura had come to the reservation to finish Charlotte Allen's biography. Certainly it wasn't any secret that she had the manuscript and journal. He could have panicked, called Laura, arranged to come to the apartment."

Suddenly Vicky jumped up. "Somebody Laura talked to must have told Toussaint about her, which means somebody knows who he is. Laura intended to see Theresa Redwing."

"She didn't show up, Vicky," Father John reminded her.

"But that was two days ago. She might've gone to talk to her after Theresa called you. And she was going to do some research at the cultural center. Maybe she found a name . . ."

"Let's go see," Father John said.

They drove separately.

They'd had a discussion in the middle of Circle Drive, and he explained they could save time if they each drove. He would go to Theresa Redwing's, she to the cultural center. Vicky agreed. She'd see him at the center in—a glance at the silver watch on her wrist—four hours.

It was logical, Father John told himself as he headed toward the mountains etched in sunlight. Laura could be hurt somewhere, and time was critical. Still he couldn't shake off the disappointment. He'd had a sense of last things all week. This would have been their last drive across the reservation together.

He found himself glancing in the rearview mirror. She was there, the sun sparkling in the Bronco's bumper. At Highway 132, he turned right and drove north. The Bronco disappeared from view.

Vicky saw the police car parked in front of the white frame house that served as the cultural center when she turned in to Fort Washakie. She parked beside it and hurried up the walk dividing a brown patch of lawn and some scraggly bushes. She stepped into the entry, made her way up the stairs, and stopped. Papers and folders littered the library, toppling over the two long tables, falling onto the chairs, skittering over the floor. *Toussaint's already been here.*

A blur of navy-blue uniforms moved past the opened door across the room—two BIA police officers. One glanced back, then started toward her, picking his way through the papers. It was Patrick Banner, the police chief's son—a younger version of the chief himself, with the same long, brown face and serious eyes, the same easy, efficient manner. "Vicky? What're you doin' here?"

She ignored the question. "What happened?"

"Somebody decided to break in last night and tear the place apart. Bunch of kids, you ask me. Nothing better to do."

"See what they've done!" Phyllis Manley edged around the door, holding out a wad of papers, a look of disbelief on the plain, round face, like a sleepwalker in the midst of some nightmare. "All the old records, the old stories, thrown about like they were nothing. Why would anybody do this?"

Vicky walked over. "Are you all right?" she said, taking Phyllis's arm and leading her carefully to one of the reading tables. She picked up the papers thrown on a chair and waited until the woman had sat down. Facing Patrick again, she said, "This could have something to do with the disappearance of a woman in Lander. Laura Simmons."

The director swiveled about. "I saw the article in this morning's paper. It's terrible. Did the police find her yet?"

"Not yet." Vicky patted Phyllis's shoulder.

"What makes you think this is related?" Patrick asked. The second officer was standing in the doorway, thumbs linked in the pockets of his uniform trousers, head bent forward as if awaiting her answer.

"Laura has some documents that belonged to the woman found by the river last week."

"The old skeleton?" This from the other officer.

"Somebody wants the documents. Whoever it is ransacked Laura's apartment. He could have thought Laura left the documents here."

"Why would anybody think such a thing?" Phyllis said, the high pitch of her voice like a wail of pain.

Patrick Banner had pulled a small notebook and pen from his jacket pocket and was jotting something down. After a moment he snapped the cover in place. "We'll let the fed know, and we'll do our own investigation. Kids like to brag. Somebody might shoot his mouth off, and we'll find the guys responsible."

The other officer had already started for the door, and Patrick followed. "Don't worry, Phyllis," he said, glancing back. "We'll keep a close eye on the place." And then they were gone. The door cracked into the quiet, rustling the papers on the floor.

Vicky cleared another chair and sat down next to the director. "Laura did some research here, didn't she?"

Phyllis nodded, a slow, jerky motion, as if her head were not firmly attached to the rest of her body. "She was here for two days, wanting to see everything on Sacajawea. We went through all the files. It took some time, I can tell you. That is one determined white woman. She just didn't want to believe that what she was looking for wasn't here."

Vicky glanced around. Laura wasn't the only one, she thought. She said, "Did Laura mention anyone she was interviewing?"

"Well"—the word elongated into two syllables— "she'd already arranged to talk to Theresa Redwing, and Robert suggested—"

"Robert?" Vicky felt her pulse quicken.

"Robert Crow Wolf." The woman's expression softened, the outrage forgotten for a half second. "He was here doing research on the agricultural history of the reservation." Her eyes had started to wander about the room; suddenly the tears were coming in long, thin streams. She pulled a tissue out of the pocket of her blue skirt and dabbed at her cheeks. "How's anybody ever gonna find any records now?"

Crow Wolf. Vicky barely knew the man. She'd seen him at powwows and other celebrations. She'd heard the gossip about how hard he'd worked for his doctorate, how proud the Shoshone elders were of him. She'd envied the man for that.

"What did he suggest to Laura?" she asked.

"Oh, he was very helpful. Suggested she talk to Willie Silver. Even called Willie himself and set up the interview for Wednesday. You know Willie?"

Vicky nodded. One of the Shoshone elders, a descendant of Sacajawea. His father had been one of the four elders that Charlotte Allen had interviewed. Willie was a drunk. Vicky hadn't suggested that Laura interview the man.

"Did Robert suggest anyone else?"

"Not so far as I know. Just Willie."

"Is Robert still here?"

"Oh, no, no." Phyllis was shaking her head. "He went back to Laramie three days ago for his classes."

"Thanks, Phyllis," Vicky said, getting to her feet. She was halfway to the door when she turned back. Phyllis sat slumped against the chair, looking as dejected as a discarded doll. "Will you be okay?"

Phyllis grabbed the edge of the table—a slow, deliberate motion—and levered herself upright. "I gotta be, don't I? I gotta get the stories back together."

Vicky eased the Bronco through Fort Washakie, then turned on to Highway 287 and pressed down on the accelerator. Willie Silver's ranch was out on Sacajawea Ridge, a good forty-five-minute drive.

167

⇒· 21 ·⇐

Highway 132 was a ragged road that shot north before bending into the east. A white frame house rose out of the expanse of plains ahead, like the last surviving tipi in an Indian village after the cavalry had swept through. Father John eased up on the accelerator and turned on to Rabbit Brush Road, then into the yard, bumping across the ridges of bare earth. As he started toward the front door it swung open.

"Come on in out of the cold." Theresa Redwing, gray hair curled tightly around her face, one hand stuffed into the pocket of the white apron tied at her waist, looked out from the shadowy interior. "I wasn't expectin' visitors," she said, letting herself down on a brown sofa with white crocheted doilies arranged along the top that reminded him of the sofas in his youth. "Always good when folks stop by."

Just as he was about to take one of the upholstered chairs against the opposite wall, a young woman with shiny black hair and a trim figure in blue jeans and white T-shirt walked out of the hallway. "You know my granddaughter Hope?" Theresa said. "She's back home from Laramie for a couple days doin' some research for the book she's writing on our ancestor."

"A dissertation, Grandmother." The woman started across the small room, hand extended. "Nice to see you again, Father." Her hand felt cool, her grip surprisingly firm. "How can we help you?"

He waited until she'd taken a straight, high-backed chair before he sat down. "I'm worried about Laura Simmons," he said, addressing the older woman. "She's missing from her apartment."

"I seen the *Gazette* this morning," Theresa said. "Sounds like that white woman's got herself some man troubles. Must be the reason she didn't come out here Thursday, like she said."

"Did you hear from her again?" Father John leaned forward.

The old woman was shaking her head. "I must've scared her off, Father. I told her about Hope here."

"Grandmother simply told her the truth." Hope stared at him with frank, steady eyes. She crossed her jeans-clad legs, letting one foot swing freely. "I know what Professor Simmons is after. She thinks she's going to find Sacajawea's memoirs. Does she really believe any Shoshone will give them to a white woman? I'm the one my people will give them to."

The words jolted him. *Toussaint will bring the memoirs tonight.* And Laura had thought she would get the memoirs. Now this young woman. "You must know the man who has the memoirs," he said. "Toussaint?"

Theresa made an impatient *hrmmmp* noise. "I told you, Father, nobody by that name. And I never heard about any memoirs either. Sacajawea told her stories, and the agent's wife wrote 'em down. What she wrote was burned up, but it don't matter. Writing them down don't make them true. Lots of folks heard the stories and passed them down. We got 'em in our hearts."

"I'm sorry, Grandmother, but you don't understand," Hope said, a calm, patient tone. "Stories that are written down while they're still fresh are more important than stories passed down orally."

"Oh, she says I don't understand." The old woman threw up both hands and spoke to some point on the side wall. "Well, we been keepin' stories for a long time without the help of historians telling us what's good and what isn't." She rearranged herself on the sofa and faced her granddaughter. "Why you wanna do what Robert Crow Wolf's doin' anyway, Hope? Why you wanna make him look like he's not special?"

"We've been over this, Grandmother." The younger woman's expression remained calm and reflective, and Father John wondered at the effort. "Robert doesn't feel that way. He's my adviser, and he's been a great help. You know that some of the elders wouldn't have talked to a woman if Robert hadn't asked them to." She lifted herself up and started backing around the chair. "I hope you'll excuse me, Father. I have some work I want to finish."

"Hope, wait." Father John was on his feet. "Laura Simmons expected to get the memoirs, and now she's missing. Twenty years ago Charlotte Allen believed she'd get the memoirs. She was murdered. Who is it that promised them to you?"

"The elders," she said.

"One of them has told you he has the memoirs?"

"I don't know who has them, Father." Calm, assured of her position. She might have been fielding the questions in an oral exam. "But I'll have them in the next day or two. Don't worry about me, Father. I can take care of myself." She gave him a slow, confident smile before she turned into the hallway.

Theresa's eyes followed the fading shush of her granddaughter's footsteps. She shook her head. "I don't know, Father. All this trouble about some memoirs that I never heard of. All Hope has to do is listen to the stories, but she says they're not good enough for her anymore." Father John walked over, took the woman's hand, and thanked her for her hospitality. "Try not to worry about her," he said, forcing a note of confidence into his tone to mask his own worry. Minutes later he was guiding the Toyota back across the yard and onto the highway, leaning onto the accelerator, an alarm sounding in his head. Unwittingly, trustingly, Hope Stockwell had come across the man who called himself Toussaint. He was here, and he knew where Laura was. They had to find him. Hope Stockwell could also be in danger.

There was something strange about the cultural center, Father John thought as he pulled into the curb. An unsettling quiet, as if the two-story, white-frame house had suddenly been vacated. He checked his watch. Four-thirty. Phyllis Manley had probably closed for the day. There was no sign of

Vicky's Bronco. The drive out to Theresa's had taken longer than he'd anticipated. Vicky could have gotten tired of waiting and gone back to Lander.

Except he knew she would wait for him here, just as she'd said. He got out of the pickup and went up the sidewalk. The door was unlocked. "Anyone here?" he called, stepping into the small entry. He took the stairs two at a time.

Phyllis Manley sat at one of the long tables in the library, stacks of papers piled in front of her. A pathway of white paper wound around the floor. She looked up out of eyes shadowed with grief and fatigue.

"What's going on?" he said, the alarm in his head as loud as a gong. Toussaint was ahead of them, a spirit darting about, striking wherever he wanted, leaving destruction behind.

"Oh, Father. You see what they did?"

"Who did this?"

"Some kids, the police say. Broke out a back window last night and got in. Pulled all the files and cartons off the shelves. Tossed everything around. I don't know how I'll ever get it back in order."

Father John felt his stomach muscles clench. This wasn't the work of kids. This was the work of a man desperate to find a journal that could link him to a twenty-year-old murder. And what he wanted was in the library at the Arapaho Museum. The man could show up there.

"May I use your phone?" He stepped over to the desk and dialed the museum's number. He waited, beating out a rhythm with his fingers on the wood. Pick up. *Pick up.* Finally Lindy's voice on the other end. "Arapaho Museum."

"Has Gianelli been there?" he said, not bothering to identify himself. She knew his voice.

"About two hours ago, Father. He got the folder okay."

Good. He could feel his muscles begin to relax. "Listen, Lindy," he said. "I want you to close the museum, lock all the doors, and go home."

"What? The elders are still here reading through some letters."

She wasn't alone. "The minute they've finished, lock up and go. If you see Father Kevin, ask him to keep an eye on the place. I'll be back as soon as possible."

He could feel the director's eyes on his back as he replaced the receiver. "You think those kids'll do the same thing to the Arapaho Museum?" she said.

He faced her. Ignoring the question, he said, "Have you seen Vicky Holden?"

"She was here earlier, Father. She left—oh, I'd say four hours ago. I can't be sure. The day has been so terrible, I'm afraid I haven't been very focused."

"Did she say where she was going?"

"I think she might've gone up to Willie Silver's place. She asked me who Laura Simmons might've talked to, and I told her about Willie."

"Where's the man live?"

"Up on Sacajawea Ridge. Take the wide dirt road off 287 just past Dinwoody Lakes. You'll see his old black truck before you see his shack back in the trees."

Forty-five minutes each way. Still, Vicky should have been back by now. He started for the door. "If she should return, ask her to wait for me here," he called over his shoulder.

The Toyota bounced over the ruts carved into the dirt road, the rear end swerving about. He was going too fast, he knew. The sun had disappeared, and thick, dark shadows drifted over the ponderosas flashing by the windows. It would be totally black in the mountains soon. He flipped on the headlights. He'd insisted they take separate vehicles. To save precious time! And now—Vicky had gone to see the same Shoshone Laura had talked to. She could be with Toussaint himself.

⇒ 22 ⇐

The headlights caught the glint of chrome as Father John rounded a curve. He slowed down. The tailgate of a black truck jutted over the dirt path, spilling into a road on the right. He turned past the truck, headlights jumping around the ponderosas. In the clearing ahead was the Bronco, parked next to a small gray shack. Vicky stood a few feet away, wrapped in the black coat, staring into the headlights, a mixture of astonishment and relief on her face. Between her and the Bronco was the large, hunched figure of a man.

Father John pulled in behind the Bronco and got out. "Any trouble?" he called, walking toward Vicky.

The man came toward him, blinking in the light. The odor of whiskey, at once sweet and bitter, floated ahead of him. "Who the hell are you?"

He brushed past the man and placed his arm around Vicky's shoulder. "Are you okay?"

"I was just leaving." She spoke slowly, defiantly.

The man threw up both hands, a gesture of surrender. "Yeah, your lady friend here was just leaving. Said she didn't want my company no more. I was just tryin' to change her mind. Hey, no offense, man."

Father John opened the Bronco door and Vicky folded herself inside. "I'll follow you out," he said as he closed the door, one eye on the Indian swaying a few feet away. The engine roared into the scattered light, the headlights flashed on, and then the Bronco was backing out, swerving around the Toyota. He waited until it had backed onto the road and started down the mountain. Then he walked past the man, got into the pickup, and followed.

When he reached 287, he saw the Bronco stopped alongside the road. He pulled in behind and walked up to the passenger side. The window was dropping. "What happened back there?" he said.

"Can we talk over some food?" Vicky's voice was low and tight.

"I'll meet you at Lana's," he told her.

What about Willie Silver?" Father John said. They

sat across from each other at a table near the window. Outside, the neon lights—Lana's Café—blinked over the parking lot. An occasional headlight flashed in the darkness of Highway 287 beyond the lot. The café was noisy, most of the tables occupied by families with young children squirming in the chairs. A group of Indian men lingered over coffee in one of the back booths. Lana herself, blond curls springing about her head, pad and pencil in hand, had taken their order: two hamburgers, two coffees.

Vicky was shaking her head slowly. "I thought I was going to have to fight my way out of there."

"He threaten you?" Father John heard the sound of his own voice, measured and tight.

Vicky glanced away, then looked back. "It hadn't reached that point yet. I was very glad to see the headlights bouncing up the road."

Father John waited as Lana delivered the plates of hamburger and poured two mugs of coffee. Then he said, "What does Willie know about Laura?"

"She came to see him Wednesday. That means Toby Becker's telling the truth that Laura was fine on Tuesday night." She drew in a long breath, then went on: "Willie says Laura was going to write the real story about Sacajawea's husband, Toussaint—what a great man he was, nobody knows the truth, that sort of thing—and he was going to help her."

"Help her?" Father John took a bite of hamburger. *Toussaint's been a great help to me.*

"Get her the real stories, even some records."

176

"What about the memoirs?"

Vicky was holding her hamburger in both hands, chewing thoughtfully. A moment passed. "He claims he knows where the memoirs are. He said he told Laura to come back Thursday and he'd give them to her. According to him, she never came back."

She set the hamburger down and stared at him. "He could be lying, John. Laura could be on the ranch somewhere. He could be holding her in an outbuilding."

"We've got to let Gianelli know." Father John got to his feet and, fishing a quarter from his jeans pocket, started toward the wall phone next to the entry. Vicky's footsteps sounded anxious behind him. He plugged the coin into the slot and tapped out the number. The bump and clatter of dishes and the sound of laughter rose from the tables. Finally the answering machine came on. He left a message.

"Let's try Eberhart." Vicky took the receiver, pushed in another quarter, and dialed a number. A half minute passed. "Detective Eberhart," she said. Then: "Bob? Have you found Laura?" In her eyes, Father John saw the answer.

"I just came from Willie Silver's ranch out on Sacajawea Ridge," Vicky hurried on. "He saw Laura Wednesday. She had agreed to meet him again on Thursday, but he says she never showed up." Vicky nodded a few times, thanked the man, and hung up.

"There's no word on her." Vicky slowly faced him. "Eberhart will contact Gianelli. They'll send somebody to talk to Willie."

Father John found another quarter and dialed the mission. He told Kevin he was running a little late. Would he take the new parents meeting?

He hung up and turned around. Vicky was leaning against the opposite wall in the narrow entry, the color leached from her face.

"You okay?" he said.

"Laura could be dead."

"Vicky, don't." He stepped over and took her arm. She was trembling. "We don't know what happened. Don't let yourself think—"

"Don't preach to me," she said. Then she reached up and laid her hand over his. "I'm sorry, John. I'm just worried about her. She would call me if she could. What did he do with her?"

"Who are you talking about?"

"Toussaint. What did he do with her?"

It had started to snow, large white flakes drifting through the headlights, like cotton falling from the trees in the summer. Vicky slowed past Ben's truck at the curb in front of the house and pulled into the driveway. The light filtering past the windows seemed dreamy and surreal in the snow. She gathered her black bag and crossed the yard, hugging her coat against her. As she let herself inside, the odor of whiskey came at her like a fist.

"Where've you been?" Ben stood in the shadows of the dining alcove beyond the living room. In his hand was a glass of amber liquid.

She slipped out of her coat and hung it in the closet next to the door. *Take your time. Stay calm.*

"You didn't answer me." His footsteps padded across the living room.

She turned slowly and, walking past him, went through the alcove into the kitchen and switched on the light. Next to the sink was an open, half-empty bottle of Jim Beam. She opened the refrigerator and took out a bottle of water.

"I called your office. You've been gone all day." Ben leaned over the counter that jutted between the kitchen and the dining alcove.

She took a sip of the cold water and faced him. "My friend Laura Simmons is in some kind of trouble." She formed the words slowly, struggling to conceal—was he too drunk to notice?—the tremor in her voice. "I've been trying to find some way to help her."

"Don't give me that bullshit." Ben set the glass down hard. A thin stream of whiskey curled over the counter. "You been out all day with him."

"What are you talking about?" She forced herself to relax her grip on the water bottle, fearing she might crush it.

"You heard me. I know what you've been up to. One of my relatives called me. You and John O'Malley were having dinner together over at Lana's, gazing into each other's eyes. A real romantic scene."

The Indians in the back booth, she thought. She hadn't paid any attention; her thoughts had been

179

filled with Laura. "Don't be ridiculous," she said. "He's a priest. We're both trying to help Laura." As she started to brush past he grabbed her, digging his fingers hard into her shoulders. The water bottle slipped from her hand and slid on the floor, sending a cold spray of icy water against her legs. "Let me go, Ben," she said, fighting back the rising panic.

Gradually—reluctantly—he released her, and she stepped into the living room. "I think you'd better leave," she said.

He was beside her, shadowing her. She moved backward, bumping into the chair at the desk. Slowly she moved around until the chair was between them. "Please go now."

"You owe me an explanation," he said in a whiskey-roughened voice. Specks of white light flashed in the dark eyes. "You keep me hanging around, thinking everything's gonna work out fine between us, and all the time you're running out with him."

"I don't have to explain my life to you. We're not married."

The muscles in his face grew rigid, the vein in the center of his forehead pulsing. "Well, that's the problem, isn't it? We need to get right to the wedding. We've been waiting around too long. Hell, I've been waiting for thirteen years. That's a long time to wait for a woman to come back to you, don't you agree?" He kicked the chair away from the desk and pulled her to him, crushing her against his chest. The heavy smell of him—perspiration and whiskey and aftershave—made her stomach turn. She forced herself not to struggle; there would be bruises if she struggled. "Let go, Ben," she said, her voice muffled against the roughness of his shirt.

"We're gonna get married again, Vicky. That's what you want, and you know it." His arms tightened around her as she fought for breath. "You'll belong to me again, and I'll take care of you. Once we're married, everything's going to work out just fine. Tell you what"—his grip seemed to relax— "first thing Monday we'll go to the courthouse and take out the license. Then we'll find a judge to do the honors."

"No, Ben." She wrenched herself free.

"That's not what you want?"

"It's not what I want."

"I get it." He threw his head back and gave a shout of laughter. "No judge for you. We eloped once, and that wasn't good enough. Right? You want a big church wedding. Yeah, I can see you coming down the aisle all dressed in white." He was smiling now, gazing off into a corner, as if the scene were already unfolding in the living room. "We'll get that priest friend of yours to do the honors. That'll be the last thing he does before he gets out of our lives."

Vicky felt her stomach turning over. She was going to be sick, she knew, and she struggled to swallow back the taste of hamburger rising in her throat. She could not end things now. Now was not the time. *When the women try to leave, that's the most dangerous time.* "You're drunk, Ben," she said. "We can discuss this tomorrow when you're sober."

"We're discussing it now. Now, Vicky." He reached out and grabbed her by the shoulders again.

"Let me go." She pulled hard, and his grip tightened, digging into her flesh. "There's not going to be a wedding, Ben!" Shouting now. "Can't you understand? It's over between us! It will always be over!"

Suddenly he released his grip, and she stumbled backward, her legs knocking against the hard edge of the desk. He stood over her, clenched fists raised above her face, and she heard the sound of screaming, wild and disembodied, like a bobcat screaming into the night, and felt herself drifting into another time, another house, with fists pounding into her body, bones cracking beneath her flesh.

⇉ 23 ⇇

The residence was quiet when Father John let himself through the front door. An oblong of light floated down the hallway, throwing shadows over the walls and staircase. He tossed his hat and jacket onto the bench, trying to shake off the uneasy feeling that had come over him as he'd watched the Bronco pull out of the parking lot at Lana's and turn in to the highway, yellow headlights shimmering in the snow. *Laura could be dead.* He could still hear the hopelessness in Vicky's voice.

"That you, John?" A chair scuffed the floor in the kitchen. Father Kevin appeared at the end of the hall, backlit by the pale light, just as Walks-On bounded past. The dog set his wet muzzle into Father John's hand. He patted him a moment, then followed the other priest back into the kitchen, where he poured himself some tepid coffee probably left over from dinner.

"How'd the meeting go?" he said, starting back down the hallway for the study.

"Pretty well." Kevin was behind him. "The couples seemed to like what I had to say about child rearing."

"Well, that's a subject we're certainly experts in. That and marital relationships." Father John sat down behind the desk in his study and turned on the lamp. Walks-On flopped beside him.

"Fortunately they had an expert speaker." Kevin took one of the twin wingback chairs facing the desk. "A child psychologist talked about rearing responsible children, so I left early. I wanted to transcribe some interviews while they're still fresh. By the way, you had some calls."

"So I see." Father John was already sorting through the stack of messages. He pulled out two from the provincial, two from Gianelli. He didn't want to hear any more about the plans for his new life. He picked up the phone and dialed Gianelli's number.

"Any news about Laura Simmons?" Father Kevin's voice punctuated the buzzing noise.

Father John shook his head.

The other priest pitched to his feet. "Beats me why anybody'd want to harm a scholar. We're a harmless bunch." He brushed the palm of his hand along the edge of the desk, announced he was going back to his computer, and backed into the hall as the answering machine came on. Father John hit the disconnect button. He found the agent's home number in a notebook in the desk drawer and dialed again.

"Ted Gianelli." The voice cut off the second ring.

"It's John. What have you heard?"

"Want the short-and-sweet answer?" A sigh came over the line. "Not one damn word. Where you been all afternoon? I want to know everything you know about the woman."

He told her what Vicky had told him. It wasn't much, he realized. He didn't know Laura Simmons at all.

"I want the rest," Gianelli said. "I spoke to Eberhart a little while ago and I was at the cultural center this afternoon. You and Vicky been snooping around, playing detective all day. So let's have it. What'd you find out?"

Father John took a sip of coffee. He told the agent about Willie Silver. "Vicky thinks Laura could be on the ranch someplace," he said.

"BIA boys are already on the way. We'll check it out." There was the sound of a pen clicking in the background. "Anything else?"

Father John exhaled a long breath, then began explaining his theory: someone called Toussaint had promised to give Charlotte Allen Sacajawea's memoirs. Charlotte had written about him in the journal. Laura was also looking for the memoirs. The man had murdered Charlotte, and now he wanted the journal, the only link between him and the woman.

"Sacajawea's memoirs," the agent said, a musing tone. "Valuable document, right?"

"Priceless."

And then Father John remembered Hope Stockwell. "Look, Ted," he said. "There's a young Shoshone graduate student, Hope Stockwell, who's convinced she's about to get the memoirs. Maybe someone wanted to make sure the memoirs stayed with the Shoshones. Maybe that's why Charlotte Allen was killed and Laura Simmons has disappeared."

"Yeah, maybe." A note of skepticism in the agent's voice. "Or maybe we've just got us a violent boyfriend who got carried away." He let out a long sigh. "Until we find Laura Simmons, we don't know what we've got. I'll let you know if I hear anything," he said before the line went dead.

As Father John set the receiver in the cradle, the phone started ringing. He let it ring. One, two, three times, feeling the same dread he'd felt two weeks earlier. Finally he answered.

"What's going on out there!" The provincial's words burst over the line like buckshot.

"What are you talking about?"

"Don't play dumb with me, O'Malley. I know

185

what you're up to, and frankly I'm outraged. I want a straight answer."

Father John set both elbows on the desk. "Tell me what this is about, Bill, and I'll do my best."

"You hear that?" The voice drifted away. A machine was rattling in the background. "The fax has been clogged the last two hours, letter after letter from people with names like Yellowtail and Standing Bull and Elkman and Knows-His-Horse. Don't tell me you didn't put your Arapaho friends up to this."

He understood. Howard Elkman had mentioned something about calling his boss. He said, "I won't tell you I didn't put them up to this."

"This has your historian's fingerprints all over it. The letters are coming with letters from 1910."

"What?"

"That's right. You're very clever, digging in the archives for a situation similar to your own. Sure enough, you found one. The Arapahos didn't want their favorite priest transferred in 1910, one Father Perelli, so they deluged the provincial's office with letters. Probably took a couple of weeks to arrive. We're more fortunate. We have fax machines, so the letters can arrive immediately."

Father John threw his head back and laughed. He'd badly underestimated the elders, and Lindy Meadows, for that matter. *The elders are interested in some letters,* she'd told him. While she was going through the files, looking for documents for Laura Simmons, she must have come across the letters about Father Perelli. She'd obviously called Howard Elkman, who, along with other elders, had spent the last two days at the museum reading through them. He'd thought the elders were interested in Arapaho history. Well, he'd been right, in a way.

"I'm glad you find this humorous." The provincial's voice again.

"What happened, Bill?"

"What do you mean?"

"The letter-writing campaign in 1910."

"You know perfectly well what happened. The provincial backed down. Father Perelli spent the rest of his days out there in that godforsaken place. I thought I was doing you a favor by getting you back on the track you never should've fallen off of in the first place." The line went quiet with anger and frustration. "I expect you in Milwaukee next Tuesday."

Father John replaced the receiver and leaned back in the chair, lifting the front legs off the floor. He ran a hand over the dog's soft fur and sipped at the last of the coffee, trying to ignore the reminder always in the shadows of his mind. *This is not whiskey, not the same at all.* It was his decision, was it not? He was a free man, he'd taken the vows freely. For better or worse, he'd promised. I will trust in you, Lord, he'd promised.

The phone was jangling again. Perhaps someone needing a priest, he thought as he lifted the receiver. "Father O'Malley," he said. Instantly he knew that Vicky was on the other end, even before he heard the sound of her voice.

It came like a sob. "I'm sorry. I don't know who else to call."

"I'm on the way," he said.

≫· 24 ·≪

The Toyota skidded through the fresh snow on Rendezvous Road. There were no other vehicles in sight, only the pristine whiteness wrapping around the pickup and the tunnel of headlights ahead. He fought against the images crowding into his mind; he didn't want them. Vicky walking into the living room; Ben Holden waiting. *Dear Lord, don't let him have been drinking!* Vicky telling him it was over. She was so small and soft, and Ben Holden, my God—what had he done to her?

He swung right onto the highway, sending the pickup skidding toward the ditch. He let up on the gas and turned in to the skid until the front end pointed west, then accelerated again. He had to think rationally. She had called. She was alive. Maybe Ben hadn't hurt her. But the pain in her voice! He would always hear the pain, he knew. In the middle of the night, in the midst of prayer and meetings and classes, the unexpected sound of her pain would come.

He banked south into Lander, the snow lighter now, faint traces of dark asphalt punctuating the whiteness. Another couple of turns and he was in front of the small house where she lived, slamming out the door and running up the snowy sidewalk. He pounded on the door, then opened it.

He saw her the instant he stepped inside— huddled on the floor beside the desk, as if she'd slid down the wall, the phone on the carpet beside her, crumpled tissues scattered about. He crossed the small room in a couple of steps and went down on one knee, his eyes running over her face—the hollow spaces beneath her cheekbones, the shape of her mouth and slant of her jaw. There were no bruises or cuts, as far as he could see, only a membrane of moisture clouding the coppery tones of her skin.

"What did he do to you?" he said. His voice was tight with anger.

She lifted both hands to her face, shreds of white tissue curling in her fingers. "I was so scared." The words came in a whisper; he had to lean closer to catch them.

"Vicky, did he hurt you?" He placed his arms around her shoulders and reined her to him.

"I'm okay." She was crying softly into the front of his jacket. "He's gone now, probably over at the Highway Lounge getting drunker."

"You've got to tell me," he said. "Did he hit you?"

He heard the effort for control in the sharp intakes of her breath. "I saw his fists." Her voice was muffled against him, as if she were sheltering from some imaginary shadow of Ben Holden in the room. "He was so angry, and his fists came up. I could feel them pounding on me. I could taste the blood in my mouth. Everything was spinning around. I couldn't see in the blackness. It was just like before, back in that other time. Everything the same, except that, all of a sudden, he turned and stomped out."

"Did he hit you?" White anger, like an electrical charge burned through him.

"No. No." She was shivering, as if cold had become a permanent condition. "God, I don't know what made him stop. He never stopped before."

Father John didn't say anything, aware of the slight weight of her leaning into his chest, the faint smell of sage in her hair. Finally he said, "You're all right, then? He didn't touch you?"

She pulled away and blew her nose into a tissue. There was a soft finality to the sound. Then she tugged at the neckline of her dark blue sweater until the rounded ridge of her shoulder was exposed. He stared in disbelief at the purplish marks—fingerprints—imprinted in her skin, the anger rising again, swift and certain as an arrow at his heart.

He grabbed the phone and started punching in 911.

"What are you doing?" Vicky pulled at the receiver in his hand. "You can't call anyone."

"You've been assaulted. I'm calling the police."

"The police!" She gave a shriek of pain and yanked hard on the receiver. "He grabbed me, John. That's all. He never hit me."

"He grabbed you and threatened you, Vicky.

There are bruises on your shoulder. You've been assaulted, and I'm going to call the police." He took the receiver back and started jabbing again at the numbers.

"No, John. No, please no." She slumped back against the wall, both hands covering her nose and mouth, so that her sobs came in staccato bursts, as if he had been the one who had just hurt her.

He replaced the receiver. The sobbing was less, barely audible above the sounds of a clock ticking somewhere and tires whining in the snow on the street.

"Leave me this, please, John," she said finally. "A little dignity. I don't want it all over the newspaper. Local lawyer, Eagle Shelter board member, assaulted by ex-husband, foreman at the Arapaho ranch, well known and respected in the tribe."

"You have to report this, Vicky." Father John fought for a quiet, rational tone.

She shook her head so violently that her entire body was shuddering. "Somebody would send the paper to the kids, and I don't want them to know. They never knew, and they can't find out. I can't let them find out."

"Look at me, Vicky." He took her chin into his hand and pulled her face around until her eyes found his. "Don't fool yourself anymore. Your kids know. They've always known. I don't care what you wanted to think. You have to hold him responsible for their sake, if not your own."

"You can't call the police." He could sense the

firmness in the set of her jaw. "I won't have it. You just can't, John." He saw it in an instant. It wasn't the kids she was protecting, it wasn't even her own sense of herself. It was Ben Holden. He let go of her chin. For a moment he didn't say anything, not trusting himself. "What do you want of me, Vicky?" he said finally. "What exactly do you expect?" She blinked at the harshness in his tone.

He stood up. "You knew the kind of man Ben Holden is. You knew what he'd done to you before, and you knew what was going to happen, but you went back to him any way. What if he walked in right now? Would you go back to him?"

"You don't understand." She started to get to her feet, a slow, weary movement.

"You're right. I don't understand my role in all of this." He had a sense of being outside of himself, lash-ing out at her. He kept on: "What do you want me to do? Watch you fall into his arms again, lie awake nights worrying about you, waiting for him to kill you or just hurt you enough to put you in the hospital? And then come running when you call? What is it, Vicky? I can't make you forget about Ben Holden. I can't take you away from him. I can't save you."

"Don't do this, John." The pleading note made his heart turn over. She was leaning against the wall.

He took his eyes from her, whirled around, and crossed the room.

"Where are you going?" he heard her say as he slammed out the door.

192

. . .

He drove south on Highway 287, peering through the halfmoons carved out by the windshield wipers. Ahead the red-and-blue neon sign, HIGHWAY LOUNGE, blazed through the falling snow like a beacon. Cutting in front of a semi—the blaring horn—he skidded into the parking lot, barely missing two pickups parked in front of the log building. He let up on the gas, slowed the Toyota past a row of pickups and trucks, and stopped next to Ben Holden's truck. The muffled beat of country music pounded through the log walls as he headed back to the entrance.

The air inside was foggy with smoke. Conversations buzzed beneath the music thumping out of speakers in the far corners. The stale odors of whiskey and beer penetrated the fog, stinging his nose and mouth, his lungs. He scanned the clots of people huddled in the booths along the sidewalls. A man and woman were moving across the bare wood floor, holding each other up in a drunken pastiche of a dance. Across the lounge, cowboys ranged along the bar, gripping beer bottles. COORS DRAFT blinked in the mirror overhead. Ben Holden was alone at the far end of the bar.

Father John walked past the swaying, lurching couple, the thud of his boots against the floor out of sync with the music's rhythm. Ben Holden turned slightly as he approached—was he expecting him? —Father John reached out and took a fistful of the man's plaid shirt. He shoved him backward, pushing him into the wall, bracing himself for the fists sure to lash out in defense.

"You want a piece of somebody, Holden? How about somebody your own size?" He tightened his hold on the shirt, leaning his fist into the man's chest.

"Vicky's okay, isn't she?" The man's voice was sharp with panic. "Tell me she's okay. I didn't want to hit her. I didn't hit her, did I? Oh, God, tell me I didn't hurt her."

"You hurt her, all right."

The other man's face began to crumble—a slow breaking into sobs. Father John felt him buckling beneath his grip, muscles and tendons and joints collapsing like those of a marionette. He grabbed him under both arms, holding him upright against the wall, steadying him.

"I never meant to hurt her." The sobs were loud and uncontrollable, bursting from a deep, hidden place—the remorse-laden sobs of the confessional. Father John had heard them before. "I wanted her to come back to me. I wanted us to be together like a real family, the way we used to be. Just Vicky and me and the kids, that's how it was supposed to be, but I let her down again. I hurt her. I didn't wanna do that."

Father John stepped back, his gaze fixed on the man leaning on the bar now, hands flat, a half-filled glass of whiskey at his fingertips. The sounds of a country band crashed around them. We've both let her down, he thought. We've both hurt her. A couple of alcoholics, battling their own demons. And he more at fault than Ben Holden. A priest. How could he have ever allowed her any hope that he could be the man she needed?

"Any trouble between you and Ben, Father?" A burly man was beside him, thumbs linked in the side pockets of his blue jeans. He looked like a breed, black, straight hair slicked back, a light-complected, pockmarked face.

"Ben's gonna need a ride back to the Arapaho ranch," Father John said.

"Hey, Buster." The man shouted past him at an Indian halfway down the bar, his arm around the waist of a thin girl with long black hair and a tight blue sweater that draped partway off one shoulder. "You goin' back to the ranch tonight?" A glance at Father John: "Buster works up there."

The Indian drew the girl closer and kissed the bare shoulder. "Sure ain't plannin' on it, Wily," he said. "Besides I just got here."

"Plans just changed." This from the burly man. "Ben here needs a ride." He turned to Ben. "Let's have the keys. Don't want anybody suing the place 'cause you run 'em down."

Ben fumbled in his jeans pocket and set a ring of keys on the bar, which the man tossed along the polished wood to the other Indian. "Okay, Father," the burly man said. "I'll make sure ol' Ben here gets home safe and sound."

"Thanks." Father John said.

The music was still pounding, the couple still

clinging together on the dance floor, when he stepped back outside into the snow.

Wedges of snow flew out from the Toyota as he plunged north, trying to put as much space as he could between him and the lounge and the whiskey. He could taste the whiskey—I *could taste the blood.* Dear Lord, the burden of the past. Would they never be free? He held the accelerator down, ignoring the lift and sway of the rear tires. He had wanted to stay at the bar. One shot was all he needed, and the warmth would have spread into the nucleus of every cell, calming and focusing his mind. Everything would have fallen into place.

Stay away from the liquor, lad. His father's voice. *It's the devil's own curse.* He'd been three sheets to the wind, his father, when he'd dispensed that piece of wisdom, spilling another two fingers of whiskey into his glass.

He might have been drunk himself tonight, he thought, lashing out at Vicky. Except that when he was drunk he didn't go to bars looking for a fight. He'd been a quiet drunk, sunk in an armchair in his room, grading papers for some history class, sipping at the whiskey. How ironic, he thought. He could control his anger better when he was drunk. What had he been thinking, confronting a man like Ben Holden, who rode herd all day, branded cattle, every muscle a sinew of steel?

He grimaced at what might have happened. The news paper headline: MISSION PRIEST ARRESTED IN

BAR FIGHT. He'd lived with humiliation before, but only in the eyes of his fellow priests, a few of his students. That was hard enough. His drunken bouts had never been broadcast to the public.

All of a sudden he understood why Vicky had grabbed the receiver. The humiliation! It was too much to bear.

He drove on, a homing pigeon, the route imprinted in his soul, only half-aware of the familiar swells of the earth beneath the snow. Gradually he began to feel calmer, enveloped in the vast white spaces and the endless black sky. His thoughts were steadier now. He'd lashed out at Vicky, he realized, because he couldn't do anything else. Just as Ben Holden had lashed out, because he couldn't do any thing else. He and Ben Holden, paired failures at love.

He turned in to the mission grounds and left the Toyota next to the Harley. Snow lined the folds of the bike's cover. Inside the residence, he headed for the kitchen, where he started a fresh pot of coffee brewing even before he took off his jacket and hat. The house was quiet; Kevin could be asleep over his computer. When the coffee was ready, he topped off a mug and headed for the study, where he stood at the window a long while, sipping at the hot liquid, trying to quench the thirst.

He could break the vows; he wouldn't be the first priest to break his vows. He could stay here, he and Vicky together. He could find other work; he was a good counselor. He shoved the thought away. Help me, Lord, he prayed. I am weak, and the temptation is strong.

The clock on the mantel in the living room had chimed once—or was it two times?—when he'd finished off the pot of coffee and started up the stairs. He was halfway up when he remembered the phone. He went back, grabbed it from the hall table, and carried it up the steps as far as the cord would stretch. He would hear it ring if anyone needed a priest tonight.

⇒ 25 ⇐

There were more worshipers than usual crowding the little church: elders and grandmothers, gray-haired couples, young parents and kids wedged into the pews and standing at the back. The musicians huddled in a circle to the left of the altar, voices rising over the *thud-thud-thud* of the drum. Father Kevin sat in the front pew, head bowed in prayer.

It was his last Sunday Mass at St. Francis. Father John offered the Mass for the people, that they would be safe in God's care. For Laura Simmons, that she would be found safe. For Charlotte Allen, that she would have peace. For Vicky. For himself. He said the prayers out loud, reverently, quietly. The prophet Jeremiah: "I will bring you back to the place from which I exiled you." And the gospel: "Jesus told the parable about a man who went on a journey . . ."

He'd written a homily, but he left his notes on the

lectern and walked into the aisle. An expectant quiet filled the church. He looked around the congregation, memorizing the brown, upturned faces. He thanked them for all they'd given him. He promised to come back for a visit—for many visits, he hoped. He told them he would always keep them in his prayers and asked them to pray for him. Then he walked back to the altar and began the Eucharistic prayers. As he raised the bread and wine overhead—behold, the body and blood of Christ— he knew that he would have to leave this place. He was a priest. "I will go, Lord, if you send me."

The crowd in Eagle Hall seemed even larger. A paper banner hung from the wall opposite the entrance: GOOD LUCK, FATHER JOHN. WE WILL MISS YOU. Below the banner were long tables laden with chicken, Indian stew, fried bread, potato salad, red and green Jell-O, and cake. A line moved slowly past; other people had already filled their plates and were seated at the tables set up around the hall.

Father John made his way among them, talking with different families, thanking them for coming. Father Kevin, he saw, was doing the same. He half expected the new pastor to whip out his tape recorder and settle at one of the tables where the elders were gathered. He saw Howard Elkman across the hall, waving, and he walked over. "Thank you," he said, taking the vacant chair next to the old man. "You gave it a heck of a good shot."

Howard folded his arms across the white braids

hanging down his red shirt and leaned back, studying him. "What I wanna know is, how come it didn't work?"

"The provincial's a stubborn man," Father John said. He stopped himself from saying that it didn't make any difference. He had decided to go.

Howard wadded up a napkin and tossed it across the table. His gaze took in the other elders—Roger Bancroft, Elton Knows-His-Horse—at the adjacent table. "Used to be tribal elders had something to say about the holy men we got around here. There's some things your boss don't understand, and he sure don't know what stubborn is." The old man slowly raised himself to his feet. Picking up the empty mug in front of him, he walked stiffly over to the coffeepot on one of the food tables.

Father John resumed his rounds, shaking hands with the other elders, patting the toddlers on their heads. "You goin' away?" Bobby Red Owl ran over and tugged at his pant leg.

He lifted the child up to eye level. "I'm coming back to see you." Then he hoisted him overhead until he almost touched the ceiling. "I expect one of these days you'll be this tall."

The little boy surveyed the floor far below and giggled. "I'll be a giant," he said.

As Father John set him back down he thought he saw Vicky at the food table, but it was someone else. He'd looked for her at Mass. Had he really thought she might come? After all he'd said last night? He would call and apologize the moment the feast ended. He didn't want to leave this way.

He made his way over to the table where Alva Running Bull was sitting alone. "How is everything?" he asked, dropping onto the chair beside her.

The woman's dark eyes flickered in comprehension. "Fine. Fine." She threw a glance toward her husband, standing with a group of men near the door.

She's walking on eggshells, Father John thought. In his mind he saw Vicky, slumped against the wall. *She has to leave him,* Vicky had said. *Even Sacajawea left.* What had he done? Alva had made up her mind to get a divorce, then she'd come to him for help. What had he said? What inadvertent remark had shot like an arrow into the woman's heart and caused her to change her mind?

He leaned closer, his voice low: "Promise me, Alva, that if you feel the tension starting to build, you'll get away."

"I'm sure things are gonna be fine." Alva's eyes slid toward the door again.

"You'll call the Eagle Shelter?"

"Oh, Father. You worry too much." Her voice trembled.

"Promise me, Alva."

The woman bent over, lifted the floppy, rug-like bag from the floor, and patted at the folds. "Next time Lester gets drunk and starts after me, I won't be the one goin' anywhere. I got me a gun."

Father John sat back against the chair, his eyes locked on the woman. Dear Lord, he thought, what kind of counselor misses all the signs?

"Listen to me, Alva . . ."

A small girl rushed around the table and began pulling at Alva's skirt, begging for more cookies. "You've had enough," the woman said.

"We have to talk," Father John hurried on. "Can you stay after the feast?"

She was shaking her head, patting the child's shoulder. "Don't let me hear no more about cookies." Her eyes skittered again to the door.

"When can you come? First thing in the morning?"

Slowly the woman turned toward him and nodded.

By the time Father John left the hall, the only people still there were Elena and some of the other grandmothers, cleaning up the tables. He walked back to the residence, taking a diagonal path through the snow that glistened like diamonds in the sun. At his desk in the study, he tapped out Vicky's number. An answering machine again. He asked her to call him.

Suddenly it occurred to him that Ben might have fought off his driver and gone back for her. He flinched at the idea. Surely she wouldn't go with him—unless . . . unless he forced her. A sinking feeling washed over him. He called her office. Another answering machine.

He tried her again in the afternoon after the liturgy meeting, and later in the evening, the minute he'd returned from the AA meeting. The last time he tried, it was ten-thirty, the *click-click* of Father Kevin's printer upstairs echoing through the quiet of the old house. Still no answer. A new thought had begun to shadow him, chilling him to the bone. What if Toussaint thought Laura had entrusted the journal to her friend? He could have come for Vicky.

Father John picked up the phone again and dialed Gianelli's number. After one ring, the agent was on the line, sleepiness in his voice. Father John asked about Laura.

"Told you I'd call first news we get."

"I'm worried about Vicky," Father John said. "I've been trying to reach her most of the day. She's not at home or at the office. She's Laura's friend, and she was on the res yesterday looking for Toussaint . . ." He let the conclusion hang in the air.

The agent drew in a long breath. "I'll ask the Lander PD to check out her house and office."

"Something else." Father John hesitated, reluctant to divulge her secret. Finally he said, "The BIA police better send someone out to talk to Ben."

Another sigh drifted over the line. "Vicky having trouble with her ex?"

Father John didn't say anything. After a half second the agent's voice broke the quiet. "Sit tight, John. We'll find her."

Father John set the receiver down, every muscle tense with alarm. Charlotte Allen wasn't found for twenty years, and Laura Simmons was still missing. How long would it take to find Vicky?

He waited by the phone, drinking a pot of coffee,

watching the shadows merging beyond the light from the desk lamp. It was after midnight when the phone rang.

Gianelli's voice: "Lander police say the house and office are undisturbed. No sign of a break-in or anything out of the ordinary. The Bronco isn't around. Ben Holden says he hasn't seen her since last night. You got him plenty worried, though. He's likely to go out looking for her."

My God, Father John thought. Vicky had probably gone off somewhere to get away from him, and now he'd sent the man after her.

"Look, John"—a comforting tone—"let's not jump to conclusions. Most likely Vicky'll be in her office tomorrow morning. You can ask her where she went, but if she has any sense, she'll tell you it's none of your business."

The agent was right. What did he want? To keep her safe, to control her? He was the same as Ben Holden, he thought as he hung up.

The red numbers on the nightstand clock winked 3:10 when he sat up in bed, half-asleep, trying to place the noise. Part of a dream, he decided. He'd been dreaming since he fell into bed, crazy dreams that he knew made no sense even while they cascaded through his subconscious. The noise came again. It was outside.

He was wide-awake now. He got out of bed and walked over to the window. The mission slumbered in the snow; circles of yellow light floated down from the street lamps. Nothing out of the ordinary, except for the tracks of a fox crossing Circle Drive and disappearing among the cottonwoods. An animal, that was all.

He started to turn away when he saw the light, like that of a firefly batting against the library window in the museum. He pulled on his blue jeans and ran down the hall, stopping at the phone to call 911 and report a prowler before he headed downstairs, taking the steps two at a time. He threw on his jacket and was out the door, running through the snow to the museum.

➤ 26 ❮

The pinprick of light was still jumping in the library window as Father John ran up the porch steps and grabbed the doorknob. It froze in his hand. The prowler must have broken in through the back. He drew the master key out of his jeans pocket and pushed it into the shadowy slot, leaning into the door, then stepped inside. In the sliver of light from the street lamps, he could make out the broken window beyond the staircase next to the rear door. Tiny shards of glass glistened like icicles around the perimeter of the frame. Footprints marked the pieces of glass scattered about the floor.

He moved along the wall on the left until his fingers found the light switch. He flipped it up. Light cascaded along the corridor, like water

205

tumbling down a mountainside. He held his breath, listening for the faintest noise in the quiet. Nothing but the tinkling of broken glass in the drafty entry. He walked slowly to the library and stepped through the open door, flipping on the light as he went. The fluorescent bulb flickered a half instant, then burst into a preternatural white light that shoved the cartons and stacks into the shadows.

The library looked the same as it had when he'd found Vicky and Laura almost a week earlier, except for the carton balancing partway off a shelf. The prowler had just gotten started, he thought. Another few minutes—he shuddered at the thought of documents and records from the past strewn about.

A loud scraping noise came from the entry. He stepped back into the corridor just as a figure dressed in black with the wide shoulders and slim waist of a man, a dark ski mask pulled over his face, threw himself out of a shadowy corner. He had walked right past the prowler! The man bolted toward the rear door, head thrust forward, as if some force were propelling him faster than his feet could get a purchase.

"Stop!" Father John ran down the corridor. The man was already fumbling with the bolt, yanking on the knob. Suddenly the door flew open, and he was gone.

Father John ran after him through the snow on the grounds behind the school. The man raced ahead, kicking back white, puffy clouds. Except for the whoosh of footsteps and the sound of his own breathing, there was only silence. The figure veered toward the river, weaving and dodging among the long shadows of the cottonwoods until the shadows bluffed together, a gathering darkness outside the scrim of light.

Father John stopped. He stood absolutely still, his breath hard in his throat. From somewhere ahead came a faint, labored chuffing noise, like that of a small bellows. And then, only the rustle of snow dropping from the trees.

He turned back. Pain stitched his ribs together; his breath came in sharp gulps. He wasn't in as good shape as he imagined. He entered through the rear door, then threw the bolt. There was the sound of an engine cutting off in front. Red-and-blue lights flashed through the windows, creating a colored mosaic on the wood floor. He crossed the entry and walked outside just as two Wind River police officers rushed up the steps, Walks-On trailing along, sniffing and licking at one of the officer's hands. He must have left the residence door ajar, and the dog had nosed his way out.

"What's going on, Father?" the first officer said. He held a long, black flashlight that shot a column of yellow light over the porch.

"Someone broke in. He just ran out the back."

"You run him off?" the other officer asked.

"I tried to catch him."

"He might've had a weapon, Father." Both men were shaking their heads. "What direction was he goin'?"

"Toward the river."

"Maybe we can head him off," the first officer said. As if they were yoked together, they swung around and hurried down the steps past the dog, who sauntered over to Father John and licked his hand.

"Some watchdog you are," he said, rubbing the dog's neck. The passenger door was still swinging shut as the patrol car backed up. It cut a half turn, then started around Circle Drive.

Father John went back inside. The thump of his boots and the click of the dog's paws on the wood floor resounded through the corridor. In the storeroom, he found a large sheet of cardboard and a staple gun. He laid the cardboard over the broken window and shot in the staples. If Toussaint came back, he'd kick out the cardboard in two seconds, but it was the best he could do until Leonard, the caretaker, could replace the windowpane tomorrow.

He walked back to the library, Walks-On at his heels, and checked the cartons on the shelves, removing the lids, reassuring himself that the contents had not been disturbed. Then he checked the boxes stacked along the wall, the yellowed pages nestled quietly inside. "How fragile, the past," he said out loud. Then he realized he was philosophizing with a dog. He headed outside, feeling almost sick with relief that Toussaint hadn't had the time to accomplish whatever he'd intended to do.

He locked the front door, aware for the first time

of the icy temperature. Tires thudded through the snow behind him, and he turned in to the yellow headlights and followed Walks-On down the steps as the police car pulled to a stop. The officers jumped out.

"Sorry, Father," the first officer said. "We missed the guy."

"Saw his tracks." The other officer now. "He made it to a vehicle he'd left over on Mission Road. Vehicle's gone. Any idea who he is?"

Father John nodded. "The same guy who ransacked the cultural center yesterday. He's after some documents I gave to Gianelli."

The first officer snorted. "Well, he should've broke into the FBI office."

"The agent will want to know about the break-in here," Father John said.

"We'll take care of it, Father." The first officer opened the passenger door and folded himself back inside. His partner was already behind the wheel. The engine spurted into life, wipers slashing back and forth as the car backed up, then stopped. The driver leaned out the opened window. "We'll keep an eye on the mission tonight, Father, in case the guy comes back. He doesn't know the materials he's after don't reside here anymore."

Father John waited, one hand on the dog's head, until the police car had wound out of the mission grounds and disappeared past the cottonwoods. The taillights glowed red in the darkness, like two cigarettes burning down.

"Learned something about your new master," he told the dog as they started for the residence. "Father Kevin McBride can sleep through anything."

⇒• 27 •⇐

"I'm not letting go of this gun, Father."

Alva had taken one of the side chairs, and Father John had pulled the other around a stack of boxes and sat down across from her, trying not to bump the woman's stick-thin legs clad in blue jeans. She gripped the floppy bag with one hand and brushed back a strand of black hair with the other. Her red coat draped open over a blouse the caramel color of her long, smooth neck. She was an attractive woman, he thought, despite the worry lines fanning from the dark eyes and the thin mouth set somewhere between apprehension and determination.

"Why did you buy it, Alva?" he probed. "Is Lester drinking again?" The man wasn't at last night's AA meeting. He wondered if Lester was still going to the anger therapy group.

Alva stared off at an angle beyond his shoulder, as if she'd anticipated the questions and prepared the answers, which she knew by rote. "He's trying to stay sober. He's been goin' to anger therapy, but the trucking company he started driving for is cutting back, and he's gonna get cut."

And then he'll get drunk. Father John knew the

pattern. Such a thin line between sobriety and drunkenness, and losing a job was the perfect excuse to step over. He'd been wanting a drink since the provincial had called to say his replacement was on the way. The woman stiffened at the crack of the front door shutting, the footsteps in the corridor. Her eyes skittered to the door, as if Lester might walk in.

Father John leaned over and patted Alva's arm. "Father Kevin," he said. Beneath the folds of her coat sleeve, he could sense her muscles begin to relax.

"Shooting Lester won't solve any problems," he began, searching for the logic to change her mind.

"He comes at me—"

He interrupted. "He'll take the gun away, Alva. You'll only give him a weapon to use against you."

The woman flinched, as if he'd tossed her a fastball she wasn't expecting. Then she issued what passed as a laugh and shook her head. "Not if I shoot him first."

Father John kept his eyes on hers. Another tack, another stab at logic: "If you shoot Lester, Alva, you'll go to prison."

"Nobody's gonna send me to prison for protecting myself." The line of her mouth tightened.

"Prisons are full of battered women who bought guns to protect themselves." The logic, the relentless logic. "You're no different from them."

She shifted against the back rungs of the chair, suppressing a shudder, and he pressed on. "What about your children? You have to think about them."

Suddenly the woman's face started to crumble, like spider cracks running through glass, and she began to sob. "It's not that I wanna hurt Lester, Father. I love him and the kids."

"I know." His voice was gentle. "You'd better let me have the gun."

She hesitated. Then, dropping her head, she fumbled at the bag. She reached inside and slowly pulled on an object that bulged through the fabric like a snake wiggling forward. "I just want us to be a real family again." She had the pistol out now, a black metal tube shape lying loosely in her hand. "I just don't want him to hurt me anymore."

He reached over and took the gun. It felt cold and inert against his palm, an instrument of death. He got up and put it inside an empty desk drawer. "You have the number for the Eagle Shelter, don't you?"

The woman was already on her feet, eyes glistening like black stones just beneath the surface of a river. "I don't know if I can get me and the kids away before . . ."

The thought hung between them and, for half a second, Father John wondered if he'd done the right thing, taking the only protection she had. He'd laid out the most logical scenarios, but events didn't always unfold logically, not with drunks. He was playing the odds, gambling with the woman's life.

"Look, Alva," he began, searching for the words to allay his own fears as much as hers. "I'll call Lester this evening and ask him to stop by."

Tomorrow he was leaving. "He can talk to Father Kevin about some of the pressures he's under right now."

Alva nodded and started backing toward the door, clutching the floppy bag to her chest. A small figure, almost childlike, nodding, thanking him. She was glad to get rid of the gun, she said. What a worry, always watching the bag so the kids wouldn't get it. Her hand fumbled for the knob and opened the door behind her. Yes, a good thing he'd talked her into giving it up. She never wanted it anyway. She stood in the doorway, nothing between her and a man's drunken rage. The image of Vicky slumped against the wall flashed in his mind. And Ben had stopped! What if Lester didn't stop?

"Thank you, Father," she said again as she turned in to the corridor.

"Alva."

The pencil-thin fingers wrapped around the edge of the door. She looked back.

"Maybe you should take the kids and go to your sister's for a few days until Lester gets a better handle on things."

She stared at him with blank disbelief. "I don't think I'd better be tryin' to leave right now," she said, closing the door behind her.

Father John sank into his chair behind the desk and tried Vicky's office. The secretary was expecting her at any minute, she said, a note of worry running through the explanation. It matched his own.

"Ask her to call me the minute she gets in," he

213

said. Then he called Lindy.

"Father John! What happened here?" There was a breathless anxiety in the curator's voice. "The window's broken; there's glass all over."

He told her about the prowler. Then: "I want you to close the museum for a few days." Toussaint could return. He didn't want the young woman there.

"What? I can't do that. The elders are coming to look at more letters."

"Call them and explain that they'll have to wait a couple days."

"But you're leaving tomorrow."

"Lindy, I know what you're trying to do, and believe me, I'm grateful, but the provincial has already gotten enough old letters. They haven't changed his mind. We have to lock up the museum for a while."

There was a long, considered silence at the other end. Finally the woman said, "The elders are already on their way. I'll close down at noon, okay?"

He said that was okay and hung up. He'd just started to pack the last drawer in his desk when Kevin walked in. "Hear we had some excitement here last night," he said.

"Unfortunately the prowler eluded my grasp," Father John said. He'd missed the other priest at breakfast this morning. He'd come over to the office early to finish packing and wait for Alva.

"Well, if you'd wakened me, I'm sure the two of us could've collared him."

214

"Oh, I'm sure. I'll remember that if he comes back tonight." He hoped Toussaint wouldn't be back.

"Prowlers, missing professors." Kevin was shaking his head. "The provincial told me this was a quiet backwater. I'd get a lot of work done on my book." He threw up both hands and, still shaking his head, turned back in to the corridor.

Father John resumed packing the box—the last of his personal things in the office—and was stretching a length of brown tape over the tops when the phone started jangling. He reached across the desk and grabbed the receiver.

"Father O'Malley," he said, expecting to hear Vicky's voice. He tucked the receiver against his shoulder and smoothed down the tape.

"We just got a call from the BIA boys. Some Indian kid was riding his pony out on Sacajawea Ridge and spotted a blue SAAB." Gianelli's voice was so quiet, he let go of the tape and pressed the receiver hard against his ear.

"The police found Laura Simmons."

The screeching noise came again, like the cry of an animal out of the darkness. Vicky pushed back the quilt and waved one hand at the nightstand table. Something hard thudded on the floor. She forced her eyes open. The screeching had stopped. A band of sunshine lay across the tangled quilt and ran up the side of the far wall, illuminating the familiar pink flowers in the wallpaper. She felt herself relaxing again, moving back into sleep, a sense of warmth enveloping her. No one knew she was at Aunt Rose's.

She'd packed a nightgown, a little makeup, a shirt and blue jeans and driven across the reservation in the middle of the night. Fled back to the reservation, just as she'd done in the past when the world was too frightening, too overpowering. Once she'd fled the reservation for the same reasons, but even then she'd come back. After ten years in Denver, she'd come back. Ben would start thinking about that. He'd be knocking at Aunt Rose's door sooner or later, begging, pleading. He was sorry; he loved her. She knew it all by heart.

Just as she'd scrunched up the pillow and burrowed into it, there was a soft rapping on the door. It creaked open. "Your secretary called." Aunt Rose's voice was low and comforting. "Third time this morning. Seems real worried. I finally told her you were here, just so she'll quit worrying. Told her you'd call back."

Vicky was fully awake now. As she pushed herself upright against the headboard, she caught the frozen shock in the old woman's expression. Instinctively her hand flew to the bruises on her shoulder, but it was too late. Aunt Rose was across the small room, prying her fingers free, eyes fastened on the purplish-blue marks, the angry imprints in her flesh.

"Ben did this to you." The rage in her aunt's voice surprised her. It was the same rage she'd heard in John O'Malley's, and in that moment she knew:

they both loved her.

"We had an argument," she said.

Aunt Rose plopped down beside her, sending waves of motion through the mattress, and Vicky felt her face in the old woman's hands, the gentle fingers probing the skin of her cheeks, chin, neck. One arm was lifted up, turned, scrutinized, then the other, as if she were an accident victim and Aunt Rose the emergency-room doctor.

"It's okay," she said, and winced at her own words. How many women had sat across her desk, fingering the bruises running along their cheeks, dabbing at the swollen, blackened eyes, and said, "It's okay. He don't mean to hurt me. He loves me"? And she had said it was never okay.

"He didn't hit me, Aunt," she hurried on. "He grabbed me, that's all." An assault, she knew. John O'Malley was right. It didn't matter, because she could never report it, and that was something John O'Malley would never understand.

"I'll call the office," she said, slipping out of bed, away from the old woman's gaze. She shrugged on the wool robe, worn soft over the years, that Aunt Rose had wordlessly laid over the foot of the bed Saturday night. She'd probably known then. She hadn't said anything yesterday, but Vicky had felt the knowing eyes on her at breakfast and later when she'd sat wrapped in a quilt on the sofa, unable to get warm, staring out the window at the blue gray bulge of mountains and the ragged scar of Sacajawea Ridge, wondering: How many knew about your

217

hidden life? Captain Clark, surely, his knowing eyes following you through the days. *The captain had intervened on one occasion; he thought Toussaint might kill her.*

Now Vicky padded down the short hallway into the kitchen. The cold linoleum floor against her feet brought a flood of pleasant memories from childhood. Aunt Rose was her mother's sister, which meant, in the Arapaho Way, she was also her mother. Aunt Rose's home was the same as her own. She was safe here; she belonged. She picked up the phone and tapped out the familiar number.

"Vicky Holden's office." Laola's voice slammed the memories into a far corner of her mind. She heard herself asking about the day's schedule, giving instructions. Cancel this, cancel that. She wasn't ready to face the world yet; she didn't know how she would make her way. Wes Nelson had called again from Denver. He wanted her answer.

"I've been thinking," the secretary went on. "If you go to that Denver firm"—a pause—"maybe I could go with you?" Vicky felt the muscles in her stomach clench at the idea of the young Arapaho woman adrift in the city.

She said, "We'll talk about it later."

There was a moment of disappointed silence before Laola said, "Ben's been calling. Says he's worried about you. Says to tell you—"

"I know what he said."

"Father John, too."

"What?"

218

"Called a couple times. Wants you to call him right away."

Vicky thanked her and hung up. She'd been certain that John O'Malley would never call again.

She lifted a mug out of the cabinet above the phone and poured herself some of the coffee Aunt Rose had probably brewed a couple hours ago. The pungent odor had wafted into her dream, she realized now. She was seated on the cold, hard ground, watching the men dance around the campfire, booted legs rising and falling against the flickering flame, and someone—a dark, bearded man—handed her a hot tin mug. She held the mug in the flaps of the blanket wrapped about her shoulders to keep from burning her hands and dipped her face toward the steam, her heart beating in rhythm to the pounding boots: love, fear, love, fear.

"You stay as long as you want," Aunt Rose said.

Vicky whirled about. She hadn't heard the old woman enter the kitchen, but she'd already set a box of cereal and a carton of milk next to the bowl on the table. Vicky sat down and sipped at the hot coffee, still trying to separate herself from the dream. "I should get back to the office," she said.

"Let it wait." Aunt Rose sat at the end of the table; her hand, soft as rose petals, reached out and covered hers. "You take all the time you need to decide about Ben."

Vicky met the other woman's eyes. Aunt Rose had always loved Ben. Everybody loved Ben, but they didn't know the Ben she knew. She said, "It can't work between us anymore."

"I thought maybe he was changed," Aunt Rose said.

"We were both wrong, Aunt."

She watched the old woman push herself to her feet, pour a cup of coffee, and settle back into the chair. The barrage of well-meaning, prying questions was about to begin. In an effort to head them off, she said, "I've been worried about a friend who's missing in Lander."

"That history lady going around the res asking a lot of questions about Sacajawea." Aunt Rose gave a nod of understanding. "I seen the newspaper. Sounds like she had some kind of row with her boyfriend, just like . . ." She left the thought unspoken.

"There's another possibility," Vicky said hurriedly. "Laura could've run into the man who killed another professor twenty years ago."

"You talkin' about the skeleton Father John found by the river?"

Vicky nodded. "They were both doing research on Sacajawea. Laura came here to finish the biography the other professor had started. She thinks Sacajawea's memoirs are here somewhere, and a man named Toussaint knows where they are."

"She go see Anna Scott?"

"Who?" Vicky couldn't place the name.

"Old Shoshone lady used to collect all sorts of stories from the older generation before the Shoshones got around to starting the cultural center. Probably told most the stuff to the people at the center, but she might've kept some of it here." She made a little fist and tapped the side of her head.

"Where does Anna Scott live?"

"Up in Casper with her daughter. Got real sick twelve, thirteen years ago, so her daughter come and got her. I hear she's still going on. Too tough to die, that old woman."

Vicky got to her feet. On the counter near the phone she found a pencil and a stack of notecards. "What's the daughter's name?" she asked.

Aunt Rose shifted in her chair and threw her head back, as if she might pull the name from the ceiling. "Let's see. Something like Earlene, Eileen, Emmaline. That's it, Emmaline Scott. Married a white man in Casper with a name that sounded like a girl's." She dropped her head and snapped her fingers. "Emmaline Kay, that's her name."

Vicky wrote the name on a notecard. She doubted that Laura had gone to Casper; there hadn't been time. But if the woman had been collecting bits of Shoshone history, surely Charlotte Allen would have talked to her. And yet—Anna Scott's name wasn't in the journal. Still, Anna Scott could know Toussaint. And she might know about the memoirs.

The phone started screeching again. Vicky picked up the receiver and handed it across the counter. "How's it goin'?" Aunt Rose said after a moment. Her tone was light, as if everything here was fine. Why wouldn't it be the same at the caller's house?

"You don't say." A darker note. "When d'ya hear

221

about that?"

Suddenly the woman pressed the receiver into her stomach and said, "Moccasin telegraph's got some news, Vicky. Police found a body."

Vicky gripped the hard edge of the counter. "Where, Aunt? Where did they find it?"

"Buried in some trees out by the road just past Dinwoody Lakes," she said. "Couple miles up Sacajawea Ridge."

Vicky said, "I've got to call the police."

A moment passed as Aunt Rose concluded the call, then handed her the receiver. She tapped out Eberhart's number. An unfamiliar voice sounded at the other end. Sorry, the detective wasn't in. Did she want to leave a message?

Vicky gave her name and told the operator that she was a lawyer and a friend of the missing Laura Simmons. She'd just heard that a woman's body had been found on the res.

There was a brief pause, then: "Eberhart's at the site."

≫· 28 ·≪

Father John spotted the white police cars in the distance as he came around a sharp curve. He let up on the accelerator, keeping his eye on the cars and the dark uniforms moving among the ponderosas on the slope below the road. As he swung downhill onto the path the pickup bed reared off the ground, then settled back, tires kicking up a cloud of dust and snow. The police cars were nudged at the edge of the trees. Beside them was the coroner's wagon.

He pulled in behind the last car, jumped out, and started running down the snow-scarred hill toward the figures in the trees. And then he saw it, almost completely hidden, like the remnants of an old tank—the blue SAAB with ponderosa branches piled over the roof and hood and built up along the sides. The wind burst through the trees, obscuring the sounds of voices.

Gianelli climbed toward him, digging his heels into the slippery ground. "You know Laura Simmons if you see her?" he called.

He said he would, and the agent swung around and started down the slope alongside him. "State lab people are just about to bag the body," he said.

Two men in bulky down jackets and slacks—the lab people, he guessed—were stooping over something white crumbled on the ground, like a mound of snow. A stretcher lay nearby. Suddenly one of the men straightened up and began unfolding a large, gray plastic bag. Detective Eberhart stood to one side with Chief Banner and two other Wind River police officers—a contingent of local law officers, Father John thought. He said, "What happened to her?"

"Pretty badly beaten," Gianelli said. "We won't know if the injuries caused the death until we get the autopsy results. You want my opinion, they caused it all right." He jammed both hands into his pockets and spurted ahead.

"Hold on," he called to the man with the gray bag. The man looked up, surprise on the pale, pinched face. Eberhart and Banner and the other officers stepped back, forming a corridor as Father John walked closer, his gaze on the coat bunched around the thin legs, the shoeless feet and torn hose, the fine-boned hands thrown back and opened in supplication, the blond hair falling around the sides of the smashed and swollen face.

He dropped to his knees and made the sign of the cross over the lifeless body. "Dear Lord, take care of this woman. Have mercy on her soul, and forgive whatever sins she may have committed in this life, and take her to Yourself." He stayed on his knees a moment—they might have been alone, he and the dead woman. The only sounds the wind rustling in the trees. Finally he pushed to his feet. "It's Laura Simmons," he said to Gianelli.

The agent was shaking his head. "God, what a mess. Looks like she was beaten in the car. Front seat's covered with dried blood. Then the killer dragged the body down here and started to bury her. Either he didn't have the tools, or the ground was just too damned hard, so he piled some brush over her and made a half-assed attempt to hide the car. Left tracks all over the place. We should have some good prints. Expect we'll have enough evidence to charge Toby Becker."

It made sense, Father John thought. His theory—his and Vicky's—was logical, and logic had nothing to do with something like this. What was it Banner always said? Look at the most obvious. The killer's usually standing in front of your face. Becker was the most obvious. And yet—

"Look, Ted," he said as they walked back up the hill. "Laura could have met with Toussaint."

"Toussaint!" The agent stopped and turned toward him. The stale odor of coffee and fatigue vaporized between them. "There's nobody with that name within a hundred miles—a thousand miles. Maybe we've got two historians working on the same biography who turn up beaten to death. But we've got a boyfriend with a history of battering Laura Simmons. Who knows? Maybe Charlotte Allen had a boyfriend, too. Maybe that's what these women had in common. If you've got something else, John, other than a vague theory you and Vicky cooked up, let me have it. I need an actual name, something definite."

They reached the top of the slope, then cut around a windblown snowdrift with stalks of dead grasses and thistles poking through. "By the way," Gianelli went on, "I tried to reach Vicky this morning. Secretary said she didn't know when she'd be in. You heard anything from her?"

Father John began shaking his head, aware of the little knot of worry in the pit of his stomach. "I haven't seen her since Saturday night," he said, half to himself. "She was very upset." Suddenly he knew where she had gone.

He rounded the hood of the pickup and called

back to the agent standing at the edge of the road. "I'll tell her about Laura."

Father John jammed down on the accelerator and turned south on 287, hardly aware of the ponderosa slopes flashing by, the white plains rolling away from the highway. A left turn, heading east now, the sun glistening on the hood. Five miles later he saw the white frame house ahead, just off Ethete Road. The Bronco was parked at the side.

As he slowed for the turn into the yard, Vicky came out the front door and headed around the corner, the long black coat sweeping around her. He could tell by the slope of her shoulders that she had already heard. She grabbed the door handle on the Bronco, then swung around, her eyes watchful as he pulled in behind and got out.

"It's Laura, isn't it?" she said, walking toward him.

He told her that he'd identified her, that the body had probably been removed by now.

Vicky's face dropped into both hands and her shoulders caved forward, shaking with silent sobs. He placed his arms around her. "I'm so sorry," he said, holding her gently.

After a moment she stepped back. "How bad was it?"

When he didn't answer, she raised a fist to her mouth and gave another sob. "Toby Becker did that to her." She spoke slowly, an automatic response. Her voice was shaking with the cold.

"Can we go inside?"

Vicky threw a wary glance at the house. He understood. What would Aunt Rose make of the fact that he was the one who had come for her, instead of Ben?

Taking her arm, he led her around to the passenger side of the Toyota. After she'd slipped onto the seat, he got in behind the wheel. A remnant of warm air still clung to the cab. He started the motor and waited until the hot air began to pulsate through the vents. "You'll feel warm in a moment," he said.

"You think so?" She was still shivering. He fought against the urge to reach for her again. "I've been trying to call you," he said. "I know."

"I want to apologize for the other night."

"You said the truth. No need to apologize for the truth."

"I had no right."

"You have every right, John. I've given you the right over the last few years, haven't I? I would have called you before you left. I didn't want things to end like that." She slid sideways toward the door and stared at some point beyond the windshield. "Laura was defenseless. How could she defend herself against a man like Toby Becker, unless she had a gun."

Father John winced at the thought. He looked away, staring out his window at the plains folding into a sky striped gray and blue. He'd talked Alva out of the gun to keep her from shooting Lester.

What if Lester attacked her again? Suddenly he was aware of the silence between them, of Vicky's eyes on him.

"What is it?" she said.

He brought his eyes back to hers. Then he told her he'd taken Alva's gun and put it in his desk drawer for safe keeping.

She cupped a hand over her mouth. "Oh, my God," she said. "I had no idea she was so desperate. It could have been Alva out on Sacajawea Ridge." She went quiet a second. "It could have been me. Lester wouldn't mean to do it, of course. And Ben would never mean to do it. You know that, don't you?" He could see that she was fighting for control.

"I know you can't report Ben." He hesitated, then forced himself to go on. "But you have to leave him."

She smiled. "Well, you know everything, then, don't you, John O'Malley? And just when you're about to go away."

Now it was his turn to remain quiet. Finally he said, "Gianelli will have an arrest warrant for Toby Becker as soon as he gets the lab report on some prints. He agrees with you that Becker probably killed her."

"And you? What do you think?"

"I'm not sure it matters." Father John grasped the rim of the wheel with one hand and let his gaze rest on the dull metal of the Bronco's bumper. "All we have is a theory that two historians, twenty years apart, ran into the same man who promised them some important evidence, then killed them. Not exactly enough to send Gianelli's investigation into a different direction. 'Give me a name,' he told me."

"Maybe our theory's just a good excuse for you and me . . ." Vicky hesitated, letting her voice trail off. After a couple seconds she went on: "We've spent a lot of time together working on different things. It's probably why you want to go."

"Is that what you think? That I want to go?"

"I don't know what to think. I don't know why you're going."

"You know," he said, and he saw in her eyes that she did know. He was a priest. He allowed the thought to rest silently between them.

After a long moment she said, "We may be able to get the name of Toussaint."

He exhaled a long breath. So this was not the end, this was not all there would be.

She was hurrying on: "There was a Shoshone woman here twenty years ago, a kind of unofficial tribal historian. Her name is Anna Scott. Charlotte Allen could have talked to her."

The name wasn't in the journal, and he said so.

Vicky shook her head. "Charlotte casually mentioned other people. 'Drove around the res today. Talked with a couple elders at the café,' that sort of thing. She carefully wrote down the names of people who gave her information. It may be a long shot, John, but we came up with nothing on Saturday, and now Laura's dead. I'd like to find the bastard who killed her. Maybe Anna Scott didn't give Charlotte any new information, but who knows what kind of information Charlotte may have given her?"

"Where does she live?" The name was unfamiliar. He'd never met the woman on the res, but there were many people he'd never met. He would never meet them.

"She's with her daughter in Casper." A second passed. "Would you like to take the Bronco?"

"The Toyota's already warmed up," he said, ramming the gear into reverse.

⇒ 29 ⇐

They went over the theory as they drove north on Highway 26, climbing out of what the Shoshones called "the warm valley." It was snowing lightly, drops of moisture flecking the windshield. Father John turned up the heat to keep the cold at bay. Still Vicky hugged her black coat around her, as if no amount of warm air could dissipate the cold. *Idomeneo* floated softly out of the tape player on the seat between them.

"It's preposterous," Vicky said. "The only evidence we have is a name in Charlotte Allen's journal. Toussaint. Obviously she wanted to protect his real identity. It could be anyone. How can we ever prove who she was referring to?" She hesitated, then plunged on. "We know Toby Becker was stalking Laura. He probably came back Wednesday night and flew into another rage when she told him to leave.

He started hitting her. Forced her into her own car. Drove her to Sacajawea Ridge, hitting her as he drove." A note of hysteria seeped into her voice. "She was pleading with him the whole time—"

"Don't, Vicky," Father John said, glancing over. She held his gaze a half second before turning to the window. The Neptune chorus floated between them. Outside the plains stretched away from the highway, shimmering silver in the snow. The sky was an endless patchwork of blue and gray floating above them.

She could be right, he thought, watching the asphalt coming toward them like a conveyor belt. Except for the patterns. Patterns were never random. There was always logic in them, if only he could grasp the logic.

A couple of miles passed before he said, "Both Laura and Charlotte wanted the memoirs." Thinking out loud now. "They were beaten to death. The killer buried Charlotte and left her car on Sacajawea Ridge to throw everyone off. Maybe he didn't have time to take Laura's body somewhere else, so he tried to bury her on the ridge. He hid her car there." He glanced over at Vicky. "It was the same man," he said.

Vicky remained quiet, watching out her window. After a moment he felt her eyes on him. "Toussaint could have been waiting for Laura when she got back to the apartment Wednesday night. He must've demanded the journal, and when she told him she didn't have it, he went berserk and attacked her. He tore her things apart looking for it. After he'd killed her, he went to the cultural center thinking she'd left it there."

"He broke into the museum last night," Father John said. He told her what happened.

"He might've killed you, John." There was a hint of panic in her voice. "He's already killed twice."

"The point is, Vicky," he said, coming back to the logic before it melted into the shadows of his mind, like Toussaint in the cottonwoods, "he doesn't know where the journal is, which means Laura didn't tell him. Why not? Why didn't she give it to him? Maybe she'd be alive."

He glanced over again, this time catching the mixture of astonishment and comprehension in her face. "Laura wanted the memoirs, John." She spoke slowly, testing the idea. "She was obsessed with the memoirs, and she was convinced Toussaint had them. She could have tried to bargain with him— the journal he wanted so desperately for the memoirs. That's when he flew into a rage."

It could have been like that, Father John thought. And yet, and yet . . . something bothered him, a missing piece of logic. Gradually the logic began to emerge in the patterns. Toussaint had killed Charlotte Allen on the day she'd expected to get the memoirs; he'd killed Laura when she'd demanded the memoirs.

He struck the steering wheel with his fist. He should have seen it. Why hadn't he seen it? He was a historian. He said, "Suppose the memoirs don't exist, Vicky. Suppose Toussaint forged them."

"I don't understand," she said impatiently. "Charlotte Allen believed—"

"The will to believe," he said. "The memoirs would be an incredible find, if they were real. They would make the reputation of any historian who found them. And they existed once. The agent's wife did record the stories of the old woman who said she was Sacajawea. But Theresa Redwing said no one in her family had heard of the memoirs surviving the agency fire. The Shoshones still had the stories. Only the historians wanted the written memoirs, a reality Toussaint obviously understood." He looked over. In her eyes, he saw the logic of his argument.

"Charlotte Allen would have insisted on having the memoirs authenticated," he hurried on, warming to the argument. "The notebook dated, the handwriting compared to samples of other writings by the agent's wife. No historian would take a chance on publishing a fake document."

Mozart, rational and measured, filled the silence between them. "When Toussaint wouldn't agree," Vicky said finally, "Charlotte realized the memoirs he'd given her were fake. But that doesn't explain why he killed her, John. He could have walked away."

"Yes, he could have."

A semi blurred past in the other lane, a roar of dust and moisture that spattered the windshield and obliterated the music. He turned on the wipers and washed out two half circles. They were on the outskirts of Casper now, rolling with the other pickups and cars past fast food outlets, gas stations, warehouses, and assorted motels and garages. He swung right onto a flat cement apron and stopped next to a gas pump.

While he filled the pickup, Vicky went inside to call Emmaline Kay, Anna Scott's daughter. He could see Vicky's image in the plate-glass window, head tilted sideways, receiver pressed into the black hair. She was still on the phone when he went inside and handed the clerk a couple of bills—the last of the gas money for the month. At least there'd be half a tank left for Kevin. He collected the change and waited until Vicky hung up.

"Anna Scott's in a nursing home," she said as they crossed the pavement outside. A freezing breeze swept between the building and the row of gas pumps. He opened the Toyota door. "Her daughter's going to meet us there," she said, sliding onto the seat.

Northern Acres sat back from the street beyond a swath of freeze-dried lawn and neatly trimmed evergreen bushes. Father John followed Vicky into the glass-fronted entry, where a stout woman with gray hair and a round, brown face rose from one of the upholstered chairs pushed against a sidewall. She wore a brown corduroy jacket and blue jeans, as if she'd spent the morning riding across a pasture, which, he thought, might be the case.

"I'm Emmaline Kay," she said, walking over,

giving them a steady, dark-eyed look. "You must be Vicky Holden and Father John from St. Francis. I've heard about you, Father." A nod in his direction. "Oh, don't look so surprised. Phone company could learn a thing or two from the moccasin telegraph." She babbled on, telling him about his own life: the people liked him, didn't want him to leave, what was the matter with the higher-ups that don't know their feet from the ground they're walkin' on, and why would they ever send that young priest rides around on some kind of motorcycle asking a lot of questions.

Vicky interrupted: "Could we meet your mother, Emmaline?"

"Oh, sure." The woman shrugged. "This way." She waved them into the corridor on the far side of the reception desk. "Mom was real glad she was getting some visitors from the reservation," she said, looking back over one thick shoulder. "Nobody comes to see her anymore. 'Course her old friends are dead, and everybody else probably thinks Mom's dead."

The corridor was long and wide, a succession of doors that opened onto tiny rooms with white-haired occupants slumped in overstuffed chairs or propped up in white-sheeted beds. No different from the nursing homes he'd visited in Lander and Riverton, Father John thought. The same television noise, the clinking dishes in a dining room somewhere, the faint antiseptic odor. It was the people who were different, filled with different stories of the past. He would miss his visits with the old people.

Emmaline made an abrupt swing through one of the doors. "Visitors are here," she called, a loud, cheerful voice.

Father John followed Vicky into the room with a narrow bed in the center and a window that gave out over a patch of wintery grass. A tiny woman sat primly in an upholstered chair, hands clasped in the lap of her pink dress, gray hair pinned back along the sides, the toes of her black oxfords barely touching the floor. Emmaline was already making the introductions: Vicky Holden, the lawyer I told you about; Father John, the mission priest.

The old woman gestured toward two wooden chairs wedged between the window and the bed. "Have a seat," she said in a tone not meant to be challenged.

"Thank you for seeing us, Grandmother," Vicky said as she took one of the chairs Father John pushed into a small circle facing the old woman. Emmaline took the other. He stood behind Vicky.

"Come see me anytime," Anna Scott said. "I like to hear all about the reservation." She leaned so far forward that Father John braced himself to reach over and catch her. "Who's that white woman they found murdered up on Sacajawea Ridge?"

"How'd you hear about that?" Emmaline's eyes opened wide in surprise.

"I got TV." Anna tilted her head toward the TV set almost hidden behind the door. "Whadd'ya think

I'm doing here all day, vegetating?" She waved a bony hand at Vicky. "They know who she was yet?"

"Laura Simmons," Vicky said. "A friend of mine from Colorado. She was a history professor, Grandmother. She'd come here to research Sacajawea."

The old woman settled back into the cushions. "You don't say. Just like that other professor come from Colorado twenty years ago and got herself murdered. Everybody thought she wandered off in the mountains like Sacajawea and got lost. 'Course Sacajawea never got herself lost."

Her daughter laid a hand on the woman's shoulder. "Now, Mom, don't get yourself excited." She glanced up at Father John. "Mom's blood pressure isn't good, you know."

"You're the priest that found her, aren't you, Father?" The old woman shook free of her daughter's hand.

That was right, he told her. Did she know Charlotte Allen?

"Of course I knew Charlotte." The woman shifted her gaze around the room, remembering. "Short white woman, not very big around, with brown hair. Pretty good-looking, for a white woman, and very smart, I'd say. Drove out to the ranch two, three times to ask me about Sacajawea. Said she already heard the stories I told her. She was looking for something written down that was gonna prove Sacajawea was really buried here."

Anna Scott nodded slowly, the memories flooding over her now. "I knew what she was after. Used to be a notebook with Sacajawea's stories that the agent's wife wrote down. Only one that ever wrote 'em down. All the Indians kept the stories in their heads." She lifted an index finger and traced out a circle in the gray hair. "Some historians come around a long time after and wrote down what the Indians said, but Charlotte said them stories wasn't good enough. They was written down too late, wasn't fresh enough. She wanted the notebook, all right. Only problem was, the agent's wife had put it in the agency, and it burned down. Would've been better if she'd just kept it under her mattress. I remember sayin', 'Charlotte, you think that notebook's just been waiting for you? If it was around, I would've written about it myself.'"

"A man convinced her the memoirs survived," Vicky said.

"Oh, yeah." The old woman shrugged. "Charlotte believed somebody was gonna get her the evidence. Imagine, a smart woman falling for a line like that. Well"—another shrug—"I figured she wanted to believe 'cause she wanted that evidence so bad. It must've left a sour taste in her mouth. She kept on thinking it was gonna come to her."

"Grandmother," Vicky said, a persistent tone, "do you know who the man was?"

Anna shook her head. Vicky glanced up at Father John. Disappointment mapped her face.

"I remember asking two, three times," Anna Scott went on. "She always told me she didn't want anybody to know he had the evidence. I said, 'Char-

238

lotte, why's he gonna give *you* this precious thing?' And she said"—the head still shaking—" 'Anna,' she said, 'you wouldn't understand.' "

"She was in love with him," Vicky said.

Anna smiled. "She thought I didn't understand. She thought I was never in love with a man, wanting to believe all his promises. How'd she think I got myself Emmaline here?" She reached across the armrest and patted her daughter's hand.

"Thank you, Grandmother," Vicky said as she got to her feet. There was a mixture of discouragement and fatigue in the way she moved.

Father John reached over and took the old woman's hand. It was light as a leaf. "You've both been very kind," he said, nodding toward Emmaline.

"You don't have to go." Anna Scott scooted forward in the chair. "I like to talk to people."

He wanted to tell her he'd be back, but that wasn't true. Tomorrow he would be gone. "I'm sorry," he said, part of his mind already at the mission. He'd left Kevin alone again, and for what? A wild-goose chase to prove an unprovable theory. The man in Charlotte Allen's journal was a phantom.

Just as he started for the door, where Vicky stood waiting, Anna Scott said, "I got my suspicions."

He turned back. Vicky had moved beside him. "About the man?" she asked.

"Now, Mom," Emmaline said. "You shouldn't be spreading gossip."

The old woman jerked her head toward her

daughter. I like gossip. You hear lots of things, see things, too, if you just keep your eyes and ears open, and you know what? Most the time they're true. I seen something in Charlotte when she got to talking about the people she met on the res. Something come into her eyes, and her voice went kind of soft whenever she talked about the student that was doin' research for his dissertation, and I remember thinking, Yeah, she's got herself in a tizzy about him, no matter he's a lot younger'n her. He's the one told her he's gonna get her the precious evidence. Oh, and he was handsome all right, that Shoshone, all muscles and a smile that, I tell ya, it'd make your heart leap around."

"Robert Crow Wolf." Vicky said the name so quietly, Father John wondered if he'd heard correctly.

"How'd you know?" The woman flinched at the stolen punch line.

"I didn't," Vicky said. "Until this moment."

⇒ 30 ⇐

"Do you know Crow Wolf?" Father John heard the sound of his own voice over the soft music— Verdi now, *La Traviata*. He took his eyes from the highway a half second and looked over at Vicky. She'd been so quiet since they'd left Casper, he wondered if she'd fallen asleep.

"I've met him several times. A handsome and charming man, the kind women always like, at first.

240

Twenty years ago he was probably even more attractive. A young graduate student, making himself an expert on the early days of the reservation. Yes," she went on in a musing tone, "I can understand what Charlotte saw in him for a while."

"What are you saying?" Dried stalks poked out of the snow in the barrow ditch, marking the edge of the asphalt. Snow fluttered in the headlights.

Vicky exhaled a long, quiet breath. "Charlotte probably came to her senses. Sometimes it takes a while to see that a handsome, brilliant, charming man may not be all he seems. She probably took a closer look and saw someone ten years younger and still in graduate school. After all, she was a professor. And . . ." She hesitated. "She was white; he was Indian. It might have been a passionate love affair, John, but Charlotte didn't see 'future' written on it. A good reason to keep the affair secret."

The logic was locked into place now, Father John thought, the patterns a seamless whole. "Crow Wolf must've hit upon the idea of the memoirs when Charlotte tried to break things off. She never mentioned Toussaint in the journal until he brought up Sacajawea's memoirs. And then she wrote it down." He smiled at the consistency of it; of course, a historian would keep a record of something as important as the memoirs, even if she'd kept the name of the source in her own code.

"He could have loved her," Vicky said.

The idea surprised him, shaded the logical propositions ever so slightly. He'd assumed Crow

Wolf was only using the woman, an older, established scholar in a position to further his own career. An attractive woman willing to get involved with him. He hadn't thought Crow Wolf might have fallen in love with her.

"The man never would have taken such a gamble if he hadn't been desperate to hold on to her," Vicky was saying. "He made up a story about the memoirs surviving the agency fire, hoping that if he held on to Charlotte long enough, she'd decide to stay with him. He must've copied a lot of information into an old notebook and told her it was the memoirs."

She sighed, an expulsion of air, and went on: "He's not the first man to promise the moon to keep a woman from leaving. Who knows what lies Sacajawea's husband fed her to get her to stay with him? You've got to hand it to men like that. They can be very persuasive."

That was true, Father John thought. Crow Wolf had even persuaded Charlotte that he intended to give her the memoirs, instead of publishing them himself.

"Oh, I can imagine what happened," Vicky continued. He winced at the realization that she was talking about herself now. "Oh, how he loved her. No one would ever love her the way he did. They were meant to be together, two halves of a half-consumed peach. She was his woman. What more could she ask? And all the time the tension was building because he knew she was leaving. Finally he exploded. And he got away with it, John, for twenty years. He would have gotten away with it forever if he hadn't panicked when Laura showed up with the journal. He had no idea what Charlotte might have written."

Father John was quiet a moment. Riverton lay ahead, like a miniature Christmas village blinking in the snow. "When I asked Theresa if she'd talk to Laura, she already knew Laura was on the res looking for information on Sacajawea. Phyllis Manley had called her after Laura came into the cultural center. Theresa must've called her granddaughter, and—

"Hope told Robert." Vicky finished the thought. "He had no idea of what was in the journal. But he knew that Charlotte's body had been found. He must have figured that sooner or later Laura might connect him to Charlotte's murder and turn the journal over to the fed. He had to get the journal."

She shifted forward on the seat. "My God, John. Now Crow Wolf's promised the memoirs to Hope Stockwell. What if they've been having an affair, and she's decided to break it off? He could be using the same excuse to keep her."

Hope Stockwell. Father John could see the young woman. Beautiful, hopeful, ambitious. And trusting. She might not even think of authenticating the memoirs that came from a scholar like Crow Wolf. But if she did . . .

"We have to see Gianelli," he said. "We have a name now."

The snow was lighter as he drove through the

243

wide, flat streets of Riverton and turned onto the slick pavement of a fast-food restaurant. Inside Vicky went to the order counter while he found the phone in the corridor near the rest rooms. He dropped a quarter into the slot and dialed Gianelli's number. In the background was a clatter of dishes, a medley of shouts. Finally the ringing stopped.

He hung up on the answering machine and tried the agent's home number. The phone rang into a vacuum. He pushed the disconnect lever. Vicky was at his shoulder, holding a large white food bag. "Gianelli's not in," he told her, fishing another quarter out of his jeans pocket and dialing Banner. The operator picked up on the first ring. He identified himself and asked for the police chief. A hollow sound came on the line followed by the familiar voice: "What's going on, John?"

"Vicky and I . . ." He paused. They had a theory, but what proof did they have? An old woman's suspicions that Charlotte Allen had been involved with Robert Crow Wolf? Their own suspicions that the Shoshone was the man Charlotte wrote about in her journal? It didn't add up to proof that Crow Wolf had killed the woman. It certainly didn't prove he'd killed Laura.

Before he could go on, the chief said, "Gianelli's already filled me in on that crazy theory you and Vicky came up with about some guy named Toussaint."

"Robert Crow Wolf killed Charlotte Allen and Laura Simmons," he said.

A whistle of exasperation sailed over the line. "Robert Crow Wolf never killed anybody. He's a good man, John, one of the best. So what if he might've known the victims? They're all historians."

"It's more than that." Father John could tell by the exasperation in Vicky's eyes that she was following the conversation. "Crow Wolf made promises to Charlotte that he couldn't deliver. She challenged him, and he killed her. He killed Laura because he thought she had the evidence to connect him to the murder."

"Look, John, you're way off the track. Crow Wolf might have a reputation for liking the ladies, but he's no murderer. Gianelli got some lab reports this afternoon. Toby Becker's fingerprints are all over the Simmons car. The fed flew out of here about an hour ago with a warrant for the man's arrest. Said he wanted to bring the bastard back. Took a real personal interest. You know he's got four daughters, and he wants to protect 'em from slimeballs like Becker. He'll bring Becker back tomorrow."

"Fingerprints!" Father John shouted. "Becker was her boyfriend. Of course his fingerprints are in her car." Vicky shook her head and looked away. He went on, making an effort to lower his voice. "Crow Wolf probably wore gloves when he drove Laura out to Sacajawea Ridge and beat her to death."

A low sucking noise punctuated the silence at the other end, as if the chief had just taken a drink of something hot. "I'm sorry, John. Crow Wolf isn't on the res. He lives in Laramie."

"He's here, Banner. He's still trying to find Charlotte Allen's journal. He's involved with Hope Stockwell, and she could be in danger. You could pick him up, ask him some questions, keep him from harming anyone else." Father John felt his stomach muscles tightening. What if Hope tried to end the affair tonight? "We can be at the police department within the hour. We'll fill you in on the details."

"You mean, fill me in on your theory? I can't haul Robert Crow Wolf in on some vague theory. What kind of hard evidence are you talking about?"

No evidence. No fingerprints. Nothing written down. Just a series of propositions that yielded a simple, elegantly logical conclusion. "Believe me, Banner, it makes sense."

There was another sigh edged with exasperation. "It's already been one hell of a long day, John. Two bad accidents, couple assaults. I was just heading out the door when you called, and the minute I hang up, I'm going home. Maybe priests and lawyers work all the time, but I like to go home once in a while. Take your theory to the fed when he gets back tomorrow. He's gonna tell you he's got the Simmons case wrapped up."

Father John set the receiver in its cradle and lifted the phone book attached to a metal chain. He flipped through the white pages. "We've got to warn Hope," he said, taking in the number. He fished another quarter out of his jeans pocket and started dialing.

"Let me talk to her." Vicky took the receiver from his hand. A moment passed. "Grandmother," she said, "it's Vicky Holden. Is Hope there?" She glanced up, giving him a half smile of success. Then: "Hope, I'm a friend of Laura Simmons. I have to talk to you about something very important." Another moment of silence before she went on: "Tonight, Hope. We have to talk tonight. I'll be there in forty minutes."

She hung up slowly and turned to him. "She's waiting for an important call, probably from Crow Wolf."

Father John nodded. "We'll get over there right away. I have to call Kevin first." He plugged another quarter into the slot.

"Kevin? What's he have to do with Crow Wolf?"

"Crow Wolf could show up again looking for the journal," he explained. The phone was ringing; he could imagine the shrill sound echoing through the quiet of the administration building. He was about to hang up and try the residence when the buzzing stopped.

"St. Francis Mission." Father John felt a surge of relief at the sound of Kevin's voice.

"It's John," he said. "Everything okay?"

"Sure." The other priest sounded tense.

"Make sure Leonard locked up the museum," Father John said. "If he's still around, ask him to stay until I get back."

"He's already left." The tense voice again.

"Are you sure everything's okay?"

There was a pause. "When will you get back?"

"As soon as I can." Father John replaced the receiver again, an uneasy feeling gnawing at him.

"What is it?" Vicky asked as they walked through the dining area and out the glass doors. The snow licked at his face. *Think logically.* "Kevin's been handling things by himself most of the day," he said. "He's probably tired."

"It'll take some time to convince Hope that Robert Crow Wolf isn't who she thinks he is," Vicky said as she climbed into the Toyota. "I know you want to get back to the mission. Just take me to the Bronco. I'll drive over to see Hope."

He walked around and got in behind the wheel, the uneasiness chafing like a bur in his skin. "Are you sure?" he said, turning the ignition. The engine spurted into life.

"I'm sure."

He pulled into the traffic and after several miles headed west on Seventeen Mile Road. She'd handed him a hamburger, which he munched as he drove. Except for the lights twinkling from the occasional house by the road, they were surrounded by the flat, white plains.

"Suppose Hope won't listen to me," Vicky said.

It was possible, he thought, chewing on the lukewarm beef. Banner called the idea crazy; Gianelli would probably say the same thing tomorrow. "We need evidence," he reminded her.

Yes, she understood all about evidence. She was a lawyer, had he forgotten? She took a bite of her own hamburger. After a moment she said, "If I can get Hope to admit that Crow Wolf is the one who promised her the Sacajawea memoirs, it would support our theory."

"It's not physical evidence." Father John turned right on Ethete Road.

"It's something, John," Vicky said as he slowed, pulled into the yard, and stopped behind the Bronco. A mantle of white draped over the hood and windows. The house was dark.

"Aunt Rose's bingo night," Vicky said, gathering up the remains of their meal and crumpling the bag. She gripped the door handle and got out. Then she leaned back. "What time does your plane leave tomorrow?"

His plane. He'd forgotten about his plane. He was packed; he was ready to go. "Five in the afternoon," he said.

"I can meet you at Gianelli's office in the morning. Call me as soon as you get ahold of him."

He promised.

He waited until the Bronco's taillights flicked on before he started to back out.

⇒ 31 ⇐

Vicky eased the Bronco to a stop in front of Theresa Redwing's stoop and hurried up the snow-slicked steps. The front door flew back as she was about to knock. A young woman stood in the opening, a small figure framed by the light shining behind her.

"Oh! I thought you were someone else," she said in a voice airy with disappointment.

"You must be Hope," Vicky said.

The door opened wider, and Theresa Redwing sidled next to her granddaughter. "I told Hope I didn't want her going nowhere till she seen you. Arapaho lawyer drives all the way out here to tell her something, it's gotta be important." The woman reached down and took Hope's hand, leading her back into the room. Vicky followed.

"You sit down right over there." Theresa gestured with her chin at an easy chair and closed the door. "The two of you can have a good talk while I get us some coffee. Cold night like this, you can use some hot coffee." Her eyes stayed on Vicky a moment before she disappeared into the kitchen beyond the small living room.

Vicky glanced at the young woman, who was truly beautiful, she thought, with thick, glossy hair framing an almost perfect face, a coppery complexion, and dark, almond shaped eyes that watched her with a mixture of distrust and annoyance. "You could be in danger, Hope," she said softly. She didn't want to alarm Theresa. "What?" Hope pulled back the sleeve of her red cable-knit sweater and stared pointedly at her watch. "Whatever it is you're talking about, you'd better tell me. I don't have a lot of time. I'm expecting a call."

"From Robert Crow Wolf?"

Hope's head snapped back. Vicky caught the effort just below the surface in the blank, unreadable expression. She pushed on: "He's promised you the Sacajawea memoirs, hasn't he?" A leading question, she knew, but this wasn't the courtroom.

"Suppose he has." Hope moved past her and plopped down on the sofa.

"When did he promise them?" Vicky perched on the chair across from the young woman. She might have been her own daughter, only a few years older than Susan. "After you decided to break off a relationship with him?"

"My relationship with Robert is none of your business." The dark eyes blazed with indignation.

"You're not the first woman he promised the memoirs," Vicky said. "He's used them as an excuse before to get what he wanted."

Hope met her gaze. "I have a right to the memoirs," she said. "I'm the one who's descended from Sacajawea, not your white friend. I don't care what she told you. Robert never had any intention of turning the memoirs over to her."

"He's a dangerous man," Vicky said. Her throat felt tight and dry. She *had* to make the woman understand. "He promised Charlotte Allen the memoirs twenty years ago. He promised Laura the same thing. Both women were beaten to death."

Hope let out a high-pitched laugh, an imitation of merriment. "You're saying Robert beat someone to death? That's ridiculous. He's the kindest, gentlest . . ." The faintest hint of a blush came into the dark

251

cheeks. "The most handsome, brilliant man I'll ever meet." Suddenly the girl's tone dropped a couple of notes. "If you want to know who killed your friend, try her boyfriend, the guy the police allowed to drive out of here free as a bird and go back to Colorado. He's the one who killed her."

"What about Charlotte Allen?"

"How do I know what happened twenty years ago? Maybe she had a boyfriend."

"Exactly."

"Well, it wasn't Robert. He was at Berkeley then."

"He was on the res that fall, researching his dissertation."

Surprise flickered in the blank eyes. *Hope Stockwell didn't know everything about Robert Crow Wolf.* Vicky pushed on: "He's a historian. Why would you ever suppose that he'd turn Sacajawea's memoirs over to you instead of publishing them himself if the memoirs really existed?"

The young woman drew her lips into a tight line, grabbing a half second, Vicky thought, to consider the answer she'd probably used to convince herself. "It's simple," she said finally. "Robert's already made his reputation, and now it's my turn. The Sacajawea memoirs will jump-start my career. I'll be like a bronco bursting out of the chute, is the way he puts it. My dissertation will be published, no question about it, and I'll have my choice of teaching positions on the best history faculties in the country." She held up the palms of her hands, as if to ward off any disagreement. "Besides, Robert and

I are in love."

"The Sacajawea memoirs don't exist," Vicky said.

"I told her that." Theresa crossed the room and set a plate with three mugs on the table in front of the sofa. "If those memoirs had gotten out of that fire, folks would've heard about it sooner or later. None of the descendants could've kept a secret bottled up for a hundred years." She handed around the mugs filled with coffee. Steam licked at the rims. Then she sat down on the sofa next to her granddaughter.

"Robert's a scholar, Grandmother," Hope said in a respectful tone. "He's been doing research on the reservation for a long time. He's found a lot of documents no one else ever discovered."

"He's telling you a big story 'cause he wants you to keep on with him," Theresa said. "A man old enough to be your father, and he's already had himself a couple wives and a lot of girlfriends. He's probably got a girlfriend in every little town between here and Laramie. You know what's good for you, you won't have nothing more to do with him." She took a long drink of coffee, staring at her granddaughter over the mug.

"Grandmother, please. You don't understand how things are today."

"And what's that supposed to mean? You think I wasn't young and pretty like you once upon a time? That I don't know how an old stallion can sidle up to a young filly and make her all jittery with the wanting? Oh, I knew all about smooth-talking, good-looking guys making all sorts of empty promises before I figured things out and settled down with the real good man that was your grandfather. Don't tell me, young lady, that I don't know about Robert Crow Wolf and his like."

"They aren't empty promises, Grandmother." Vicky heard the struggle for respect now in the young woman's tone. "Robert's gone to get the memoirs. I expect to hear from him at any moment, and this whole conversation will be meaningless." Hope got to her feet. Locking eyes with Vicky, she said, "I really have nothing more to say to you."

"Hope!" Theresa scooted forward, as if she might bolt off the sofa. "I won't have such rudeness here. It's not our way."

Slowly Vicky rose out of the chair. "Robert Crow Wolf is lying to you, Hope," she said. "He's after Charlotte Allen's journal because it incriminates him in her murder. He beat Laura to death trying to find out where she'd hidden it. He's still looking for it. Sooner or later Robert's going to be charged with two homicides. He's desperate. There's no telling what he might do to try and save himself. You must stay clear of him."

"This is crazy." Hope edged back toward the shadowy hallway next to the kitchen. "You're talking crazy. I don't want to hear any more."

"Please trust me," Vicky said. "I'm telling you the truth."

"Shut up! Shut up!" The young woman clapped her hands over her ears, turned, and fled into the hallway. There was the hard crack of a door shutting.

"What should we do?" Theresa said, almost in a whisper. The old woman had pushed herself upright. She stood wedged between the sofa and the coffee table, the color drained from her face.

"Try to talk to her, Grandmother," Vicky said. "And don't let Robert Crow Wolf into the house."

Vicky's hands trembled against the cold steering wheel as she backed out of the yard. She felt limp with frustration. She shifted into forward and drove into the snow falling on Rabbit Brush Road. Hope had convinced herself she was in love with the man who could give her the memoirs. She didn't want to hear the truth. She wanted to believe. The will to believe, John O'Malley called it.

How many times, Vicky thought, had she seen the truth and turned away? The years when Ben had stumbled into the house, spinning out some wild story about a sick calf that needed tending, the smells of whiskey and another woman on his clothes and skin and breath? Still she had believed.

She had believed him again. Not because she still loved him. Because she'd wanted to put the broken pieces of their family back together. Because she'd wanted to belong somewhere again.

She eased up on the accelerator. A thin film of snow lay over the asphalt that disappeared into the darkness beyond the headlights. Despite the heat from the vents, she felt chilled. If only Theresa could convince Hope not to see Robert tonight! Gianelli would be back tomorrow, and she and John O'Malley would go over everything with him. Gianelli was a logical, rational man—he and John O'Malley, she thought, two of a kind. Solid and dependable. He'd see the logic.

And then? Vicky gripped the wheel hard, fighting the trembling that wouldn't stop. And then Robert Crow Wolf would walk away, because there was no evidence. He'd have a dozen stories, all plausible, to explain why he couldn't have killed Laura. Unless he were to confess.

Vicky laughed out loud, surprised at the sound of her voice against the hum of the engine and the kerplunk of the tires on the slick asphalt. Robert Crow Wolf would never confess. He'd gotten away with murder for twenty years and he'd get away with it again.

She gripped the wheel hard, the tips of her fingers digging through her gloves into her palms. Robert Crow Wolf was still looking for the journal. He was picking it up tonight, Hope had said. She'd meant the memoirs, but it was the journal Crow Wolf intended to get tonight. Suddenly Vicky realized where he would go to look for it.

She pushed down on the accelerator; the Bronco shimmied on the wet asphalt. A mile passed, then another. She could feel her heart jumping in her chest as she turned south onto 132 and drove on. Darkness swam outside the windows. On Seventeen Mile Road she turned east, her thoughts collapsed into a pinprick of determination. She had to get to St. Francis Mission before Robert Crow Wolf showed up. She had to warn John O'Malley.

⇒· 32 ·⇐

Father John slowed the Toyota through the balloons of light filtering over Circle Drive. There were no cars or pickups about. The mission had that vacant feeling of evening, after Elena and Leonard and Lindy and all the volunteers had gone home and before people arrived for whatever meeting happened to be scheduled. He never minded the quiet. Dinner in the kitchen, talking over the day with the other priest, when there was another priest, or listening to an opera alone.

He parked next to the Harley and started up the sidewalk. The house was swallowed in darkness, yet Kevin was obviously here. Maybe watching television, he thought as he stepped inside. He hung up his jacket and glanced into the living room. The TV was off; no sign of Kevin.

In the kitchen he found Walks-On curled on his blanket in the corner. The dog raised his head and gave him a sleepy appraisal before nestling back down. On the table between the two place settings was a sheet of paper: Elena's instructions for dinner. Odors of tomatoes and onions and stewed beef rose from a pan on the stove. Kevin hadn't yet eaten.

He retraced his steps down the hall, climbed the

stairs, and knocked on the other priest's door. There was only stillness. He knocked again, then looked inside. The room of a tidy man: the narrow bed tightly made; blankets tucked under the mattress military style; the cleared dresser, as if any articles that might have occupied the surface had recently been swept away; a pyramid of papers, folders, and small notebooks stacked in the center of the desk next to the computer and printer.

He closed the door and hurried back downstairs and, shrugging into his jacket as he went, headed across the grounds. Something was wrong; the bitter taste of it rose in his throat. Kevin had been at the mission an hour ago; he'd probably answered the phone in the administration building.

He took the steps two at a time. The front door was unlocked, a good sign that Kevin was still here. He hurried down the shadowy corridor toward the light leaking from the office at the far end. "Kevin?" he called.

The office mimicked the other priest's bedroom: papers neatly arranged on the desk next to a closed laptop; a row of books perfectly upright on the shelf. He walked back to the door leading to his own office and flipped the light. Everything just as he'd left it this morning.

He could feel the muscles constricting in his arms. His hands balled into fists, the taste in his mouth now so bitter he could hardly swallow. What had happened to Kevin? Why hadn't he locked up when he left? He started for the front door, then stopped.

He'd left Alva's revolver in the desk! He crossed to it and yanked open the drawer. The gun was still there, black metal gleaming in the light. He ran his fingertips lightly over the cold surface, then shut the drawer and went back outside, leaving the lights on. If anyone was about, he wanted the lights on.

The church was dark, but Kevin could be inside praying or meditating, Father John told himself. He unlocked the door and went in. The same routine: flipping on the lights, walking down the aisle, checking the empty pews for some sign of the other priest. The red votive light blinked in front of the tanned hide tabernacle to the left of the altar.

After checking the sacristy—no one there—he let himself out. The lights blazing through the stained-glass windows mingled with the lights from the administration building. The mission was coming alive.

He strode down the center of Circle Drive to the hulking, stone-block museum at the end of the curve. His boots thumped into the silence as he came up the steps and crossed the porch. He was about to insert the key when he realized the door was slightly ajar. He stepped inside. He was not alone; he could feel another presence, as real as the lattices of light over the entry.

He started down the corridor, all of his senses alert now, watching, waiting for someone to jump out of the triangular shadows floating in the corners. Even before he reached the end of the corridor, he saw that the library door was also ajar. He moved slowly along the wall until he could see most of the room. Light filtered through the windows and glowed around the papers, the upended, smashed cartons, the bookshelves toppled onto the floor. Father Kevin was in one of the chairs, his leather jacket unsnapped, a wild look of surprise visible in the shadowed contours of his face. Seated across from him was an Indian he knew, Robert Crow Wolf, one arm extended over the table, a finger cocked on the trigger of a silver pistol.

"Come in, Father O'Malley." The Shoshone's tone was quiet and confident, hinting of amusement. "We've been awaiting your arrival."

"In the dark, Crow Wolf?" Father John walked in and reached for the light switch.

"I wouldn't do that."

He dropped his hand.

The Indian gave a bark of laughter. "I have the wolf gifts, Father O'Malley. I can see my enemy in the dark. Besides, it would never do for someone to happen by and pay us a little visit before we finish our business."

"What is it you want?" Father John kept his voice calm.

Another loud noise that passed for laughter. "In the interest of good manners, I will assume you don't know. I have reason to believe that Laura Simmons left a document here. It belongs to me, and I simply came to retrieve it."

"You could have asked, Crow Wolf." Father John gestured at the papers creeping over the table and littering the floor.

"Oh, but I did ask. Unfortunately Father Kevin here maintains he doesn't know what I'm talking about."

"He's torn up the place." Father Kevin sounded amazingly calm and determined for a man held at gunpoint. "He's crazy."

"Crazy?" Crow Wolf seemed to find the epithet amusing. "I prefer to think of myself as cunning as a wolf."

"Mad as a hare." Kevin tilted his hand toward the upended shelves. "Nobody sane does this to historical records."

The Shoshone shrugged. He turned slightly and raised his gun until Father John could see that it was pointed straight at his heart. "Perhaps you'll be good enough to give me the documents Laura stashed here."

"What if I don't, Crow Wolf? Will you kill us, too? Just like you murdered Charlotte Allen and Laura Simmons?"

Crow Wolf's hand twitched; the gun seemed to jump, then steadied. "You've got the story all wrong, Father O'Malley. I'm not a murderer."

Father John saw the look of recognition in Kevin's eyes. The other priest had also recognized the undertones of self absolution and excuses in counseling sessions, in the confessional. *I'm not a bad person.* He said: "You had an affair with Charlotte Allen, and you went to Laura Simmons's apartment the night she disappeared. Both women were beaten to death."

The Shoshone kept his gaze on the pistol extended in front of him. Finally he said, "It wasn't my fault Charlotte died. She hit her head against the table leg. It was an accident."

"An accident? You were beating her at the time."

The man jumped from his chair, the gun shaking in his hand. "She said she was leaving me." It was a scream that bounced around the walls and the toppled shelves. "After everything she'd promised. She was going to get me a position at CU, and we were going to be together. Lies! All lies! Oh, I should've known I couldn't trust her. She insisted on keeping our relationship secret. Gave me a big story about having some boyfriend back in Colorado, but that wasn't it. That white woman just didn't want to be seen with an Indian."

"You promised her Sacajawea's memoirs, which don't happen to exist." Father John struggled to keep his gaze from the gun waving a few feet from him.

"I only wanted her!" A scream of pain. "Why didn't she understand? I gave her the notebook with the memoirs."

"They were forged."

"She could have used it. I wrote down different versions of the stories the Shoshones told years ago. Nobody would've questioned the notebook. But, oh, no, she had to make sure it was real. She wanted to give it to the experts. I tried to tell her it wasn't necessary." The man's voice shifted into a sobbing, pleading tone. "I tried everything. I loved that woman, and she was going to ruin me. She said I'd forged historical documents. I'd never teach in any history department. I didn't mean to hurt her, but she fell and hit her head. Nobody would've believed it was an accident. I would've gone to prison. What university would want me after that? I had to bury her and make it look like she'd taken off on a hike in the mountains. She was always going hiking alone. Nobody questioned that she got lost, until Laura Simmons . . ." He spit out the name. "She shows up here with Charlotte's journal. Jesus, I never knew she was keeping a journal, writing everything down, keeping a record, when all the time she kept saying to me"—he switched into a falsetto voice—" 'We must keep this a secret, my darling.' "

The man was waving the gun in a frantic, jerky motion. "Enough of this," he shouted. "Just give me the damn journal."

"Is that what you said to Laura before you beat her to death?"

"You're trying my patience, O'Malley. I'm not one of your penitents sobbing out my sins in the confessional. I'm the one who was sinned against, not those two bitches. If Laura Simmons had left the journal in her apartment when I sent her out to Willie's ranch, I could've gotten it. I wouldn't have had to go back there Wednesday night and try to reason with the woman. She thought she was so clever. Cleverer than any Indian. 'I'll make you a deal, Robert,' she said. 'You'll give me Sacajawea's memoirs and I'll give you the journal.' She was gurgling in her own blood and she still believed the memoirs were real."

Father Kevin levered himself slowly upright. "You killed two women over memoirs that don't exist?"

"Oh, they existed, all right," Crow Wolf said. "As real as a vicious hound dog in their minds. It didn't give either of those bitches any rest, yapping and chewing at them all the time." He was shaking his head. "It was beautiful. They wanted those memoirs to be real so they could be real."

"What happened to Laura, Crow Wolf?" Father John asked. "Another accident while you were beating her up?"

"Why the hell should I tell you all this?" A look of panic and alarm crossed the man's face.

"Perhaps you want to unburden your conscience and change your life," Father Kevin said. "Surely you don't want any other murders on your conscience."

"I'm not a murderer!" Crow Wolf shouted. "I would've given Laura the damn memoirs if I'd had them. What do I care about some woman's story? Let the female historians write their revisionist history, I don't give a damn. I only wanted the journal. It's about my life; it's mine. She should have given it to me, but, no, she had to see the memoirs before she'd tell me where she'd put the journal. And she was going to have to make certain they were legitimate, of course. She shouldn't have done that to me."

"So you started beating her," Father John said. The words were constricted with anger.

"She should've told me. All she had to do was tell me, but she wanted those memoirs more than she wanted to live. What happened was her fault, the stupid bitch."

"So you made it look as if Laura had disappeared, just like Charlotte," Father John said. "You tried to bury her and hide her car."

"It would've worked, too, if some nosy Indian kid hadn't gone out riding and found the SAAB." The pistol swayed back and forth. "You've stalled long enough, O'Malley. I want the journal now."

Father John drew in a long breath and exhaled slowly. "What if I were to tell you, Crow Wolf, that I've already given the journal to the FBI?"

"Well, I'd have to shoot you both, wouldn't I? I can see the newspaper headlines: 'Mission burglarized. Two priests shot to death.' Must've surprised the poor burglar who had no other choice but to kill them."

"My God," Father Kevin said. "The man is really crazy."

"Just give me the journal."

"I told you I gave it to the fed."

Crow Wolf raised the gun. "Now look what you've done, Father. You've forced me to kill you and your friend. Believe me when I say I don't want to do this." There was the slightest twitch in the finger looped around the trigger. "I'm certainly not a murderer, but you've given me no choice."

"Wait," Father John said. His mind raced for some way to buy time, to give him and Kevin a chance to catch Crow Wolf off guard. "The FBI doesn't have the journal yet."

"You're lying. You'd swear your own mother was a whore to save your skins."

"I called the agent today after I found the journal," Father John said, the words tumbling out. "He was on his way to Colorado to arrest Laura's boyfriend."

A little smile played in the Shoshone's eyes. "Perfect," he said.

"He'll be by tomorrow for the journal."

"I still say you're lying." A hint of uncertainty clung to the Indian's words.

"If you use that gun, Crow Wolf, you'll never get what you want. You can tear the whole mission apart, but I guarantee you won't find it. The agent knows where I put it. He'll have it in his hands tomorrow."

Crow Wolf drew back a few inches, as if he needed more space to consider the possibility. Finally he said, "You have one second to tell me where it is."

"Not until we have a deal."

The gun started waving again. "Seems to me you're not in any position to make deals." He snorted. "Too bad Laura wasn't clever enough to figure that out."

"It's simple, Crow Wolf," Father John said. "Charlotte Allen's journal for our lives. I tell you where the journal is, and we walk out of here." The words sounded hollow in his own ears. He was grasping. He pushed on: "You can go and get it. End of story."

"What do you think I am? Some dumb Indian? I'm not letting you and your friend out of my sight until I have it."

"He'll kill us." Father Kevin gripped the edge of the table.

"That's the chance you'll have to take," Crow Wolf said. "We're wasting time. Where is it?" He shot another glance about the room.

The man's crazy, Father John thought. Get him outside. Look for the chance. It was then that he saw the way. Alva's gun was in his desk. If he could get to his desk . . . He said, "The journal's in my office."

"Lead the way, O'Malley." Crow Wolf motioned toward the door. "I'll be right behind you. Don't try any tricks, unless you want a bullet in your spine."

Father John turned slowly and walked through the door. The corridor reverberated to the sounds of their footsteps. He stepped out onto the porch and waited a half second until Kevin was at his side, then they walked in tandem down the steps and started along Circle Drive. The cold air bit at his face and hands. He could hear the raspy breathing noise behind them.

Suddenly a shadow darted through the snow. Walks-On! He'd left the front door ajar. The dog stopped a few feet away, then threw himself forward, barking and growling.

"Call him off!" Crow Wolf shouted.

Father John grabbed the dog's collar. "It's okay,

boy," he said firmly. He patted the dog's head. "Sit," he ordered.

The dog dropped onto his rear hunches, a low growl rumbling in his throat.

"Keep going." The gun jabbed into Father John's spine. They started around the wide curve in Circle Drive. Father John felt his heart lurch. In front of the administration building, almost hidden in the shadows, was Vicky's Bronco. My God—the thought flashed like lightning in his mind—if Crow Wolf finds her here, he'll kill her, too.

Father John veered sideways into the snowy field bounded by Circle Drive. Kevin stayed in step, as if he'd also seen the Bronco.

"Where you going?" The jab of the gun again.

"To my office."

"Don't bullshit me, O'Malley. The office is up ahead in the administration building."

"The journal's in my office at the house," Father John said, keeping a matter-of-fact tone.

⇒· 33 ·⇐

John? Where are you?" Vicky shut the heavy wooden door and started down the corridor. The sound of her footsteps clacked into the silence that lay like a shroud over the administration building. Light cascaded around her, bouncing off the whitewashed walls and glinting in the framed glass over the portraits lining the walls.

"John?" she called again, easing toward his office, scarcely breathing, half expecting Crow Wolf to jump from the shadows. She stopped in the doorway, stunned at the evidence that John O'Malley was leaving. The surface of his desk was clear, so unlike the logical chaos of papers and folders she was accustomed to seeing here. Boxes were stacked about the floor, brown tape wrapped over the tops. One box was still open, and she could see the stack of books inside. The shelves behind his desk were empty.

A dog was barking somewhere outside. She whirled back into the corridor. How could she have been so stupid? The whole mission was lit up like a Christmas tree, but she'd gone to his office, assuming he'd be here. Crow Wolf wasn't stupid. He'd figured out that Laura had probably left the journal in the museum. He could be there now. Oh, God, she thought, let John be at the residence.

She was halfway down the front steps when she saw the three men coming along Circle Drive, then suddenly turning in to the field. John O'Malley was ahead; she knew by the slope of his shoulders, the way he walked and held his head, as familiar as a glimpse of her own image passing in a store window. Another man—the new priest—walked beside him, and behind them, Crow Wolf: the thick shoulders, the barely controlled rage in the jerky steps.

Vicky flattened herself against the cold, rough stucco wall and slid into the shadows. The barking was frantic now, and she realized Walks-On was sitting in the snow close to the museum. John and the others had already crossed the field. It was then, as they came into a circle of light, that she saw Crow Wolf had something in his hand. Jabbing, jabbing—a gun!—into John O'Malley's back. She heard herself gasp into the cold air. *Don't let him die.*

Think! Father John told himself as they started up the sidewalk to the residence, the gun scraping the knobs of his spine. He could hear the tension in the Indian's quick gulps of breath. A misstep, a stumble, and the tension would explode.

He opened the door and walked into the study on the left. Walks-On was howling, like the sound of a wolf floating through the night. Kevin was so close behind him he could see the shadow of his shoulder. He reached over and turned the knob on the desk lamp. For a half second he caught Kevin's eye, and he knew the other priest understood. They would both die if they didn't get the gun.

"The journal, O'Malley." Crow Wolf made a sharp hissing noise. "Get me the fuckin' journal."

"Hold on, you'll get it." Father John lifted one of the boxes he'd been packing and set it on the desk. As he pulled open the flaps he saw Kevin inching closer to the Indian's right. He reached slowly inside, easing around the corner of the desk toward the Indian's left, and began removing books and piling them next to the box.

"Come on, come on." Crow Wolf's voice was nervous. He jerked the gun toward the carton.

Father John lifted out the large box of opera tapes he'd carefully packed in bubble wrap and strapped with large slabs of brown tape. He set the box next to the pile of books, turning sideways toward the man. "There it is," he said.

It was only an instant, a flash of time, but it was what he'd been watching for. Crow Wolf dropped his gaze to the box, and Father John rammed into the man, sending him rearing backward. The pistol fell, and out of the corner of his eye Father John saw Kevin diving toward the gun. Then, a flash of movement: the Indian's boot rising and crashing into Kevin's head, and Kevin dropping onto the carpet.

Father John slammed a fist into the Indian's jaw, then landed another blow at the man's chest as they stumbled backward, knocking over one of the wingback chairs, Crow Wolf sloping against the wall, gasping for short, hard breaths. Then, like a volcano erupting molten fire, he reared upward, shouting and slashing out, a fury of fists flying at Father John's head and chest. He ducked sideways, managing a few more blows into the Indian's hard flesh, but the man kept coming. A disembodied voice—it might have been from a loudspeaker somewhere—shouting, "I'll kill you, I'll kill you," and then Father John felt the pain sear his jaw as he caught an uppercut. He reeled back against the hard edge of the desk, struggling for the breath stopped in his chest.

The Indian swooped downward, then snapped upright. He was gripping the pistol in both hands, moving slowly backward now, taking careful, steady aim, and Father John could see the blackness of the nozzle pointed at his heart. "You've done enough, Crow Wolf," he said. Pain ripped through his jaw. "Take the package and leave."

The Indian was gasping, his chest rising and falling, his hands shaking. "Leave you to tell your lies to the FBI?"

"What difference would it make?" Keep him talking, Father John was thinking. Appeal to the man's reason, his logic. "Without the journal, there's nothing to link you to Charlotte. You can take the package and walk out of here. It's over, Crow Wolf. You're free and clear. Why risk any more murders?"

The Indian seemed to consider this a moment. His hands steadied, the gun held in place. "Why should I take the chance? With you and this other priest"—a quick nod toward the crumpled form of Father Kevin—"out of the way, no one will ever know."

The Indian planted his boots and crouched slightly, the gun rising a quarter inch. Father John closed his eyes. "Lord, have mercy on us," he said as the room crashed around him.

His eyes snapped open, the noise still reverberating off the walls and furniture. The Shoshone was staggering backward, face fixed in astonishment, the whites of his eyes narrowed into slits, arms dangling at his side like ropes hanging from the branch of a tree. A circle of blood soaked into the man's white shirt and was widening into the open front of his sheepskin jacket. The pistol slid out of his hand and clacked against the chair leg as the man folded onto the floor.

Father John wheeled around. Vicky was standing in the doorway, still pointing a pistol at the Indian, as if she expected him to rise up and come at her. He walked over and took the gun—Alva's gun, he knew, by the contours of the black handle. He set the gun on the desk before he took her in his arms and held her. He could feel her trembling against him.

After a moment he let her go and knelt beside Kevin, checking for a pulse in the priest's neck. He was alive. A red bruise was rising over his cheekbone. "Kevin," he said, gripping his shoulders. The man's eyelids fluttered, his jaw relaxed as if he were trying to speak. "Wake up, Kevin," Father John said again, shaking him lightly.

The eyelids opened, then dropped, then opened again. "What happened?" he asked in a groggy, disconnected voice. He began struggling to push himself upright.

"Don't move," Father John said. The frenzied noise of the dog barking and yelping outside mimicked the turmoil in his own mind. "I'll call an ambulance."

He got to his feet and stepped over to the crumpled form of the Shoshone. Blood covered the front of the jacket and spattered the wall and carpet. It seeped from the man's nose and the corners of his slackened mouth. He went down on one knee and found the inert carotid artery. "He's dead," he said. There was no response, and he looked over at the doorway. Vicky was gone.

<h1 style="text-align:center">⇒ 34 ⇐</h1>

Father John picked up the phone and punched in 911. "There's been a shooting at St. Francis Mission," he told the operator. "Get an ambulance over here right away." He slammed down the receiver without waiting for a response, told the priest still slumped against the desk that he'd be right back, and bolted for the front door.

Outside, the grounds were quiet, a collage of light and shadow from the blazing windows and the circles of light under the street lamps. He ran across the field. Vicky's Bronco was still in front of the administration building. He knew where she'd gone.

He turned in to Circle Drive, then in to the narrow alley that separated the church from the administration building. The moon hung just above the trees, lighting up the snow. The small, dark figure was running through the shadows ahead toward the banks of the Little Wind River. Walks-On ran alongside, looping about, barking, barking.

"Vicky," he called. He ran faster, his boots pounding into the ice just beneath the thin surface of snow.

She turned in to the trees and disappeared in the

mesh of shadows and moonlight. As she angled right he made a sharp right turn and came around in front of her. "Stop, Vicky," he said, taking hold of her. Walks-On jumped against them, yelping and barking. She struggled out of his arms, but he grabbed her again, holding her tightly now. "Stop, stop," he said close to her ear, his voice quiet. Gradually he felt her body give in to a kind of sustained shuddering.

"What have I done, John?" She was crying. "Oh, my God, what have I done?"

"You saved my life," he said. "You saved all of our lives. He would've killed us."

"But I've killed *him*!" She pulled back and threw her face up into the moonlight. Tears streaked her cheeks. He brushed his hand lightly over one side of her face, then the other.

From the distance, far beyond the trees, came the faintest sound of sirens as he put his arm around her again and led her to the fallen log where they'd sat many times, discussed many things in the past. For the first time he was aware of the cold biting at his skin. His jaw throbbed. He lowered her onto the log and sat down beside her. "Look," he said, "I'm as much to blame as you are. If I'd gotten to Alva's gun, I might have been the one—" He felt as if his heart could no longer beat.

She shook her head. "I saw you going to the residence. I saw that Crow Wolf had a gun on you, so I went back into your office. I found the gun in the desk drawer. I heard the shouting and banging as I ran to the residence. Walks On was going crazy, racing around, barking. I was afraid Crow Wolf had already killed you. I went inside. All I could see was Crow Wolf crouching, pointing the gun at you." She grabbed his shirt and held on, as if she were holding herself upright.

"I could feel the blows." She was sobbing. "I could taste the blood in my mouth. And there was a loud noise, and I jerked backward. And I knew I'd killed him." She sank her face into both hands, still sobbing, the sounds coming from some deep reservoir of grief.

"Vicky, Vicky." He pulled her to him again, saying her name over and over. Finally he said, "Try not to judge yourself. God is our judge, and He is merciful."

The sirens were louder, a well of noise and red-and-blue lights flickering through the trees. "Come on," he said, pulling her up beside him. "We have to go back now."

Okay, let's have the whole story." Art Banner sat back against a kitchen chair and took a long sip from a mug of the coffee that Father John had brewed thirty minutes earlier. Two other BIA police officers leaned against the counter, drinking from their own mugs. Father Kevin shifted in the chair next to the chief. A large white bandage applied by the ambulance attendants spread across one cheek and into his hairline. There was a hush of voices in the study where the other officers were examining the crime scene, then a sharp bang, as if the police photographer had knocked the package of tapes off the desk.

Father John glanced sideways at Vicky sitting beside him across from the two men. Her face was blanched and constricted, her eyes vacant. She was still in shock; he knew the signs: the fixed stare, the short, quick gasps. Her hand was like ice under his. The mug in front of her sat untouched. He took a gulp of his own coffee, wanting it to be whiskey. He badly needed a shot. God, one shot, that was all. "Can't we go over things tomorrow, Banner?" he said. "We've been through enough tonight."

Suddenly Kevin jerked upright, as if he'd just sprung awake. He started fumbling inside the pocket of the leather jacket hanging from the back of his chair. "Maybe we don't have to go over anything," he said, bringing out the small, shiny tape recorder and laying it on the table. "It might all be here," he said.

The kitchen went quiet a moment, as if time had stopped. Banner flexed his fingers and picked up the recorder. "Well, well," he said. "What do we have here?"

The priest's bruised face broke into a slow, painful smile. "If I got lucky tonight, I may have an interview with a murderer who confessed to two homicides and was about to shoot John and me."

Father John stared at the other priest. "How did you manage that?"

Kevin shrugged, then winced as if the effort had

reminded him of the boot kick he'd taken. "Crow Wolf walked into the office just as I was about to leave and introduced himself. I was glad to meet a Shoshone historian. Naturally I invited him to take a seat. I was even thinking about putting on a pot of coffee, expecting to have a good talk about the early days on the res."

He said "res," Father John thought, as if he'd been around for a long time.

"Next thing I know, he's holding a gun. I swear I don't even know which pocket he pulled it from. He demanded I take him to the library and give him some journal. I didn't know what he was talking about." He drew in a long breath. "That's when you called, John. I tried to signal you that things weren't right here."

"I missed it," Father John said. Somehow he'd missed all the signals tonight. Surely there was a moment—when was it?—when he might have taken the Indian's gun.

"I said to Crow Wolf," Father Kevin went on, " 'It's cold out there, man. I need my jacket.' So I took my jacket from the back of the chair and put it on. I expected him to check the pockets, but he didn't say a word."

"Must've figured a priest wasn't carrying a gun," the chief said.

"Yeah, well, he didn't figure on a tape recorder." Kevin gave a snort of laughter. "I managed to flip on the switch while we were walking across the grounds. Somewhere in front of the church, I believe. From there on"—he nodded at the chief—"we could have the entire conversation. It's a marvelous piece of equipment, very sensitive."

The chief was turning the small block of metal over in his hand. "The fed's gonna love this," he said. Then he looked up at Vicky. "Since when are you in the habit of carrying a revolver?"

Father John felt the little shiver in Vicky's hand. "It's not mine," she said, her voice so quiet that the kitchen stayed silent a moment after she'd spoken.

"She found it in my desk drawer." Father John locked eyes with the chief. "It belongs to Alva Running Bull. I was keeping it for her."

"So she wouldn't kill Lester." One of the officers at the counter spoke up. "The bastard deserves it."

Banner threw a cautionary glance at his men, then turned his gaze back to Vicky. "Okay, so you took the gun . . ."

"I saw that Crow Wolf had a gun on John and Kevin," Vicky said, her voice still quiet. "I went into the office and found the gun."

"Why didn't you call us right then?"

"There was no time, Banner." Vehemence seeped into her voice. "He'd killed two women. He killed my friend for the journal he thought was here. All I could think of was that the minute he found out John didn't have the journal, he was going to kill him. I had to stop him." Suddenly she dipped her face into her hands. Tears wound through her fingers. After a moment she looked up. "I thought I could make him drop his gun. I didn't mean to kill him."

"We tried to get the gun," Kevin said. "For a couple of Irish lads, we're lousy street fighters."

Banner laughed. "You're just out of practice,"

"It's all on the tape." Father John locked eyes with the chief. "Why don't you and Gianelli listen to it and ask the rest of your questions tomorrow."

Banner nodded slowly as he pushed himself out of the chair. "The agent's gonna want to see everybody soon's he gets back." Turning to Vicky, he said, "You probably shouldn't be driving. How about we give you a ride home?"

"I'll see that she gets home," Father John said.

Father John drove the Bronco west on Seventeen Mile Road, glancing every minute or so at Vicky huddled in the passenger seat, the way she'd huddled on the living-room sofa for the last two hours until the fleet of state crime lab and BIA officials had finally ferried out a stretcher with Crow Wolf's corpse zipped in a gray bag. He'd divided his time between sitting with her, trying to get her to drink some water, answering questions in the study, and refilling his own mug in the kitchen. His thirst was boundless, unquenchable. He'd brewed a second pot and gulped it down.

As he came around a jog the Toyota's headlights behind them flashed in the rearview mirror, blinding him for a half second. Kevin was behind them. He adjusted the mirror and glanced over at Vicky again. In the glimmer of the dashboard lights, her eyes looked bruised and puffy from crying, but, oddly, her expression seemed more peaceful. She seemed to have gone off somewhere far away. "Are you asleep?" His voice was soft.

"No." Vicky shifted in the seat and laid her head back. A moment passed before she said, "Ironic, isn't it? I always feared that one day I'd shoot Ben. So I left him, before it could happen. Now I've shot someone else."

"He was a killer."

"And I'm a lawyer. I believe in due process and all that, not in summary execution."

"That's not the way it was," he told her. "Try to think about what actually happened. Don't make it into something else."

She seemed to shrink inside the black coat, going off again into that place within herself. A good mile of highway unfolded ahead before she said, "We've been through a hell of a lot together, John O'Malley. But neither of us ever killed anybody before."

He reached over and took her hand again. It felt warmer, but the Bronco was warm, heat pouring from the vents. "In time—"

"Don't tell me how time heals everything. It's not true, and you know it."

"Well," he began, another tack. "Perhaps, in time, we'll learn to live with it."

She turned his hand over, gripping it so hard he could feel the tiny pinch of her nails against his palm. "I don't want to be alone tonight, John."

He let his hand remain in hers. He didn't say

anything for a long time, guiding the Bronco with his other hand into the fastness of the plains. The mountains rose ahead, massive black shadows. They might have been the only people in the world, he thought, except for the headlights dancing intermittently in the rearview mirror. Several minutes passed. "I'm going to take you to Aunt Rose's," he said.

⇒ 35 ⇐

That's some bruise you got there, Father John." Alva Running Bull leaned forward and reached out a hand, tracing in the air the eggplant-colored tender spot below his lip. Lester rearranged his weight on the chair beside her, embarrassment and concern mingling in the man's face. "Bet that hurts." Alva again.

It hurts, he thought. He said, "Looks like I'll survive."

"Oh, yeah, mostly we survive." The woman laced her fingers over the floppy bag in her lap.

"I don't hit you anymore, Alva." Lester was staring at the floor, hands folded between his knees. "You don't have to be afraid anymore."

"I know," the woman said.

"You didn't have to go get a gun."

"I was worried there for a while last week, when you started acting weird. I could tell; I can always tell."

"What's bothering you, Lester?" Father John tried

to bring the counseling session back to the source of the rage that exploded into fists pounding on flesh.

Lester exhaled a long sigh and drew himself upright. "The job, you know. Looks like the boss might lay some people off. First ones to go are Indians."

"How are you dealing with that?" Father John prodded, hoping the man would realize that he had managed to deal with the rage.

"Went back to the anger therapy, talked about what was going on."

"Did it help?"

"Yeah," Alva said. "It helped a lot. Lester got calmer." She turned to her husband. "I wasn't gonna shoot you. I just wanted to make you stop if, you know, if. . ." She hesitated, then looked back at Father John. "Anyway, good thing that gun was here."

That was true. He and Kevin and Vicky were alive, but Vicky—he hadn't been able to reach her all week. She was nowhere. Not at Aunt Rose's, at the office, at home. And she hadn't returned his calls. He didn't blame her. He could not be the man she needed. The realization came over him at the oddest times—during Mass, meetings, counseling sessions. Each time it seemed brand-new.

"Thank you, Father." Alva was gathering her floppy rug bag and levering herself to her feet. Her husband was standing beside her, one hand on her elbow, steadying her rise. Another crisis averted, Father John thought. Another stressful period navigated successfully. But the next one was always ahead. What might it bring? He could feel his jaw throbbing again. The woman was still tiptoeing through a minefield.

Father John followed the couple into the corridor and held the front door as they filed through. Suddenly Alva stopped and looked back. "See you next week, then, Father?"

"Yes," he said. The assurance seemed to give her a renewed sense of confidence. She crooked one hand into her husband's arm and allowed him to lead her down the steps toward a brown pickup.

Father John stepped out on the stoop and drew in the pristine air, filling his lungs. A cold breeze plucked at his shirtsleeves. He felt invigorated by the cold, the blue sky, and the bright sun flooding the plains and melting the snow. Or was it still the effects of the call from the provincial the previous Tuesday, scarcely an hour before Kevin was set to take him to the airport—the other priest most likely at the wheel of the Toyota. He'd finished packing his belongings—books, tapes, and papers in boxes stacked and ready to be picked up by UPS. Everything in his room—a few changes of clothes, his clericals and shaving kit, some more books—in the duffel bag that he would carry.

"Well, you won this round, John," the provincial had said. "The conference—"

"The Jesuit conference?" He wasn't sure he'd heard correctly.

"They didn't appreciate all those faxes any more

than I did." Dear Lord, Father John remembered thinking. Howard Elkman had gone over the provincial's head. "The conference decided you should stay there awhile longer, if that's what you want," the provincial went on. "Is that what you really want?"

Father John remembered the space that had opened on the line, awaiting his response. *I will go, Lord, if you send me.* His voice, when he finally spoke, had been quiet. "I'd like to stay."

"You know my concern." The familiar, warning tone. "You say the woman's gone back to her husband, is that right?"

Father John had remained quiet a moment. Vicky had left Ben before, and she had gone back to him. "I don't know her plans."

That had elicited a long pause on the other end of the line. Finally the provincial said, "I want you to think about your decision."

"I've already thought about it."

"I trust there won't be any problems."

"No more than usual."

"Is that supposed to allay my worries?"

"I'll notify you of the first problems that arise, Bill."

"I'm not leaving you out there much longer," the provincial had told him after another pause. "You know that, don't you?"

He knew that. At any moment the phone might ring again, and on the other end would be Bill Rutherford, an old friend from seminary days, his boss now, issuing the logical, peremptory order. No amount of letters from the elders, no pleas about unfinished business would change the decision. It would be the time, in the Arapaho way of time, and he would be ready.

Now he drew in another long breath, taking into himself the open spaces beyond the ring of cottonwoods and the ridge of mountains shimmering in the sun. He was at St. Francis now. And so was Kevin McBride.

He went back inside and made his way down the corridor to the *tap-tap-tap* of computer keys. The news that he was to be the assistant pastor seemed to suit the other priest just fine. More time to finish his anthropological study, he'd told Father John, as if he believed that would be true.

Father John rapped against the doorjamb. Kevin sat hunched over the blue computer screen, fingers pounding the keyboard, an earphone running from a cord to the tiny metal tape recorder next to the computer. It was a moment before he looked up, as if there were a time lag between the knock and his awareness of it. A swollen lump and purple bruise rose under one eye. The man looked as bad as he did, Father John thought. He said, "We should be ashamed of ourselves, a couple of Irish lads getting the worst of it."

Kevin seemed to consider this. He fingered the contours of the bruise, as if he were trying to make out just how inept they really were. "We could have taken Crow Wolf." He might have believed that, too.

"We're just a little out of practice, like Chief Banner said."

"There's something I've been wondering about," Father John said, swinging a side chair over in front of the desk. He straddled it backward and laid his arms over the top. "Who do you suppose advised Howard Elkman to go over the provincial's head?"

"Well, that is a mystery, isn't it, now?" Kevin McBride sat back and folded his arms across his blue shirt. The prism of sunlight in the window reflected in the man's light blue eyes.

"I doubt very much that Lindy Meadows would know how to contact the Jesuit conference," Father John pushed on.

"I doubt it," the other priest agreed. Silence filled the space between them.

"Well, if you ever find out who the guy is," Father John said, swinging one leg over the chair and getting back to his feet, "tell him thanks for me."

Kevin said he'd be happy to do. that.

"Will you be here for a couple hours?" Father John asked.

The other priest nodded and laid one hand over the tape recorder. "Got some good stuff I'm transcribing," he said. "Did you know the Arapahos were forced to sell a lot of their land in the early 1900s?"

Yes, he knew, Father John said, although until that moment he hadn't remembered he knew. There were so many stories he'd absorbed since he'd been here, so much that had seeped into his consciousness and become as much apart of him as the color of his hair and eyes. He forgot about them.

Father John had turned in to the corridor when Kevin said, "You haven't heard from her, then?"

"No," he said, looking back. He could still see the anxiety in her face during the interviews with Gianelli and Banner. It hadn't eased, even when the U.S. attorney had ruled Crow Wolf's death a justifiable homicide in defense of others. "I'd like to make sure she's all right," he added.

"She's a tough woman, John."

"You think so?" He wasn't sure, but then, he knew her.

"She wasn't about to let Crow Wolf kill us. She's going to be fine."

"I hope you're right." Father John gave a quick wave and walked back to his office, where he retrieved his jacket and hat. Then he hurried out the door and across the grounds to where he'd left the Toyota.

Vicky stopped the Bronco at the side of the narrow path that cut through the Shoshone cemetery. She gathered the small envelope she'd folded out of blue calico and stepped out into a cold gust of wind that whistled through the plastic flowers on the graves. She started toward the center of the cemetery, the sound of her boots on the earth punctuating the quiet. Layers of mountains rose into the sky on the west, sunlight outlining the humps and ridges and long, blue shadows drifting down the slopes. In the near distance were the roofs of Fort Washakie.

She stopped at the foot of the grave with SACAJAWEA carved into the tall, granite marker. Little piles of prayer bundles, faded and soggy, were arranged on the bare-earth hump. Close to the marker were several plastic bouquets—red, yellow, blue flowers. Slowly and reverently she unfolded the calico envelope and withdrew the three small prayer bundles she'd tied out of circles of fabric. Inside each bundle were tiny stalks of wild grasses and sage, symbolizing the earth, and clippings of her hair, symbolizing her own spirit.

She leaned down and set the prayer bundles on the grave next to the others. A prayer for Laura, her friend; a prayer for Charlotte Allen; a prayer for Sacajawea. The bundles would remain here, after she had left, beseeching the Creator to remember the women. "Please take care of them," Vicky said out loud, her words caught in the breeze.

There was a growl of a motor in the quiet, and she glanced around. The red Toyota pickup was working its way up the narrow path. It stopped, and John O'Malley eased himself out from behind the wheel and started toward her.

"How are you?" he said when he reached the grave. His eyes fell for a half second on the three new prayer bundles, then met hers again.

"I'm okay," Vicky said. She saw the barely concealed question in his expression.

"I drove out to Aunt Rose's," he went on. "She said you were here."

"I wanted to pray."

He nodded. The fact that she hadn't returned his calls swept into the space between them like a cold gust of wind.

"All those interviews," she heard herself explaining. "I've needed some time alone."

"I understand."

"How are you doing?" She reached up and touched the sore spot on his chin. "That's ugly."

"So everyone's been telling me."

She took her hand away. "How's Father Kevin?"

"Same ugly condition."

Vicky shook her head, then started walking toward the Bronco. His footsteps sounded behind her. "I would've come to the mission to tell you good-bye." She spoke into the space ahead.

"Good-bye? Do you expect me to believe the moccasin telegraph doesn't reach you at Aunt Rose's?"

"I know you've been given a reprieve," she said, still looking ahead. "I'm glad you'll be here."

Vicky felt the gentle pressure of his hand on her shoulder. She stopped and faced him.

"You're taking the job in Denver." There was an unaccustomed tightness in his tone.

"It's time for me to leave, John, with the shooting and all. And the firm's made me a great offer. I'll be working on natural-resources cases that are important to my people. Laola's coming, too."

"You went to Denver once before to get away from Ben," he said. "Do you have to do this again?"

290

"Sometimes we have to leave." Vicky let her eyes rest for a moment on the granite rising out of the earth. "I've been reading about Sacajawea. Things went better for her after she got away from Toussaint. She married a Comanche, and he was a good husband to her. She lived with the Comanches until her husband died, then she returned to her own people. Sooner or later Alva will realize that she has to get away from Lester and that her life can be better. Then she'll start looking for another lawyer."

She started to turn again, but he held her in place. "That's not why you're leaving," he said.

What he said was true. This time she wasn't leaving because of Ben. In any case, Ben would be gone for a while. He'd stopped by Aunt Rose's after he'd heard about the shooting and told her he was going to enter a treatment clinic in Salt Lake City, then spend some time in Los Angeles with the kids.

"These are your people, Vicky," Father John said. His voice was soft. "You should stay. I'll tell my boss I want to go to Milwaukee."

"You, a priest, telling a lie?" She shook her head and laughed.

"I'll be sent there sooner or later anyway."

"John O'Malley, you're the one the people want here." She kept her gaze steady on his. "You have to stay, don't you understand? I have to go. Besides, I'm looking forward to some legal cases that have nothing to do with real-estate leases or divorces or"—she paused—"women with black eyes."

She shrugged away from his hand and started

291

back toward the Bronco. He walked beside her, their boots scuffing up tiny pieces of leftover snow and earth.

"You'll stop by the mission on visits home, won't you?" he said.

"Of course. I'll want to check up on you, see what kind of trouble you're in."

They walked around the Bronco to the driver's side. He held the door as she slid in. "Go in God's care, Vicky," he said.

"You, too, John O'Malley." She smiled up at him and closed the door.

Author's Note

The written records and the oral histories of the Shoshones do indeed provide different accounts of Sacajawea's life following the Lewis and Clark expedition to the Pacific Ocean in 1805-1806. The records suggest that Sacajawea was the Shoshone wife of Toussaint Charbonneau who, in 1811, accompanied him to Fort Manuel in present-day South Dakota. And she was "the wife of Charbonneau, a Snake squaw," who died at the fort in December 1812. However, neither of these records mentions Sacajawea by name.

William Clark himself believed that she had died. In 1828, he listed in a journal the names of those who had gone on the expedition. Next to Sacajawea's name he wrote "dead." However, Captain Clark also wrote "dead" next to the name of Patrick Gass, who died in 1870, after outliving the captain by three decades.

The stories passed down among the Shoshones say that the wife of Toussaint referred to in the written records was not Sacajawea but another Shoshone wife, Otter Woman. Even the records agree that Toussaint had several wives. According to the Shoshones, Sacajawea eventually left Toussaint and went south to the Staked Plains to live among the Comanches, who were related to her people. In the 1860s, she returned north and rejoined the

Shoshones. She went with them to the Wind River Reservation in 1871. The wife of the government agent did indeed record the old woman's stories of the expedition, and the "memoirs" were destroyed in an agency fire. Sacajawea died on the reservation in 1884 at the age of nearly one hundred. She is buried in the Shoshone cemetery in Fort Washakie.